BE THE FIRST TO KNOW OF A NEW RELEASE!

*Click here to signup for my newsletter.*

*Like my Facebook Page*

*Join my Facebook Group*

# WOLF'S HUNGER

## MAFIA MONSTERS SERIES

### ATLAS ROSE

1

———————

"*C**arina!*" Phantom roared.

I jerked my gaze to the Alpha, then slipped and fell, hitting the asphalt hard. But strong hands were there, scooping me up from the road and hurtling with me toward the car as the deafening sound of gunshots rang out.

Smoke stung my eyes. The white plume was choking as the fire blazed from the Wolves' strip club on the mortal side of the city, blurring the sleek black Camaro in a tear-filled haze.

Screams came. Orders were barked from Harlan, the FBI Special Agent in Charge and my goddamn boss, as almost every cop in the city descended on the burning building behind me.

But it wasn't the fire that made Harlan scream with rage…it was the body they'd found.

A body that had been alive only an hour ago.

A body that'd been clawed to death…from what looked like a Wolf.

The back window shattered with a *crack* as I reached the car. Shards of glass exploded, stinging my face and arms. I ducked, and threw my arm over my head as Church yanked open the back door and shoved me inside.

The roar of the engine was thunderous. I tried to shove upwards, tried to find Arran and Vitold in the Hummer behind us as the monstrous four-wheel drive was peppered with bullets.

"*No!*" I screamed as the Camaro's engine roared. "*ARRAN!*" I fought Church, punching and bucking my hips, trying to dislodge his weight.

But there was nothing I could do as the tires of the Camaro howled, spinning for a second until they bit and propelled us forward. "*Arran! Vitold!*" I roared and tried to lift my head.

"*Get them!*" Harlan's faint roar came through the busted window. "*Hunt them the fuck down!*"

"*Stay down!*" Phantom barked, and whipped the car toward the busy city streets of Crown City. "Stay the hell down!"

Church braced his hands on each side of me, his heavy weight almost pushing me into the seat as he shielded me with his body.

"Arran!" I raged. "Jesus Christ, *Arran.*"

"He'll be alright." Church turned his gaze to mine, the low growl vibrating from his chest. "They'll *both* be alright."

But I saw panic in those piercing blue eyes, terrifying, *unmistakable* fear.

"*What the fuck just happened?*" Phantom barked. "That *fucking* cop was alive when we left him."

The image of the crime scene techs stuffing Special Agent Murphy into the body bag returned. "He's not alive now," I murmured. "Not at all."

His hands singed from the fire, chunks of hair torn out, and his face scratched. But his organs were pooled outside his body, slipping through the jagged claw marks across his middle, a Wolf's claw marks. I should know…I'd seen more than my fair share lately.

Gutted like a fish and left in the one perfect place to set the Wolves up for his murder.

The nightclub called Wild.

Phantom worked the gears expertly, pushing the Camaro hard as the faint wail of sirens slipped through the busted window. They were hunting us, just like Harlan had commanded...like a pack of hunting dogs as we headed for the bridge and the other side of the river. The flashing glow of red and blue splashed against the roof as Church slowly eased his weight off me.

I pushed upwards as the agent in me battled the woman. *Get them to pull over. Hands in the air. Knees on the ground. If they told the truth, Harlan would believe them.*

But then I remembered the curl of my commander's lips and the way he'd looked at Phantom.

*I'd seen that look before.*

It was how he'd looked at Phantom in the meeting, right after the Alpha had hunted me along the hallways of the FBI building and claimed me in the bathroom. Harlan hated the Wolves, hated everything they were...and it showed now, burning in every command.

*"Jesus."* The word trembled on my lips as my hands started to shake. I tried to stop the panic, but the shit roared through my veins. "Jesus Christ. *Jesus Christ. Jesus Christ.*"

The Camaro coughed and surged. Phantom let out a savage snarl and gripped the wheel. "The car took a bullet, somewhere important."

I jerked my head up at the words.

Church pushed forward between the seats to look at the instrument panel. "Will we make it?"

"I'll make sure we fucking make it." My Alpha cast a look at me in the rear-view mirror.

Desperation shimmered in his eyes. The kind I hadn't seen before, as he downshifted and we hit the on-ramp to the bridge. I gripped the leather seat, holding on as the cold river wind invaded, and glanced behind us, searching the traffic for my Wolves.

Red and blue lights flashed in the distance. But I didn't care about them, not in this moment. Agony savaged me like my own terrifying beast. This was all my fault. *All because they came for me.*

A tortured sound tore free as I wrung my hands, twisting my fingers until the knuckles turned white.

*All. My. Goddamn. Fault.*

My body whipped sideways as Phantom raced around a minivan, leaving a scowling woman in our wake, until the howl of the sirens closed in. She braked hard, pulling over to the side.

They all did.

Until we were left racing to the other side of the river with almost every Crown City law enforcement officer nipping at our heels. The Camaro gave a cough…then a splutter, before we lost speed.

*"Fuck!"* Phantom punched the steering wheel.

I swallowed a whimper, watching the speedometer drop like my stomach.

This was it…

*Christ, this was it.* I lowered my hand to my gun and drew it free with a trembling hand. *Whatever happens, I'll make sure they can run. I'll make sure they--*

"Put your fucking gun away, Carina," Phantom growled and pulled his phone free. "I have a bigger weapon in mind."

He pressed the button…and the phone was answered in a heartbeat. "Mojin…we're in trouble. The bridge…the entire fucking city is after us and the Camaro's about to die. Yeah… yeah, and brother…I owe you."

He hung up, glanced at me in the rear-view mirror once more. "Hold on, Carina. Just hold the fuck on."

I opened my mouth to ask why? But the word never left my lips. I was slammed to the seat as agony roared through my chest. Darkness claimed the city, swallowing the sparkle of stars and swept the remnants of the storm away.

The bridge lights darkened around me like a candle snuffed out by the wind and darkness descended. Like a beast...*like an Unseelie.*

I slammed my hands against the seat, spearing my nails into the stitching as that sickening green glow howled to life in my chest. Below us, a towering midnight wave rose, cresting before it slammed into the port with a defining *boom!* A scream tore from me, searing all the way to my soul as we plunged into darkness.

Tires howled all around us. All I could see was Phantom and Church, their faces a mixture of horror and determination as we skidded sideways and jolted to a stop. They were out of the car in an instant, tearing the doors open, screaming at me.

But I couldn't hear a thing, only the frantic thundering of my heart...until Phantom was there, pulling me from the back seat and into his arms. I gripped my gun as that burning in my chest pushed deeper.

"I can run!" I roared.

He lowered my feet to the ground and grabbed my hand, scanning the absolute darkness with the shine of those silver eyes. "Then *run!*"

A howl tore through the blackness, and the thunder of my heart met the stampede of paws. They were a blur tearing past me...two Wolves I knew in an instant. I barely glimpsed the thick, amber-colored fur on one of the beasts, and the shimmering midnight black on the other. *Vitold. Arran.*

My heart leaped at the sight of them. *Jesus, they were alive. Thank God...thank God.*

"*Come on, Carina!*" Phantom barked.

I drove the heels of my boots into the asphalt and lunged after them. We ran through the unnatural night and raced toward the far end of the bridge. Shots rang out, but they never found us, neither did anything else. The glow ached and pulsed in my chest, driving that endless dark away. Phantom's hand around mine anchored me as the two Wolves paced beside me and Church raced ahead, his long legs striding out.

Something red shimmered in the distance, two glowing crimson eyes. I lifted my gun, pointing as that blood-red glare grew bolder and the rear end of an Escalade came into view. The Unseelie was there, striding toward us from the choking night, the glint of a Sig Sauer in each hand.

He took one look at me and the Wolves. "Keys are in the ignition. I'll give you a head start."

"Thanks, brother," Phantom dropped my hand and strode toward him, grabbing him in a man-hug. "I won't forget this."

"Good. So get gone, already." Mojin glanced toward me. "They won't wait forever."

The doors to the Escalade were opened as sickening howls shattered the night. Through the window of one of the back doors, Arran lifted his head and looked my way, long white canines peeking beneath his lips before he lifted his head and rode the rest of the shift. I climbed in, inhaling the stench of hunger and rage, and ignored the glint of silver eyes in the dark.

"*Phantom, come on!*" Church snapped, and shoved the four-wheel drive into gear.

He strode past me, yanked the front passenger door open, and climbed inside.

"The files," Church growled, and glanced his way. "We have to get the files."

One glance toward him and the Alpha nodded. "Then we need to hurry. Mojin can't hold it forever."

Tires howled as the black Escalade leaped forward, tearing from the off-ramp of the bridge and toward the Hunting Ground. People walked the streets, staring at us as we shot forward.

"Stay in the car, Carina," Arran urged.

"Like hell I will," I growled as I holstered my gun.

The sound of a roaring engine tore my thoughts from the oncoming battle. Red and blue flashed from the shot-up patrol car. The windshield was shot to hell, large holes where the rounds had torn right through. But that hadn't stopped the cop...

*"Move!"* Arran barked as the patrol car skidded sideways, coming to a stop in front of the Hunting Ground.

I shoved out of the car, leaving the door open behind me, and lunged after Arran as he raced for the rear of the club. Faint screams came from the front of the nightclub. More engines were coming, the distant roar ending suddenly as the door slammed shut behind me.

Footsteps beat like thunder in the hallway as Arran left me behind and raced for their rooms. A door opened at the opposite end of the hallway and a half-naked dancer stepped out.

"Back inside!" I yelled. "Cops are here."

She was confused for a second, until the screams from the bar registered. I left her ran to the cracked open door of the Wolves' den, and plunged through.

*"I've got the files!"* Church barked. "Let's go!"

Phantom strode out of his bedroom with a duffel bag thrown over one shoulder, carrying a semi-automatic. Death echoed in his gaze as he met mine. Death and a promise. *I won't let them hurt you.*

"We have to go." Vitold came out of the study. "We have to leave now."

The *boom* of a gunshot somewhere in the club made me flinch. Phantom curled his lips and bared his teeth. He wanted to fight and defend his territory. But this was no battle for strength, this was a fight with the law, one he wouldn't win.

"Go," Phantom commanded as terrified screams came from the front of the club. *"Now!"*

I tore my gun from my holster and followed them as they raced along the hallway once more and back outside. Red and blue flashed, mirrored in the Escalade's windows.

"Get to the car!" Phantom ordered and tore away, racing to the front of the club.

"Phantom, *no!*" I screamed.

But there was no stopping him, no stopping all of this and, as the door of the four-wheel drive slammed shut behind me, I knew my life as I'd known it was over.

Tires and sirens howled as more patrol cars descended, following a black unmarked sedan that skidded to a stop, boxing the Escalade in. The engine of the four-wheel drive roared as it charged backwards, smashing into the hood of the unmarked with a *crunch.* Brute force shattered glass and metal as Church used the car like a battering ram.

"*Carina!*" Arran howled, throwing the back door open. Desperation raged in his eyes before the first shots rang out. I tore my gaze from his, my pulse deafening inside my head.

One step and I lifted my gun.

I couldn't leave, couldn't turn away from him…not anymore.

"*Fuck!*" Arran screamed as I lunged, charging for the corner of the building as the doors to the unmarked were shoved open.

"*Police, don't move!*" came the screams.

But I didn't slow, only charged around the front of the strip club as the doors were thrown open and patrons and dancers scrambled out. I was swallowed by the rush, slammed, barged into, and knocked sideways. My arm was punched, and my gun tore free. I heard it hit the pavement with a clatter before I was elbowed hard in my side.

Agony blended with that sickening, pulsing glow in my chest. I tried to shove out my arm, tried to focus on the ground. I tried to find Phantom and as the rush of bodies slowed, he was nowhere to be seen.

"Carina!" Arran roared over the deafening noise.

He grabbed my arm and pulled me against him, desperation wild in his eyes as more police cars arrived.

*"We have to run!"* I grabbed his arm, yanking him with me.

The Escalade was abandoned as four more unmarked police cars screeched to a halt with screams of *"Police! Get down!"*

Arran gripped my hand, dragging me as we blended with the last of the partygoers running from the club. "We have to go!" he growled, scanning the terrified faces of those rushing toward us. *"Now."*

The police were everywhere, guns raised, plunging through the crowd. I caught sight of Harlan as we stumbled toward the other side of the club. Hate darkened Harlan's eyes, the kind of rage that made a home in someone. The kind of rage that made an enemy of someone…only that someone was us.

I ran, half dragged by Arran as I watched for Phantom behind us. "We have to go back. *We have to find Phantom!*"

"He'll find us!" Arran barked. "Now, *move!*"

I trusted the Wolf, trusted the Alpha, so I ran from the Hunting Ground and, as the men and women stumbled toward the bright lights of the other clubs, Arran led me into the darkness.

The kind of darkness I'd felt before.

One that made the power in my chest shiver and throb.

Arran led me down the tight space between the buildings, leaving the flickering lights behind. We exited from the rear of the Hunting Ground and kept on running. The thud of our footsteps sounded like thunder, but still we ran, hit the dip at the back of the parking lot, and speared into the darkness.

I lost my bearings as we turned and turned again, and by the time we finally slowed, we'd lost sight of the lights altogether. There were no clubs here, no glinting lights, not even the red and blue flashes accompanied by sirens.

There was just dark empty streets and towering skeletal buildings, ones that shimmered a deep steel gray.

"Shit," Arran muttered and turned, scanning the street in all directions.

"What is it?" My lungs were so damn tight, I could barely breathe.Then I caught the dark blotch of his blood on his shirt. I stepped closer, my heart hammering, and touched the warm wetness. "Arran, you're bleeding." I jerked my gaze to the silver shine of hi eyes.

I yanked on my collar and tried to find air as Arran pulled me closer and let out a low snarl. "There's no time for that. We shouldn't be here." He stumbled forward, dragging me back the way we'd come. "We have to leave, *now.*"

"Leave *where?*" I yanked my hand from him, fighting a wave of dizziness as that unseen belt around my lungs drew tighter... and that sickening green glow brightened in my chest.

"We're in Unseelie territory." Arran backed away. "This is not good...*not good at all.*"

Shadows moved as he spoke the words, spilling from darkened doorways to stain the ground.

From one of those doorways came a scream. One so faint that for a second, I thought it was the wind...until the wind howled with desperation. *"Help me! Please HELP ME!"*

"Don't listen to it." Arran shoved me behind him, his tone hardening with fear. "It's not real." He jerked his gaze toward me. "None of it is real. Get out of here, Carina...*run!*"

2

"**P**lease *help me!*" The woman's scream drifted from a hollowed out concrete building. *"He's coming for me...he's coming!"*

But that was no trick of the wind, and no whisper of the dark.

That *was* real.

*And so was she.*

I took a step forward, then glanced back the way we'd come. There were no police here, no fleeing dancers and drunken horny men. There was just us, the darkness...*and her.*

"We can't leave, Arran" I winced and wheezed. "She sounds like she's in—"

"Carina, *no.*" Arran grabbed my arm and dragged me backwards. His lips curled, and white teeth shone as he bared his teeth and shoved me. I froze at the sudden aggression and stumbled as he pushed. "*Listen* to me. We need to get out of here *now!*"

Something scared the Wolf. *No,* something *terrified him.*

Panicked glances, and wide glinting eyes as he scanned the buildings, and I stilled.

It was this place...that *unfathomable hunger* in the air. A hunger I carried with me...a hunger I couldn't escape. I'd never seen this part of the city, didn't even know something like this existed. Towering concrete was barely kissed by the silver glow of the moon. It had a feeling about it, a cold, *ominous* feeling. One that made me shiver.

But I couldn't leave, not like this. *"Is anyone there?"* I called out. *"Do you need help?"*

I waited for her to answer...waited for anything other than the chill of the air crawling up my spine.

"We need to go." Arran repeated, yanking my arm, and this time I followed, turning my back on that cold, lifeless world.

*"He's coming. He's coming and this time he's not going to stop."*

I stilled at the cry, and jerked my gaze back to the building, my heart hammering inside my chest. "I can't leave, Arran. Not until I..."

I pulled my arm from his hold and took a step toward the building, and that *need* rippled in my chest as the green glow brightened. But it wasn't just the heat of desire this time, not that burning desire...it was darker, *harder.*

My lips curled, baring my teeth as Arran let out a tortured moan. "So help me, *woman,* you have ten seconds to turn your ass around or I *will* throw you over my damn shoulder. *And I'll enjoy it."*

He was serious, *deadly serious.*

"Ten seconds, right?" I licked my lips, pushing my damn luck with the Wolf. "I'll take that." I took a step toward the darkness.

"You're gonna get us fucking killed."

"No, I won't." I took a step toward the building, sucking in as deep breaths as I could. The echo of my boots was lonely in the night as I left the asphalt behind.

The shadows trembled and lashed against the building as I got closer. Shadowed fingers crawled along the ground toward me before they curled and drew away, like this world tasted me…like it somehow *knew me.*

I licked my lips and stepped up into the gaping doorway, listening to Arran give a whimper behind me, and tried to focus on the sound of her cry. *"I'm here!"* I called. *"Tell me where you are so I can find you."*

There was no answer, nothing but that emptiness as goosebumps raced along my skin.

"Phantom's gonna be pissed," Arran warned, shaking his head.

"Then let him," I replied, and took another step.

One savage snarl, and the Wolf was with me, striding through the gaping ruins and into the empty doorway.

"See?" he barked, and grabbed my arm. "There's no one here."

But I wasn't so sure. I wasn't sure about anything. Not about this place, or this night. Gunshots still resounded in my head and Harlan's savage howls of retribution lingered at the edges. We needed to get out of here. We needed to find the others. We needed to get somewhere safe…and just *think.*

But I could no more turn my back on someone in danger than I could see the Wolves framed for a crime they didn't commit. "Talk to me." I demanded. "Tell me where you are."

A cry echoed back to me, low, choking.

That green glow pulsed inside my chest, the heavy throb swallowing the echo of my own heartbeat. Something moved in the corner of the gutted building, a blur of darkness, malevolent and malicious. Something that was birthed from the shadows with a chilling growl.

"Carina," Arran warned.

There was no fighting him this time, no tearing my arm from his hold. The Wolf lunged, grabbed me around the waist, and hauled me backwards as the thud of heavy steps grew louder…and a man stepped into the room from the darkness.

He was a beast of shadows, growing bigger and more terrifying the closer he came. "Wolf." The threatening growl resounded all around us. "You shouldn't be here...and neither should *you...Carina.*"

I flinched at the sound of my name, watching as the shadows clung to the hard planes of his face. He was breathtaking... haunting and mesmerizing. I couldn't tear my gaze away as that merciless desire inside me called to him, writhing and rubbing, making me want to sink to my knees right there in the ruins and the dark.

I'd let that beast do things to me no man should want to do...

A savage sound tore from my lips. *But he wasn't a man...was he? He was an Unseelie.*

Arran let out a low, predatory snarl and stepped forward. There was a flicker of amusement from the Unseelie in front of us as he glanced at the Wolf and me. "Easy now, Wolf."

"Shrike," Arran spoke carefully. "You scared the shit out of me."

But the brooding monster didn't offer a smile, instead he watched me with a frightening gaze. "What are you doing here?"

"There was a problem." Arran licked his lips. "The police opened fire, cops are everywhere, hunting us from the other side of the city."

The Unseelie jerked his gaze toward me, and that forbidding gaze dropped to the green glow in my chest. "And Phantom?"

"On the run, but we had to come back for the files. Then the bastards started shooting and we got separated from the pack."

"And you thought this was the safest place to come?"

The way he said it...the way he lifted his gaze to mine, left me reeling. *No,* that panicked voice whispered inside my head. *This wasn't the safest place at all.* "I heard a woman." My voice trembled. "She called out to me."

"There's no woman here," Shrike answered, those chilling black eyes glinting. "Must've been the wind."

*The wind, my ass...*

"If Phantom's in trouble, then we need to get back to him," Arran answered, prodding.

He didn't need to push any harder. I took one last glance around at the cracked concrete walls as the weighted darkness of the place grew heavy, then turned. Arran's hand found mine as we stepped out of the building and back into the empty street. But there was something not right here, something about these abandoned buildings that felt *wrong*.

"What is this place?" I glanced at the Unseelie as he followed us out into the empty street and waited for him to answer.

"A place not meant for people like you," he growled and motioned us ahead.

I opened my mouth to push the subject, until Arran gave my hand a gentle squeeze. Desperation flared in the Wolf's eyes as he gave a tiny shake of his head. I swallowed that hunter in me and let the lie be what it was. These were Immortals, and right now, I was invading their world.

I needed to remember that…if I was going to stay here.

*Stay here...with them...the Wolves.*

The events of tonight made me more determined than ever. I squeezed Arran's hand right back, reassuring him. *It's alright,* I whispered inside my head. *I've got your back.*

The faint red and blue glow of police vehicles fought through the gloom in the distance.

"This way," Shrike said, stepping behind me and heading not for the rear entrances of the clubs but to what looked like vacant lots as he pulled his phone from his pocket and made a call.

"It's me. Phantom's in trouble. Yeah, the pack. I'm with Arran and Carina. We're coming out of the portal now…*yes, all three of us.* Send Ruin, to the valley…yeah, and tell him to bring the Explorer."

*Carina.* The way he said my name made it feel so fucking

*intimate.* I didn't like that feeling...not at all. He was dangerous, this one, even more than the Vampires and the damn Wolves. He scared me and I didn't scare, not easily anyway.

Headlights cut through the night up ahead in an instant as the sound of the racing engine of a four-wheel drive surged toward us. *Jesus, that was fast.*

"Ruin will take you to the safe house," Shrike said as he slowed, then stopped. "The others will meet you there."

"Is that it?" I shook my head and slowed my steps. "There's at least ten different units out there. They'll stop us in a heartbeat in that."

"Not if I have anything to do with it," Shrike muttered, and that same unhinged look of danger shone once more.

"Let's go." Arran yanked me forward, dragging me toward the waiting car.

The air seemed to throb and hum, standing the hairs on the nape of my neck. I turned my head as I reached the open door of the Explorer and looked at the looming Unseelie. He lifted his hands into the air, and the power lines that ran on poles from the back of the Hunting Ground to the front let out a *zap*, sending neon white sparks into the night sky.

"Holy shit," I muttered, climbing into the car as Arran yanked open the passenger's door in front of me and shoved mine closed.

"Damn right, *holy shit*," the Wolf growled, and closed his door before turning to the male behind the wheel. "Get us the hell out of here, brother."

The Unseelie shoved the four-wheel drive into gear as bright sparks detonated behind us in the night with a *kaboom!*

"Chaos," Ruin murmured in a low growl. "Sometimes that's all it takes."

That green glow in my chest pulsed with the word. I felt that darkness, that seething, wretched *thing.* Chaos, Ruin called it. *But not chaos like I knew it.* This was a force, a kind of *magic.* A darkness I now felt in myself lingered in that abandoned concrete shell behind us. I looked through the window to the empty buildings behind us. "She was real."

Movement came from the driver's seat. I turned and met the Unseelie's gaze.

"What did you say?" Ruin asked before he glance right to the cop cars and rolled the Explorer over the gutter and onto the asphalt.

White sparks arced and exploded from the abandoned building next to the Hunting Ground. I watched as cops and agents ran for their lives. Still that urgency claimed me, forcing me to speak. "In that abandoned building back there, there was a woman, I heard her calling for help."

The dark Fae met my gaze in the rear-view mirror. "There's no one back there, Carina. Must've been the wind."

It was the same response Shrike had given me. A *bullshit* response, like the ones kept for mortals...only this mortal was learning to read between the lines. *Keep your head down and shut the fuck up. Listen and watch like your life depends on it...because it fucking does.*

I did just that, holding my tongue as the tires grabbed on the asphalt and the engine roared, tearing us away into the dark. In my head, all I could see was the savaged belly of Murphy and the claw marks left behind.

I lifted my gaze to the back of Arran's head. He'd been with me the entire time...*but Phantom wasn't...was he?* The sinister words lingered as I pressed my spine into the soft leather and watched the outside turn from buildings to trees. I felt numb, *disconnected.* Like tonight had been one long bad dream and I was going to wake up.

*Any second now...*

*Anyyy second...*

But I didn't wake, instead I sat there listening to the snarl of the engine and the unnatural quiet inside the car. There was no radio, no music, not even any conversation, just silence. Cold, unwelcoming silence. "Where are we going?"

"Safe house," Ruin answered, leaving even more silence in his wake.

*Safe house.* Nice. Like I was a damn criminal on the run.

I hunted people like me. I coordinated, attacked, brought them to justice. How the hell can I bring myself to justice? Phantom didn't kill Murphy. I refused to believe he had, and neither had any of the others. I'd know it if they had. Blood splatter on their clothes, to start with. *Unless they'd shifted...*

No, I refused to believe that. You couldn't fake that look of surprise on Phantom's face...

And he *had been* surprised.

It had to be another Wolf.

*The midnight-colored one from the farmhouse.* The more I thought of it, the more the memory took hold. He wasn't like the others, wasn't careful or kind. A rival. Maybe. I breathed deep and lifted my hand to the throb in my chest. It was the only throb I felt now. No more pain, no more agony.

I touched the lump on the back of my head, a remnant from the goddamn tire iron Murphy had hit me with. Even the swelling had gone now. There was no tenderness, not even a twinge in my side, only the deep green Unseelie glow that seethed in my chest. Movement came in the rear-view mirror as the Unseelie met my gaze.

He knew about the magic inside me. *They all knew.* Cold, pitch black eyes held mine before I broke the stare and looked away. I stared out the window as we left Crown City behind. We were headed to the desert foothills of the Hidden Mountains, a place notorious for people to disappear into. That was just what we wanted, wasn't it?

The Explorer climbed, winding higher and higher until we started a slow descent, but before we could hit the bottom, the Unseelie slowed the four-wheel drive and eased onto the shale shoulder of the road. Only it wasn't any shoulder, it was a track.

Deep ruts and washed out edges. I tried not to look into the drop below as our headlights carved along the side of the mountain and bled into the night. Gravel pinged as the tires slipped and caught, kicking rocks onto the underbody of the vehicle. Still we kept on going, carving our way into the night, following the thin track that cut through the brush and the bramble. The further we kept going, the more I started to worry…until the glint of soft yellow lights shone from the side of a mountain.

We headed for those lights. The road widened until I saw they came not from a house, but hollowed out caverns. "What the fuck is this place?" I muttered as the Fae pulled the four-wheel drive around and killed the engine. He glanced over his shoulder at me before I answered myself. "Yeah, I get it. The damn safe house."

Movement came from the weak yellow glow. A powerful physique was a blur of darkness, striding toward me. My heart knew who it was before it registered on my brain. I yanked the handle, shoved open the door, and all but spilled out of the vehicle, running toward the Alpha.

"Carina," Phantom growled, opening his arms wide.

I slammed into him, my chest thudding against his, my head pressed against the thunder of his heart as I wrapped my arms around him, taking in the feel of his body. "Jesus, thank God. Thank fucking God."

"Are you hurt?" Those calloused fingers slid down my back and over my body, searching everywhere he could.

"No." I shook my head against him. "I'm not hurt."

His hard exhale scattered my hair before he gently gripped my arms and pulled away. In the bright headlights of the four-wheel drive, his eyes shone silver. "I swear to you I didn't do that."

I closed my eyes for a second, rocked by the desperation inside me. I knew he didn't...I just *knew*. But to hear him say the words...was *everything*. "I know you didn't."

"Wolf." Ruin acknowledged the Alpha. "I'll organize a drop-off sometime tomorrow, after the dust settles. You going to be alright out here without a ride until then?"

Phantom gave a nod, gently pulling me forward as he shook the Fae's hand. "Yeah, we're good."

"Stay safe, brother," Ruin muttered, glancing at me before he dropped the Alpha's grip and stepped away.

I didn't like the way he looked at me. Didn't like the way those careful eyes seemed to say a lot more than his damn mouth did. Like he blamed me. Like he *despised me.* My kind. My blood. My hunger...like it was so very different from his own.

3

Movement came from every side as the Unseelie climbed into the Explorer and drove away. Tension coiled like a serpent, slithering along my spine in the fading headlights…and left me in the dark.

A low growl rippled from my right. Vitold slunk forward on one side of me, and Church on the other. But their Alpha never moved, just watched as the pack surrounded me, watching, scenting the air.

"Phantom." I glanced from Vitold to Church. "What's going on?"

A growl came from one of them, not Arran, nor the Russian. Church approached cautiously, silver eyes glinting as he came from the side.

But it wasn't a warning…it was *fear*. Vitold licked his lips. "Fae. We can smell Fae all over you, and fear."

"We got separated," Arran explained as Church stopped behind me and gripped my shoulders. "Ended up in the dark city."

There was a flared of anger in Phantom's gaze, his top lip curled and an unmerciful sound slipped free as the Alpha jerked that savage gaze from Arran to me. Dark eyes glinted as he searched mine.

Vitold pressed his face to my hair and breathed in deep. No matter how much I tried, I wasn't used to that…all the touching and the *smelling.* My body shivered as Vitold stepped closer, his gaze trailing down my body. "The dark city, not a place for someone like you to be in, Carina."

I swallowed hard. "I'm starting to get that feeling."

"You're here now," Vitold continued. "I heard you cry out as we ran, thought you caught a bullet."

He licked his lips, eyes drifting down to that low throb in my chest. I knew what this was now, knew the desperation that rode them to breaking point. "No bullet," I murmured.

"No blood," Church sighed as he slid his hands down my shoulders and then along my back.

I closed my eyes to the feel of them as Vitold brushed the back of his finger along my cheek. "Thought we were going to lose you," he growled and that finger drifted down to capture the point of my chin and tilt upwards. "Fucking mortals and their guns."

"But you didn't, did you?" The words trembled as the night turned cold against my skin.

"Not this time," Phantom growled.

I opened my eyes and stared down my nose at Vitold and Phantom behind him. "Not any time."

"Can't take that chance," Vitold growled. "Not with men who want to hurt you…or the fucking FBI."

I shivered as the air turned bitter and cold. I wasn't sure if it was from the truth or the night, either way I felt exposed now…*threatened* more than I'd ever felt before. But not from the Wolves…*never from the Wolves.*

They were the only ones I could trust. *They'd come for me.* I inhaled as the words rose. They'd come for me, protected me…*cared for me.* Vitold lowered his hands to my hips and yanked me against him. "You're safe now." He slid his hands along my back. "You're with us."

I needed this…their warmth, their touch. I exhaled hard and slow, letting the tension shudder through my body and finally ease. *Safe.* I hadn't felt safe in a very long time, certainly not this night.

"Come inside," Phantom urged. "It's warmer."

Vitold's hand slipped into mine and tugged me forward. He cut Arran a glare before following Phantom and Church. He was pissed off at Arran, making sure the Wolf fell behind us as we strode toward the hollow of a large cavern. I wanted to pull away from Vitold, wanted to glare back at him like he glared at Arran. It wasn't his fault we'd gotten separated…it was mine.

"Home sweet home." Phantom strode through the opening and moved deeper into the cave.

I inhaled the dank smell of cold earth and looked around. It was a house alright, sofas, a makeshift kitchen, even thick rugs on the compacted dirt floor. My gaze drifted to further inside the mountain, where I was guessing the bathroom and sleeping arrangements were. Very…*outdoorsy.*

"We need to figure out what the fuck happened." Phantom paced back and forth. "That bastard was alive when we left him."

Silence descended, smothering and heavy, like a weight over all of us.

The image of Murphy's body filled my mind, blackened skin, singed hair, his stomach ripped open in a savage attack. He was alive when I last saw him, screaming and raging, desperate to hurt me, taunting me with images of my father and my uncle as he lay dying in some kind of warehouse. Images that'd exonerate my father and finally expose Ruth Costello for who she really was. Images I'd been hunting for years. It was the reason I'd joined the FBI, the reason I'd followed my father into a life of truth and justice. Now my only hope for that justice was gone…along with the Wolves' nightclub in the middle of the city.

"I need a beer," Arran muttered finally, and headed toward the kitchen. "Anyone else?"

"God, yes." I swallowed a shudder. "Or something stronger, if you have it."

"We own a damn *bar*," Vitold snarled, turning to the shelves against the wall and yanking down a dust-coated bottle of Scotch. "We have a stockpile of *'something stronger'*."

"What is this place, anyway?" I asked as I looked around.

"Safe house," Vitold answered as he cracked the seal and opened the bottle.

"I got that much already."

"No," Phantom corrected. "That's what we call it, Safe House. No one can get here but for two roads you saw coming in, and you know they're not for the faint of heart. One track in, and another leading out. The open walls let the wind in and up this high, we can smell another Wolf coming for miles." Phantom turned and pierced me with that formidable stare. "You're safe here, Carina. We'll make sure of it."

I took the bottle from Vitold and raised it to my lips. *Safe.* Safe and far away from everything I knew, I swallowed, coughed, and choked, taking in gulps of air. Silver eyes shone in my mind as I swallowed. Safe…

"So, since we didn't kill that piece of shit, then *who* the hell did?" Church strode toward me and reached out, grasping the bottle and taking a deep swallow.

"The other Wolf." The words slipped free before I knew. "It has to be."

Phantom jerked his gaze toward me. "What *other Wolf?*"

I tried to put myself back at that farmhouse, tried to remember the terror pumping in my veins and the agony roaring through my head. Sparks collided in my eyes. My breaths deepened and that hunger burned as the memory came flooding back. "There was a Wolf at the farmhouse when I ran. At first, I thought it was you…"

"Describe it," Phantom ordered as he stepped closer.

Anger rippled off him in waves as he directed that focus to me. I fought the tremor in my voice and met his gaze. "Black, big, with yellow eyes that glinted silver. That's all I remember."

His lips curled, teeth bared. A spark of something terrifying glinted in his eyes.

I was reminded of how fragile my existence truly was.

"It's him." The Alpha ripped his gaze from mine and turned to Church. "It has to be."

But the blond Wolf was more careful. "We don't know that for sure."

"I *fucking know it*," Phantom insisted, and turned to pace. "It *has* to be. Who else would come here? Who else would know to come after *her?*"

One glance my way, and the Alpha stilled. "Unless it was a setup. Murphy. Harlan. It was too easy, too *neat.*"

I flinched at the words. "You think it was one of—" *us*…the word almost slipped out, "the FBI?"

"I wouldn't put it past them." Church glared at me.

I slowly shook my head. "They wouldn't do something like that."

"Wake up and smell the hate, Carina," Vitold barked. "You think we hide on our side of the river because we like it? Your kind have wanted us gone for eternity. They'd be happy if we were out here in the mountains and the trees, hidden from their precious sight for good. Don't underestimate the mortals' hate for what they don't understand, even if they do like to pretend otherwise."

The way he said it made me stiffen. Anger blazed for a second in the Wolf's eyes before Vitold exhaled hard and took a step toward me, softening his tone. "Look, I'm sorry, I forget you're…"

"What?" The word was hollow, like *I* felt hollow. "I'm what?"

"*Not* like *them*," Phantom growled. "At all. You have purpose, a little disillusioned, but you can still be saved."

"Saved." I forced the word and chuckled. "I'm so fucking far from being saved, it's a wonder I'm not finding my own silver eyes glinting in the mirror."

"And that," Phantom took a step closer, his dark eyes blazing, "is exactly why you're still here."

Still here. Still with them. Still shunned by my own family… and my own bureau.

Because I was more like them?

A cold kind of clarity cut me to the bone. The thought hadn't rocked me like it should. Alone. Abandoned…and now separated from the rest of the mortal part of the city. Phantom's phone gave a *beep* and the screen brightened.

He turned away and pulled the cell from his pocket. "Path." Then there was silence while he listened. "Come again?" he growled, and the hair rose on the nape of my neck. "False lead. So you left us for nothing? Sure, yeah, I get you. Call me if you hear anything."

Every gaze gravitated his way as Phantom let out an unmerciful snarl and hung up the phone. He just stood there, staring out into the night, until he finally turned toward us. "First they're called away on some kind of urgent mission, then Wry turns up with his damn throat ripped out. It's Finis. It has to be."

I never said a word, just watched Phantom shift into something more savage…unlike anything I'd ever seen before. Not a beast—his dark eyes glinted with rage—*an Alpha.*

"If he wants a war," Phantom promised, "then it's war he'll get."

Goosebumps raced along my arms as the energy turned predatory.

"We patrol the boundary," Church jerked his gaze to the

others, snapping into command. "Every fucking inch is to be covered." He glanced my way. "No one's getting in without our knowing."

"I'll go first." Vitold stepped forward, staring at me.

"Then me," Arran nodded to the others.

"I'll be out there." Phantom glared at Arran and worked the tension in his neck. "I need to hunt, to kill, need to damn well think."

A chill raced along my spine. Think. That's all we were going to do out here. Think and panic and wait…Vitold took a gulp of the Scotch and handed the bottle back to me. "You and me, brother. You and me."

He turned and headed for the open cavern walls with that sleek, powerful stride, until he hit the opening and lunged, disappearing into the night.

I turned away from the sight and tried to slow the thunder in my chest.

Phantom was gone in an instant, head down, fists clenched, seething hatred until he was gone as well, leaving the three of us. Church glanced from me to Arran and something unspoken passed between them before the second-in-command left, making his way deeper into the cavern, his heavy footsteps fading.

"Wry, the Wolf who was attacked at the bar, is he going to survive?" I took a step toward Arran, carrying the bottle with me.

"Survive?" His eyes sparked with fury as he stared at me. "If you call being mute for the rest of your life surviving."

*Mute*…the thought hit me hard as I thought about Walker's sister, Ebony. "It's not a life sentence."

"It is if you're a Wolf," Arran snapped, then winced. He grabbed my hips with strong hands and dragged me hard against his body. "Imagine waiting your entire young life for the moment you howled. To us, it's more than just speaking. It's the moon in our eyes and the dirt under our paws." He took a step closer and lifted his hand, placing his palm over my heart. "It's this...*thud...thud...thud.*" The throb of my heart grew stronger with the warmth of his hand.

I stared into his eyes. They were so different from me, so very different. "Tell me what I can do."

His strong hand at the small of my back pinned me in place as he rubbed his cheek against mine, his breath warm against my neck. "Stay here," he murmured. "Don't go outside, don't go anywhere. Not until we know what we're dealing with. It's going to be dangerous for you out here. We all become a little more..." he pulled away, "*uncivilized.*"

*Uncivilized.* The cold air moved in with the word, and danced across my skin. What did that even mean?

"There's plenty of water and canned food...and alcohol." Arran lowered his hands and stepped away before jerking his head deeper further along the cavern. "The bedroom's back there and a shower. You'll need to use our clothes. When it's safe, we'll go back for your things. Until then, stay inside and if anything happens, just yell, there's going to be one of us close to you at all times."

A shudder coursed through me. It was the cold, I told myself. The chilling wind that carved through the open walls of this place. Arran stepped closer and wrapped his arms around me. "It's going to be alright, just wait and see. We'll protect you here. We'll keep you safe."

A howl tore from somewhere in the night. Arran jerked his head toward the sound, nostrils flaring, senses on fire as his body tensed. "Eat," he urged, his voice more guttural now. "Try to sleep and rest. Tomorrow we'll make a plan. Tomorrow we'll figure everything out."

He dropped his arms from around my body and took a step backwards before he turned.

"Arran."

He glanced over his shoulder.

"What is it about the Fae that's so terrifying?"

There was a twitch at the corner of his mouth, his half-hearted attempt at a smile. "They're unknowable, unfathomable…*volatile chaos* at its most brutal best. You can never fully trust them, Carina. Because you will *never* truly know them."

He turned his focus to the shimmering full moon and midnight forest all around us. "Stay inside," he repeated his warning. "Eat, sleep. Try not to be scared of us."

He was gone in an instant, taking long strides before he disappeared in the same spot Vitold had, lunging into the night…and leaving me alone.

"Try not to be scared?" I flinched as another howl rocked the night. "Easier said than done."

*Volatile chaos.* I swallowed the words and looked down at the throb in my chest. Darkness swelled inside me, a different kind of darkness now. One that had known the Unseelie as he strode from the darkness in that desolate place. One that I felt changing even as I stood here.

I lifted my gaze and looked around the cavern, to the night filled with terror.

A night that should've been the start of a new path.

What was I going to do now?

"The only thing I can do," I muttered to myself. "Survive… and find the fucker who did this."

4

Strands of hair whipped my face from the blasting wind. I shuddered from the cold and wrapped my arms around my body, staring at the spot where Arran had disappeared, until I forced myself to move.

My belly let out a grumble. The gnawing ache took hold with taloned claws until I ground my teeth hard. I couldn't stomach the thought of food, not after everything that had happened tonight. Instead, I lifted the bottle to my lips and swallowed, letting the burn of that amber liquid slide all the way into the pit of my stomach as flashbacks of the last twenty-four hours returned.

*What the fuck just happened?*

Cold air chased the heat of the Scotch as I inhaled hard.

I tried to piece it all together, how we'd started at one place...and ended at another.

It was all *my stupid, fucking fault.* I pressed the bottle's rim to my lips again and swallowed. "Why the fuck did you have to go to that farmhouse, Chase? *Why?*"

The more I drank, the less it all made sense. Trembling fingers rose and brushed stray strands of hair from the corner of my mouth. Shards of glass tumbled free. Glass from the shattered window of the car. My throat tightened as the memory returned.

The nightclub.

Their home.

Their safety.

"They lost everything." For what? "Me, dipshit. They threw it all away for me."

A moan ripped free as the icy wind howled right through the cavern. The bitter stench of ozone followed. A storm was coming, bearing down on me hard and fast. I lifted the bottle and drank. I couldn't escape this storm. Couldn't bargain and plead my way out of it.

Because it wasn't just me now, was it?

*Now I was part of a pack.*

Orange lights from the lanterns splashed against the jagged edges of the rock walls. I took the Scotch and followed the glow into a darker part of the cavern. Shadows waited for me there, crouching in corners and clinging to the walls. The wind didn't howl as loud here. There were no openings in these walls that led outside.

My hand trembling as I took a swallow and looked around. "Not the Five Seasons," my words slurred. "But I've stayed in worse. Hell, I lived in worse."

In an instant, it all came rushing back. The hate. The rage. The wasted years hunting down a family for revenge, only for my father to throw it all back in my face. *You brought that thing to my home? You brought that filthy fucking dog to MY house?"*

I lifted the bottle and swallowed once more. That line of loyalty inside me was shifting, blowing away grain by grain. Maybe it'd been just sand all along? Maybe I'd built my entire fucking world on sand…and now it was crumbling, falling into the water, only to disappear.

The faint trickling of water came from the far end of the

space. I grabbed the nearest lantern and lifted it high, illuminating the shine of the water as it cascaded down the rock wall and fell, splashing the stone floor.

An old cupboard rested against the wall. I watched my step and moved closer, until I curled my fingers around the handle and yanked. There were piles of clothes, neatly folded. A few heavy jackets and jeans, some sweats and t-shirts, all separated into sections.

I knew whose they were without looking. Phantom's on top, Church's underneath, Vitold's and Arran's. *You'll need to use our clothes.* Wear their clothes, like I wore their *scents.*

My breath caught as the memory of their hands returned, running down my spine, a face pressed to my hair, a cheek pressed to mine, rubbing me...more like rubbing them *on me.* Like a marking, a warning to any other Wolf. I swallowed hard and lowered the lantern, taking another gulp of the Scotch before I set it down. "Wear their clothes. I can do that, if that's what it takes."

One glance around the darkened space and I turned back toward the tiny waterfall. Hot shower, my ass. Those Wolves ran like a damn furnace, leaving the rest of us pathetic mortal creatures to fucking freeze. I hurried to step on the backs of my heels and yank my boots off. My shirt was covered with blood splatters, my pants filthy and torn from fighting Murphy.

*Murphy.*

I yanked my shirt over my head and stumbled, then righted myself before I reached around and unhooked my bra. My nipples hardened instantly in the icy air. I shoved my pants and panties down all together, grabbed a towel and soap, and hurried over to the water.

The small stream of water was brutal. Cold splashed onto my arms as I shivered and stepped into the waterfall. I hurried, throwing soap and water across my stomach and torso and down my legs as my teeth chattered and gnashed until I could take no more. I washed my face, grabbed the soap, and stepped free. "G-god-d-damn." My feet slipped on the wet rock floor, pitching me forward. I windmilled my arms, catching the fall at the last second, and stumbled toward the cupboard.

I snatched the towel and hurried to dry, then yanked on everything I could, not caring about whose clothes they were, socks, sweats, t-shirts, and jackets, but still I shivered and shook. There wasn't a lick of warmth in this place. Cold, stony. *Alone.* "I'm ali-ive, if that c-counts."

I grabbed the lantern and pushed deeper, heading for the darkened room with the faint glow. The moment I stepped through the doorway, the chill cut to the bone. "Jesus, is there no damn fireplace here?"

I waited for an answer, but there was none, just a faint howl from somewhere far away...I turned my head at the sound. *Arran,* his name was a whisper inside my head, coming from a place deeper than thoughts and emotions—coming from a *knowing.*

*Throb.*

That ache in my chest spread out, and I looked down through the half-closed zipper of the thick, furlined jacket as the deep green glow brightened. "Just fucking great. You couldn't be something useful like warmth, or ass-kicking strength, you had to give me some primitive energy like goddamn lust."

The weak light from the lantern spilled over a makeshift bed. *Only one makeshift bed,* even if it was massive. "You've *got to be kidding.*"

Thick piles of furs were stacked high at the foot of the bed. My stomach gave another grumble as I stumbled forward and yanked what I could onto the bed, dislodging a thick layer of dust as I did. The musty scent made me sneeze. I heaved more furs across the hard base, then collapsed on top of them, sliding myself deep under the rest of the heavy furs, and lay there, shivering.

Thunder rolled from somewhere outside. The faint grumble grew louder, followed by the flicker of white light through the opening in the adjoining room. I curled my knees higher against my chest and nestled my body into the furs, fighting the tremors.

*Murphy.*

*Dead.*

*Eyes open.*

*Belly slashed.*

*If not Phantom, then who?*

That Wolf returned to my mind's eye, his deep yellow eyes and midnight fur. Not a friend, that much I knew. *Finis.* The name rolled through my head as I watched the flicker of lightning grow bolder in the entrance to the cave. The images of my father. I kept coming back to that. Did it have something to do with how Murphy was killed, or was it just by chance?

*Nothing was ever by chance.* Being an agent had taught me that. It hadn't been chance when I was at that warehouse hunting Ruth Costello. It hadn't been chance that Phantom saved me from the Unseelie and brought me to the pack.

*Then it wasn't by chance that this shit was pushed into my chest, either.* I winced at the thought as the patter of rain started, the sound so faint I missed it at first, until the drops became heavier and the snarl of thunder echoed through the mountain like a warning of its own.

I shivered under the furs, cornered by my own racing mind. *What the hell happened? How did I get here*—how did I find myself in this cavern in the middle of nowhere, *with Wolves?*

Out of control. That's how I was spiraling. Falling faster and harder, tearing out of the light and into the dark. Finding myself further away from everything I knew. Everything I was in control of, my job, my life…as pathetic as it was. I'd had structure, I'd had rules.

Rules like they stayed on their side of the river, and we stayed on ours. *Wake up and smell the hate, Carina.* Vitold's words resurfaced. *You think we hide on our side of the river because we like it? Your kind have wanted us gone for eternity. They'd be happy if we were out here in the mountains and the trees, hidden from their precious sight for good. Don't underestimate the mortals' hate for what they don't understand, even if they do like to pretend otherwise.*

Did I pretend? Had I been pretending all this time? Or had I refused to see, refused to acknowledge what was under my nose all that time? My stomach sank with the thought. My heartbeat thrummed with the thunder as pain filled me.

Lightning flashed neon white in the cavern, the brilliance spilling through the room all around me, followed by a deafening *crack right* overhead. I jumped at the sound, clawed the furs closer, and lifted my head as darkness spilled over the bed. A shadow filled the doorway. Sleek, *savage.* Midnight fur bristled over the monstrous beast.

I kicked the furs aside and shoved my body upwards to sit. *The beast was back…*IT WAS BACK!

*"PHANTOM!"* I screamed, but the sound was swallowed by a boom of thunder.

Lips curled, white teeth glinted as the Wolf took a step inside. I jerked my gaze toward the room that led outside. *"Phantom! Arran!"* Their names burned along my throat.

Lightning flashed once more, filling the cavern as the beast slunk closer. I jerked my gaze around, searching for a weapon, but finding nothing except the heavy furs on the bed as a heady waft of blood punctured the storm's bitter stench of ozone. "No." I shoved upwards, climbing to my knees. *"No!"*

The Wolf came silently closer, its head lowered and its dark amber eyes blinked as it released something from its mouth that hit the stone floor with a *splat.*

Lightning flickered once more as the beast lifted its head to watch me. Amber eyes glinted like jewels, the color so deep and pure, a memory tore free. *I licked it, so it's mine...*

My heart pounded. Panic and fear were a Molotov cocktail in my blood. I drew in hard breaths and stilled. The beast...the *Wolf.* I *knew* this Wolf, knew this man, knew the depths of those eyes...knew that intensity. "Phantom?"

Thick obsidian fur shimmered in the glow of the lightning as the Alpha shook his body, casting droplets of water to fly around the room. His white fangs were stained with blood, but his shimmering black lips never curled, never gave even a hint of aggression. I looked down at the small shadow on the floor between his paws.

Speckled brown fur and unseeing dark eyes were illuminated in the fading glow of the storm, and the blood. I saw the blood, *everywhere.*

*Crunch. Snap.*

The Wolf buckled to the floor. He whimpered and twitched, his muscles rippling and his body shaking as bones snapped and morphed into something else. Something longer, *something more human.* Sleek midnight fur glistened and sank under pale flesh as the Alpha shifted in front of me. His chest rose, then collapsed with a savage breath, and the growl that followed stood the hairs on the back of my neck.

"Don't..." he snarled, and jerked his head upwards. He was still animal in his eyes, more beast than anything else as desperation raged in his words. "*...be scared of me.*"

I shoved from the bed, tearing myself out from under the furs until my feet smacked the floor. His chest still rose and fell, his ribs expanding with each savage draw of air. "You terrified the shit out of me."

A twitch came at the corner of his mouth as those long, bloodstained canines withdrew into his gums. Neon white light flickered again and the rain still beat down, muffling the rush of his breaths as he slowly rose from the floor and straightened.

His skin glistened. Every muscle in his body flexed and shivered. His hands were at his sides, fingers curled, the tips bloody. I licked my dry lips and forced myself to remember he'd never hurt me. *Not intentionally.* "You al—"

"You went there..." he started as he took a step closer, his eyes seizing mine like a rabbit in a snare. "To the dark city."

I swallowed hard at the guttural tone. He hadn't come to me when I'd stepped out of the Explorer, not even when the others had touched and scented me. He'd just watched me, *like I was tainted.*

"Shouldn't have gone there," he repeated as he stepped closer, his gaze sinking to the glow in my chest. *Throb...throb... throb.* The ache bloomed like a disease, one that was under his command with just a goddamn look. "They could've hurt you, could've *used* you."

Images came to life inside my head, of all the ways the Fae *used* women like me. I suppressed a shudder and swallowed. "But they didn't."

Anger flared in his eyes, brighter than the electric sky. *"This time,"* he warned, those long legs slowly eating the distance between us.

I didn't move, didn't twitch, didn't even breathe. Goosebumps raced along my skin.

"Are you scared of me, Carina?"

I didn't trust myself to answer as he reached my side.

"Rethinking your choices?"

I closed my eyes, my pulse spiking as he stopped behind me and murmured against my ear. "Maybe you're thinking about the Unseelie?"

I flinched, that heat of desire burning hot. "No."

"Really? It is what you want, isn't it? Power. *Corruption.* Don't you want to be corrupted, Carina?"

The throbbing pain in my chest dulled with his words. He was scaring me now. Dredging something deeper from inside me. Something colder...something *deeper*. Something *black*. "By them? No. By you? I thought that's what we were doing..."

The guttural chuckle made me tremble. "Take off your clothes."

I stiffened at the command. That gnawing feeling smothered the ache in my chest. My breaths sped as fear swept over me. *No,* the word raced through my mind as I fought to push that darker feeling away.

"I'm not asking twice, Carina...and I'm in no mood to play your games. You come to me smelling of another male outside the pack, and I'm going to mark *every* goddamn inch of you, over...*and over again.*"

Heat bloomed between my thighs. In an instant, we were back there in the heat and the lust...*and the hunt.* My fingers trembled as I peeled the jacket from my body. "It's freezing in here."

"By the time I'm done with you, you'll be on fire."

The jacket hit the floor with a *thud.* The pullover was next, my hands shaking so bad I could barely get it over my head. Cool air invaded, sliding through the arms of the cotton t-shirt before I lowered my arms and dropped the garment.

"Pants," Phantom urged. "I'm tired of waiting."

He never touched me, never grazed my skin with the backs of those bloodied knuckles or those sinful lips. Just stood behind me barking orders like I was his to command. I closed my eyes as a wave of heat slammed into me.

*You are,* Phantom growled inside my head. *And don't you ever forget it.*

I clenched my jaw as that battleground raged inside me, that darkness...and the Unseelie desire. Both felt the same...*but were very, very different.* A seething undercurrent raged through me, a dangerous slippery slope into the bowels of destruction. Still it touched me, *stroked me,* played with me. *You need this...*

My lips curled, as my teeth bared. Socks were next as we glared at each other. I lifted my foot and yanked, sending the garments flying behind me. I saw myself in his gaze, fierce and savage, as I shoved the sweat pants to the floor and stepped out of them.

"Are you finished?" One brow rose as he growled.

"I'm naked, aren't I?" I tried to keep that sharpened edge from my tone.

Those blazing amber eyes sank lower, like he didn't hear the change in me at all. My body betrayed me, puckering and trembling, desperate for more than a glance. I clenched my fists as that ache spilled through my chest, burning like a goddamn scald.

*Fuck him,* that animal urged. *Ride him. Corrupt him. Claim him. CLAIM THEM ALL.*

I flinched, and my heart slammed against my ribs as he lifted his hand and cupped the back of my neck. His nostrils flared. A warning growl followed, grating like gravel on my skin before the rumble in his chest quieted. He lifted his gaze to look somewhere behind me and kept that focus, dragging me closer by the strength of his hand.

*Claim them...*like a beast born to be marked.

His lips claimed mine in a savage crush. I whimpered as my body yielded in an instant, and my hands lifted to the corded muscles of his arms, touching, tasting. That ravenous hunger burning in my chest took hold. He didn't know what he was doing, didn't realize this was something *other than me.*

"No," I whispered to that power watching, as Phantom froze.

"No?" the Alpha growled, his dark eyes glinting with a flicker of cruelty. "Are we back there so soon, Carina? Your pretty little mortal conscience putting up one last fight?"

But it wasn't the fight he assumed.

No, this was a battle of beasts.

Unseelie beasts inside me.

I stared into his gaze as that animal inside me shifted under my skin. His hand slipped from the back of my neck, then both hands grabbed me around the waist and lifted.

There were no words between us. Nothing that couldn't be said by his hand against my ass as he moved me to the bed. Timber groaned with our weight, the soft fur tickling my back as I sank into the thick pile.

He rose above me, his dark eyes glittering in the light, his waist trapped by the strength of my legs as he stretched my arms above my head, pulling my body taut. A wicked sound rumbled in my chest, venomous and cruel. I was animal in that moment. Wicked and vile, debased and inhuman.

I flinched with that consuming feeling, and for a moment...I was blinded by clarity.

*Fight,* part of me urged. *Fight this...thing.*

But there was another part of me that didn't want to. And it was that part which rose like the dark of night. Unfathomable. *Undeniable. Inhuman.*

Movement came from the shadows in the room. I *felt* him more than saw him. "Church?" I turned my head. Phantom gently gripped my chin and turned my focus back to him. Fear and excitement raced through my body as the Alpha lowered his head, taking my nipple into his mouth.

The stench of blood lingered on his fingers, mingling with the heady smell of the rain that beat down outside. I closed my eyes with the sensation of his lips as he claimed each breast and licked that aching throb in my chest. I didn't want to fight this...*calling.* I didn't want to fight it at all.

"Growl for me, Carina," Phantom commanded as his strong, undeniable hands pushed against the insides of my knees, opening my legs wider. "Show me some goddamn teeth."

*You want this,* that animal murmured in my head. An animal

that sounded a lot like me. *Stop fighting, Chase...you don't have to fight anymore.*

I opened my eyes and trembled under his stare as he looked down, finding my slit bare for him. That aching throb in my chest seemed to slip, beating slower now and out of time with my heart. Then Phantom stilled in an instant, his nostrils flaring as his brow furrowed, and he jerked his gaze to mine. "What are you doing?"

*Malevolence* smiled, and I smiled along with it.

A growl slipped from the corner of the room as Church came closer.

"Carina?" Phantom warned, staring down at me. "What are you doing?"

"What you told me to do, Alpha," my voice answered, my smile even wider. *"Showing a little teeth."*

That pulsing emerald green darkened to almost black. I'd wanted some kind of power I could use, some energy I could use for control. But what spilled through my mind was more violent than I could control. Energy danced across my skin as I lifted my gaze to the doorway. Arran and Vitold stood there, both men dripping water.

Still, that Unseelie power rippled outwards. Anger cut through the air. But it was more than the cold, cutting rage. It was malignant. It was *terrifying.* "I can't," I cried, and clenched my fist. "I can't stop it."

"Control the energy," Phantom urged above me. "Wield it. Use it as a weapon."

Arran and Vitold stalked closer, their silver eyes glinting in the darkness as both Wolves focused on me.

I delved into that hunger and felt it respond.

It knew me. Knew that ache that spilled from the middle of my chest.

*Both brutal and vengeful now. A weapon...*one that rose like a tsunami and swallowed me whole.

5

---

Arran turned on Vitold in an instant. White fangs shone as he bared his teeth and grabbed the Russian Wolf's shirt, dragging him closer.

Rage lashed the air, dark and dangerous, with a menacing growl. The resounding throb sent tremors through my chest to spill out into the room.

"Carina," Phantom growled as silver shone in his eyes. "You have to control this."

I closed my eyes and focused on that violence rippling inside me. Power that was changing, morphing into something bestial, something wild and untamed...something that could *never* be tamed.

*Control it?*

*Chaos.* Ruin's words surfaced. *Sometimes, that's all it takes.*

And chaos is what this was. Violence and hunger. Like a dark, beastly predator unfurling in my chest. Lust and rage, both emotions forcing me to release my legs from around Phantom's waist.

"Control it, Alpha?" my voice was predatory as I pushed up from the bed. "How about I control *you*, instead?"

Tendons in his neck bunched as one brow rose. He lifted his hand and captured the back of my neck, yanked me close, and growled, "Do you think you can, female?"

The corners of my lips twitched at the defiance. *Can and will, Wolf...*

"Do you trust me?" I asked as I stepped away from the bed, leaving the Alpha to tower over me. It was my turn to stalk them now as I flanked his side, running my fingers over the hard curve of his beautiful bare ass. "You knelt for me once before."

He jerked that savage gaze to mine as I stepped around him, ran my hand over his cock, gripped that hard length in an unmerciful hold, and whispered, "So eager to please."

Hard breaths invaded my parted lips as he searched my gaze.

He saw something inside me. *Something once hidden...but not anymore.*

"You can *never* control Unseelie, remember?" I murmured, and slowly pumped that delicious length, letting it slide along my palm, the head pushing between my finger and thumb. "Sit on the bed," I commanded.

His body trembled, sinking in front of me. I lowered my head, still keeping up that movement of my hand. My teeth grazed the skin on his shoulder. He let out a moan, half filled with desire and half with feral fury. But my teeth weren't made for such savagery, worn and blunt, my canines not nearly as terrifying as theirs.

"This is the real you, Carina," he growled, closing his eyes. "The *woman* I saw in that warehouse. *The part of you that was hiding all this time.*"

*The real me,* the woman's voice whispered inside my head. *Waiting all those years.*

"Do it," Phantom urged, blocking the sound of that voice in my head. "Bite *hard.*"

This was more than pain, more than power. *This* was a

marking, a claiming, like those Unseelie shards in my chest gave way for something more dangerous to surface.

*Mine!*

The word raged as the memory of his own fangs ached on my shoulder. I lifted my head, instinct driving me as I pumped his cock, opened my jaw wide, and *bit*.

Flesh and muscle gave way to the animalistic act. I gripped his neck, holding him in place as I drove my teeth deeper into his flesh. He threw his head backwards and moaned. That sound did things to me.

Wicked things. Vile things. Making me want to sink to my hands and knees and rut like an animal...and we were all animals this night, weren't we? *Unmerciful animals.*

The bitter tang of blood danced at the tip of my tongue as he closed his hands over mine and drove it harder until, with a guttural bark, he came. The scent of salt and sin filled my nose. I pulled away, lifting my hand to slide his cum over my breasts.

"You claimed me, Alpha. *Now I claim you.*" Heavy breaths consumed me as I licked and kissed the wound, before swallowing the metallic taste. The indentations weren't anywhere near deep enough, barely cutting the skin. I lifted my head as Phantom met my gaze and realized in an instant...it didn't matter.

Fang marks, or no fang marks, I knew him now...knew him *intimately.* I knew him *savagely.* Power flowed through me as that dark throb in my chest grew stronger, and I took in the taste of his blood on the back of my tongue.

"Arran," I murmured, and slid my hand from around the Alpha's neck. "Come to me."

I turned to the other Wolves in the room, finding the stare of each of my pack. Church, Vitold...and Arran. *My Arran.*

My bare feet were chilled by the stone floor as the dark-haired bartender came closer, snarling and barbaric, those gorgeous eyes brimming with fire and lust as he strode nearer. "Carina—" he growled.

"Kneel."

His lips curled and his teeth bared. I knew what I was saying...how I was *forcing* him to submit to me. A Wolf... powerful and predatory, one who could tear me apart in an instant. Born with teeth and claws and a belly full of rage, but he wouldn't hurt me...*not even if his life depended on it.*

I knew that now. I saw it in the silver of his eyes.

With careful steps, he came to me without so much as a snarl, and sank to his knees.

A moan tore from Vitold or Church as Arran submitted, the sound stolen by a faint rumble of thunder. I exhaled hard and looked down, watching as he ran his hands over my ass and down the backs of my thighs. One hand stopped while the other fell to the crook of my knee and lifted.

My thighs parted as my leg slid over his shoulder, the Wolf's gaze fixed between my legs.

That menacing hunger raged in my chest, violent and brutal. I wanted to mark him, wanted to take him...*while he took me.*

Phantom rose from the bed behind me as Arran gripped my hips and pulled my body closer. The tip of his tongue drove into my slit, finding that tiny nub as lust took control.

*Let me show you how it could be...with us.*

Phantom's words drifted through my head as he ran the backs of his fingers up my arms.

"You belong to us, Carina," Phantom growled as I speared my fingers through Arran's damp black curls and arched my spine. "To the pack," he finished.

I turned my head, finding the Alpha's gaze, my hand dipping with the movement as Arran moved lower, dragging his talented tongue all the way to my core.

A moan ravaged the back of my throat as Phantom gripped my jaw and kissed me hard. His tongue in my mouth and

Arran's deep in my pussy made me whimper. The tips of thick canines pressed against the tenderest part of me. I wanted to ride that wave, wanted to press his face against me until I came against his tongue. But this was more than sex, more than my own release. This was *belonging.*

My tongue danced across long, terrifying fangs before Phantom broke away.

*The pack.*

*I belonged to the pack...and after tonight, they would belong to me.*

No more running. No more leaving. I fisted Arran's hair, pulled his face from my core, and broke Phantom's kiss to stare down at the Wolf between my legs. "Give me your hand, Wolf."

He obeyed, like I knew he would. His hand rose to mine, his strong fingers unfurled as I pressed his palm to my cheek. *Abandoned.* The bitter tang of my Wolf's pain filled my nose. He'd been rejected by his mate, left with a shattered heart —until now.

Arran swallowed hard, fear shimmering in those perfect eyes. "Carina," he murmured as I tightened my grip and turned my head.

The bite was hard and fast. My teeth sank into the meat of his palm and cut deep. I closed my eyes as that animal hunger roared through me. I released my bite and licked the beads of blood as they rose. "Mine," I growled.

A tortured sound came from the Wolf as my leg slid from his shoulder and he rose, his hand still trapped in mine and his blood on the tip of my tongue. "Mine," I whispered. "I claim you, Arran, as mine."

He gripped the back of my neck and yanked me close. The kiss was hard and savage as pent-up desire spilled free. I wanted him...*craved him.* My body hummed with ferocious desire, but I wasn't done yet...not by a long shot.

I shifted my gaze to the two unclaimed Wolves in the room

and Arran eased his hold, letting me break from his kiss. "Vitold," I called. "Come to me."

The Wolf didn't move, just stood there, watching me with those glinting eyes, filled with violence. I turned to him, letting his gaze drift down my naked body. There was something between me and the Russian, some kind of magnetic pull.

*Everything alright here?* The past surfaced, and with it came the memory of Murphy's cruel, bruising grip around my arm.

It was the first time I'd seen Vitold, as the Wolf strode into the morgue, his gaze moving instantly to my ex-partner as he'd savagely pushed me against the stainless steel morgue drawer.

Vitold had come for me that day. I knew it now, just as I'd subconsciously known it then. A dangerous kind of savagery lay inside this one, unhinged and broken. I'd seen men like him before, seen them on the other side of an interrogation table. He was dangerous. *Very dangerous.* The thought sped my pulse. "Come to me, Wolf."

He moved, with careful, deliberate steps bringing him closer. The curl of his lips. The warning in his eyes. He had a beast in his soul, a terrifying, bestial thing. I held his gaze as he stood in front of me, daring me with his look.

"You want this, female?" he murmured.

I lifted my hand to cup his cheek. "I want this, Wolf," I whispered in answer. "The question is, do you? Will you submit to me, Vitold? Do you want me as I want you?"

Hard breaths blew warm against my face as he slowly nodded.

But something in my gut was strange, tingling and wretched. "Say the words," I demanded. "Say you'll submit to me." *Chaos. Sometimes, that's all it takes,* Ruin's words invaded my mind again. "Say the words…or all this is over."

His eyes glinted like razors, honed razors…

I'd backed this Wolf into a corner, a dangerous corner. Kill or be killed, the law these Wolves lived by. The thready patter of my heart filled my ears. "Say the words."

His lips curled in a chilling smile. "Fuck you, special agent."

"I'm trying to get to that part, Wolf," I whispered, and brushed my thumb across his cheek.

That cruel Unseelie darkness grew colder inside me. *Make him kneel. Fuck that wildness inside him and he will forever belong to us.*

His nostrils flared before his eyes widened. "Female—" he started.

I moved closer, until my breasts pressed against his chest. "I want you, Vitold. I want *all* of you. All that danger, all that rage. Give it to me. Give me your beast."

He froze as that cutting edge in his gaze flickered with fear. I lowered my gaze to his dripping clothes and slowly worked the buttons of his shirt. Silence filled the room. A chilling silence as the Wolf in front of me fought his own battle...

Phantom and Arran waited behind me. Could I have a pack of two? A pang of agony tore through my chest. *No.* The answer was no. I wouldn't allow it. I pushed his shirt from his chest and dropped it to the floor.

His pants were next. My fingers worked the button. Still, he stood there unmoving, those piercing eyes boring into mine, until trembling words spilled free. "I want you."

My fingers stilled as I lifted my gaze to his.

He sucked in one shuddering breath, then slowly sank to his knees, holding my gaze until he hit the floor. Power surged through me at the sight...and that dangerous part inside me smiled. I moved closer, driving my fingers through his hair, and pressed his face against my belly. "And I am yours, Vitold. I am *all* yours."

He tilted his face and lifted his hand, cupping my breast. Warmth danced across my skin as he kissed and nuzzled. Three Wolves...*and they were the easy ones.* I shifted my gaze to Church as Vitold lowered his hand between my legs. Thick, calloused fingers pushed in, sliding all the way inside me.

I rocked my hips as he fucked me with his fingers, my gaze finding the towering blond Adonis standing at the foot of the bed, watching us. But the heat of Vitold's touch took hold, and after Arran's tongue, I was too far gone, unable to hold my own selfish desire at bay.

I tore my gaze to the Wolf in front of me and lashed out, grasping hold of Vitold's wrist. Fire licked between my thighs as he stroked deeper, his thumb dancing around my clit until a shudder tore free.

"Cum for me, Carina," Vitold whispered. "Let me watch while you climax around my fingers."

My hand moved with the movements...*in and out...in and out,* until I was lost in the sensation, swept away in that surge of *need.* Fuck me, he was good...so good—my breath caught, I stopped his hand as I clenched and pulsed, my eyelids fluttering.

"Christ almighty, you're beautiful," Vitold growled, driving me closer to the edge. "I want to burn this image into my mind. You're so eager to cum, aren't you? *So fucking eager."*

*"Oh God."* My breaths raced and my pulse was frantic as I dug my nails into his shoulders and held him against my body.

That animal inside me purred as Vitold slipped his fingers free, my own release slick and shiny over his fingers as he slipped them into his mouth. Aftershocks pulsed in my core at the sight.

"I *will* fuck you again, and again, Carina," he promised, and lifted his hand to me. "And I *will* be merciless."

I wanted that, more than anything. These Wolves made me feel alive. I gripped his fingers, the scent of my desire still on them. I opened my mouth and pressed his wrist between my teeth, my jaw aching as I bore down.

Vitold let out a guttural growl and closed his eyes as that dangerous power spilled from my chest and swept through the room. I felt Vitold...felt them all, like brands on my soul, markings that would forever be part of who I was.

But I wasn't complete...*not yet.* I turned to the darkness and to my unclaimed Wolf, lifting my hand. "Church."

The towering blond's eyes were wide and glassy. Terrified and tortured, he stared at me with so much desperation it hurt to see. He swallowed hard as I took a step closer and lifted my hand. "Come to m—"

"I can't," he growled, and shook his head, taking a step backwards as he looked at Vitold, then to Phantom. "I just can't." Then he spun on his heel and lunged away.

He was gone in an instant, with barely a sound, a shadow tearing through the faint flickering glow of the storm. An ache filled my chest as I stared after him. I'd failed...*failed the pack.*

"Give him time." Phantom spoke from the other side of the bed. "He'll come around."

I stared after the Wolf and wasn't sure if time was the problem. Pain had echoed in the Wolf's eyes. Pain like I'd never seen before. My heart ached at the thought of him out there.

"Phantom's right," Vitold agreed as he rose. "He *will* come to you."

I jerked my gaze to Vitold, then turned to the Alpha, standing there naked on the other side of the bed. "And if he doesn't?"

There was no answer, none Phantom could give me, at least.

"We just have to trust he knows what's good for the pack," Vitold answered, and dragged the back of his knuckles along my arm. "Until then..."

I lifted my arms, letting the Wolf grasp me by the waist and carry me to the pile of furs on the bed. My body was on automatic, hardening and puckering as I knelt on the bed and Vitold lowered his mouth to my breast.

There was no more waiting now, no more aching, just

hunger…consuming, controlling. Sleek muscles flexed as Arran crawled closer and reached for me.

"Mine," I whispered. "I claim you *all* as mine."

But my gaze was drawn to the doorway and the darkness outside as Arran lifted me, curling my legs until I straddled him.

The head of his cock pressed against my entrance before he slowly thrust inside. I closed my eyes and exhaled hard. Jesus Christ, it was like coming home. "Mine." I rode his length, driving it deeper inside me. *"Mine!"*

"Ours," Vitold insisted, and pressed his hand between my shoulders, forcing me down until I kissed Arran. One stroke of his fingers and he rubbed slickness against that hard ring of muscle in my ass. *"All ours."*

I closed my eyes and trembled, rising up on my knees only to slide back down, and with each movement, Vitold pressed his finger against my opening, until he finally pushed inside.

Stars sparkled in Arran's midnight eyes as Vitold pushed in deeper, until I was lost in the burn around my ass and that delicious heat in my core.

Hard breaths came as Arran gripped my hips, driving me down harder. I splayed my palms flat against the furs, my breasts smashed against Arran as I let out a whimper and opened my legs wider. "Just—" I started.

"Fuck her," Phantom growled behind me.

I turned my head, meeting the Alpha's gaze. "That is what you said to me, isn't it, Carina?" Phantom's eyes glinted with desire. *"It's just sex?"*

"No," the word was a rush of breath. "Not anymore."

One corner of the Alpha's lips curled as he watched over my shoulder while Vitold worked saliva onto his fingers and brushed it over the head of his cock. "Fuck her, Wolf." He lifted his gaze to Arran beneath me. "Make her scream with ecstasy."

I closed my eyes with the pressure, my fingers fisting the fur above Arran's head.

"Jesus fucking Christ," Arran growled as my body tightened. Vitold's hand never moved, pressing against my shoulders as he pushed in and slid out, working his way inside my body with smooth, savage hunger until he slid all the way in.

I was filled with them. Claimed by them. Stretched and starving…like I'd never been sated before.

We rutted like animals.

Savage animals.

I was tethered to that feeling, claimed by their hunger…and my own.

"Christ, you're beautiful," Phantom hissed. "Just like this…*always like this.*"

I lowered my head, my hair falling across my face as my breaths came hard and fast, tearing free as Vitold and Arran matched their pace, until I didn't know *who was riding who.*

The pressure between my shoulders eased. Instead, Vitold reached under my arm and grasped my breast, lifting my torso until my spine curled and I stared into Arran's eyes. He was close, his brow furrowed with that steely look of determination.

I slowed the thrusts, making them harder and deeper, driving both Arran and Vitold deeper inside me until that consuming wave of desire teetered in front of me.

"Look at him," Vitold growled in my ear. "Feel both of us claiming your body. Fuck, you feel so good."

The slick slap of our bodies grew louder as Vitold fisted my hair. He was strong…*so unbelievably strong,* bouncing me as I was impaled by the head of his cock. I couldn't stop my body from clenching as I cried out and climaxed.

Arran gave a grunt of release that turned into a long growl. I felt him twitch, since I was stretched to capacity, before warmth followed. His chest rose with massive breaths that matched my own.

Vitold was next, driving harder and deeper as Arran watched us. I arched my back, lifting my hand up and behind to grasp the back of his neck. He spoke to me in Russian, growling and gasping, the words growing strained as he gave one ferocious thrust and moaned.

I collapsed back down against Arran. My chest was on fire, my body humming and spent. Arms wrapped around me, cradling me until I was nestled between them.

Sleep was far away from me, but still I closed my eyes, waiting for my soul to find my body once more. Thick furs were pulled over me as the heat of desire slowly ebbed.

"Sleep, Carina," Phantom directed. "You're ours now, so sleep."

I focused on deep breaths before I finally opened my eyes. But it wasn't the Alpha I sought in the darkness. It was that faint flicker of lightning…and the darkened doorway where I'd last seen Church.

6

---

## PHANTOM

*He's coming...he's coming...PHANTOM, HE'S COMING!*

I jolted awake, her scream ringing in my ears, and for a second, I was trapped there, in the darkness, staring at the abandoned refrigeration container in the middle of nowhere... with the last memory of my sister.

A bead of sweat ran across my brow and down my temple before falling behind my ear. I lifted my hand and swiped the slick from my skin, my pulse thundering in my ears. *Fuck me...this shit never gets any easier.* The slow rhythmic sound of breaths filled the cavern room. Steady breaths...*Carina's breaths.*

It's not happening.

Not again.

*I won't let it.*

*I'd kill her before I let Finis touch her.*

She let out a tiny moan and shifted, turning over to press her ass against my thigh. I turned my head, breathing in the scent of sex and cum, the scents of my pack were all over her. *But not mine.* I licked my lips and rolled onto my side, still haunted by that unshakable ache of desperation.

*Protect her...whatever it takes.*

I lightly dragged my fingers along her bare arm and over the sweet curve of her ass.

Memories of last night slipped in. Savage and haunting, a woman consumed by lust and *something else.* It was that something else that made me still, my fingers stopped at the crest of her ass, that *something else* that made me uneasy.

*Chaos magic.* I knew the touch of Unseelie when I felt it, and she was touched…more than just the Fae shards in her chest, more than what that bastard had done to her in the warehouse. I swallowed as uncertainty reared its ugly head. *What the fuck happened to you, Carina?*

I knew the instant she awoke, knew the change in her breathing and the spike of her pulse. "This is what's going to happen now," I whispered, pushing the doubt aside as she opened her eyes. "First, you're going to ache when you move, then from that ache, you're going to be invaded by memories of what happened last night. You're going to want to feel weird about it, but instead of that, I propose something else."

There was silence, then a husky, "I'm listening."

The corners of my lips twitched. "I propose we don't stop," I suggested, pressing my cock against the crease of her ass and burying my face in her hair. "How about that? We don't ever stop."

I slowly thrust forward, pressing my cock between her thighs, rocking my hips as I curled my arm around and cupped her breast.

"I'm a little sore," she cautioned.

"I'll make you feel good." I rubbed her breasts, rolling her nipples between my finger and thumb. "How about that, special agent?"

Memories pushed in, unwanted memories. Gunshots and shattered glass. Her screams…ones that warped and echoed inside my head. I'd heard too many screams lately…*far too many.*

She moaned with the sensations from her breasts, the sound

dragging me back to her, to her heat and desire. I brushed my hand against the Unseelie shards in her chest.

"I'd like that," she answered. "But I really need a shower. I don't suppose there's a hot spring here somewhere? That damn water's icy."

The crystal shards hummed and burned under my fingers, stinging as I stilled. "I think I can fix that." I thrust my cock between her thighs. "It's a two-birds-one-stone kind of thing." I pulled away and rolled, pushing myself from the pile of furs until I stood, and lifted my hand to her.

She rolled toward me and smiled, her cheeks reddening as she scooted from the bed and rose. My damn pulse sped at the sight of her, cheeks ruddy, flesh nearly raw. I licked my lips and fought the need to push her back against the furs. I wanted her wet...inside and out...*dripping.* I led her out of the bedroom to where the icy mountain water spilled down the smooth stone, stopping to grab the soap and some towels.

"I thought you were taking me to where it's warmer," she protested, but following.

"Oh, it'll be warmer," I promised. "Trust me."

The splash was icy as I stepped into the spray and turned. She winced, clenched her jaw, and followed me in. "Only 'cause I'm desperate."

A chuckle rumbled in the back of my throat. I shielded her with my body, pulled her against me, and ran the soap along her arm. "Remember the last time I showered you?"

She lifted her head, those piercing eyes boring into mine. "Wolf, that's something I'll *never* forget."

She captured me, this woman. She owned me with a goddamn look...trapped me with a fucking smile. "Let's see if we can improve that memory," I recommended, and soaped my hand before running it down her breast.

She lifted her arms, winding them around my neck as I explored every inch of her under the guise of cleanliness. Soap slid over her breasts, her stomach, and between her thighs. Movement came from the doorway. I didn't need to turn my head to know who it was.

Church strode in and made his way to the kitchen, carrying freshly caught meat as his way of an apology. I licked my lips, turning the soap to my own body, until she lowered her arms.

"My turn," she demanded, holding out her hand.

*It's always your turn, female.* The words slipped through my head. I let her take what she wanted, let her explore where she wanted, while she put the events of last night in the right order.

She belonged to the pack now, all four of us.

"Phantom…" she started, and lifted her gaze to mine. "About last night."

"What about last night?"

Her cheeks reddened and her lips pursed, but there was a flicker of pain in her eyes. *Ah, so this wasn't about the sex.*

"I upset Church," she forced out.

"You did exactly what we needed. Church…" Flickers of memories came flooding back, the abandoned refrigeration container, my sister's screams…and a young male Wolf…*close to death.* "He'll come around."

Her hands stilled on my stomach as the scent of cooking meat drifted into the room.

"We all have our demons, Carina." I lowered my gaze to the faint green glow in her chest. "Every single one of us, it's just that some take a bigger piece of our soul."

I took the soap from her hand and cast it through the air, letting it hit the floor and slide to a stop. *What the fuck happened last night?* The question roared in my mind as I wound my hand around her neck and pulled her closer. I felt it in her now, that Unseelie taint. *Chaos magic.* Dangerous magic.

"The Unseelie you saw in the Dark City. Have you met him before?" Fear trembled deep inside me as I stared into her eyes.

If she lied, I'd know it.

*If she lied, then this was all changed.*

I'd kill Shrike…brother or no brother.

The allegiance would be broken.

My pulse sped as her brow furrowed and those brown eyes darkened. "No," she answered. "Should I have?"

I had to remember who she was…had to remember that she didn't belong in our world. I had to remember that she was an innocent here, even if the kind of magic she conjured last night *can't belong to someone untouched by an Unseelie.*

I lowered my head and kissed her hard, my own beast a snarling, savage thing inside my head. *Finis…*the bastard invaded. *Can't let him get to her. Can't let him touch her like he—*the kiss turned savage until her moan of desire turned to one of pain.

I pulled away. I caught the wince before she lifted her fingers to her mouth. "A little forceful this morning, huh?"

"I'm sorry, Carina." Rage burned inside as I lifted my hand and touched the swell of her lip. "Please forgive me."

She said nothing, but the sweet, bitter scent of confusion flooded the air.

*Fucking idiot.* I kissed her gently, licking the swollen flesh until she opened her mouth to mine and moaned. I needed her, like I'd never needed anything before in my life.

That fucking terrified me.

She moaned as my fangs grew longer, grazing her tongue as she licked mine. She wanted the Alpha in me, wanted that possessive power, that brutal, bottomless hunger. I broke the kiss and lowered my head, nuzzling that sensitive spot behind her ear. She groaned, her hands sliding around my back, pulling her body hard against mine.

I dipped, grabbed her hips, and lifted, letting her wrap those legs around my waist. "I can't lose you." My cock found her entrance before I thrust in hard, leaving her to gasp in shock. "I *won't* lose you."

A whimper tore from her as I slammed my hips against hers. My beast surfaced, savage and unmerciful, the glint of rage in his eyes. *I'll fucking kill them all,* he promised as I thrust again. *I'll kill every last one of them.* I couldn't get enough. Her body, her spirit...*her fragile mortal life.*

Her hands slid upwards, winding around my shoulders as she held on. "I'm h-here," she whimpered around the savage thrusts. "I'm n-never l-leaving you again."

I closed my eyes as the marking scar ached on my shoulder. *Her marking. She belongs to us...and we belong to her.* I speared my cock into her delicious heat, relishing the feel of her muscles tightening before her low, guttural moan of release.

My climax a second later was brutal and unmerciful, tearing something deep from me to spill deep inside her.

She wound her arms around me and held on tight. Her hard breaths blew against my neck. "Never leaving you." She kissed the marking scar. "Whatever happens," she lifted her gaze and turned her head until her gaze met mine. "We handle it together, side by side."

A tremor coursed through my chest at the words. But there was a hardness in her gaze, that savage *chaos* that reigned. She wasn't fragile, not like the velvet petals of a flower...*no, she was fragile like a bomb.*

"Whatever happens," I repeated, inhaling the mountain air. But even as I said the words, some cold whisper of fate rose inside me, chilling me to the bone.

The heady smell of meat wafted deeper into the cavern. Carina lowered her head, her hair slick and wet against my skin, but her belly rumbled and howled. She was hungry...*no, she was starving.*

Instinct roared to the surface. The need to protect and provide for this woman was like a fucking locomotive tearing through my veins. My beast sniffed her desire, forcing me to lower her feet to the floor and bend my head to her.

Her scent filled my nose, but still, *he* wanted more, leaving that possessive rumble to spill through my chest. "You're hungry," I stated, my voice low and bestial.

She jerked her gaze to mine, sensing him. A flicker of fear came in her eyes, before it was gone. "Yeah, I guess I am."

I turned from her, stepped from the icy water, and headed toward the stash of clothes we had here. The piles of towels were tucked away in the cupboard, not as thick or lush as the ones back home, but for now, they'd do.

I grabbed the top one and turned back as she followed me, wrapping her arms around herself, her teeth chattering as the freezing water dripped down her body. "That water is f-fucking f-freezing."

I wrapped her in the towel and pulled her against me, rubbing her back until she was mostly dry. "Smells like there's a fire. Come on, let's get you dry and warm."

I yanked sweats and a shirt from the pile. They were Arran's, smaller and warmer than the rest of ours, and held them out as she dropped the towel and lifted her arms. My scent was all over her, even as I slid Arran's shirt down her outstretched arms and over her head. "We need to protect ourselves out here, you understand that, right?"

My heart thundered when she lifted her head, meeting my gaze as I tugged the garment down. "Harlan will come for us."

I smoothed the fabric over her hips. "He can fucking try."

We stilled, staring into each other's eyes, knowing there was no way out of this...not anymore.

Movement came from the corner of the room. Vitold strode inside, gnawing on a bone. "Church has outdone himself." He stopped, mouth open, and glanced from Carina to me. "You okay?"

"Fine," she answered, grabbing the sweatpants from my hand and slipping them on, yanking the tie tight around her waist.

"The perimeter?" I asked him as I watched her.

"Secure," Vitold answered. "Everything alright?"

"Why does everyone keep asking me that?." I mirrored her words as my cell vibrated and buzzed on top of the stack of towels.

I strode forward and snatched it, winced at the caller ID, and answered with a cold, "Brother."

"Everything alright there?" Shrike's stony tone slipped through the speaker.

I watched Carina as she finished adjusting the clothes and lifted her gaze to mine. *How do you know her, Fae? How do you know the woman who's stealing my heart? Tell me now.* "All quiet here."

"That's good," the Unseelie commander replied. "For one of us, at least. The city is under siege, Wolf. The FBI, they've infested the clubs and the bars...and they made their way across the river. But that's not the only thing. There's word your territory is unprotected and Phantom, word is spreading fast."

Carina's brow furrowed.

"Did you hear what I said, Phantom?" the Unseelie growled.

"I heard you," I answered coldly.

"This damn kid of yours. He...he's struggling, Wolf. Won't eat, won't sleep, won't goddamn heal. He keeps tearing at the walls and my men. We can't watch him constantly *and* protect our damn territory." *You mean the Dark City, right? With the secrets and lies...and the power.* "He needs a doctor, one of your kind."

"Take him to the Darkness. I'll have one of our men waiting," I answered, but even as I said the words, I felt the beast writhing under my skin, baring his teeth. "Then you'll need to bring him here."

"I have a bad feeling about this, Wolf."

"So do I, brother," I sighed. "*So do I.*"

I lowered the phone and ended the call.

"News?" Carina asked.

"Nothing good," I answered, grabbing black cargos and a shirt. "Harlan is making his presence known, but you don't need to worry about that. My focus is on keeping you safe."

"And finding that Wolf…Finis?"

I stiffened, just the sound of his name on her lips almost bringing me undone. I swallowed and took a step closer. "He can't get to you, not now…not ever. I'll make it so you don't have to worry about him ever again."

*Once and for all…*

"And Wry?" she asked, even now she cared about the pack before herself. "Will he be alright?"

My throat tightened as I nodded. I swallowed the hard lump in the back of my throat. "Sure he will." I forced a smile, unable to hold her gaze, and looked at Vitold.

I couldn't look at her…and lie.

7

---

He wouldn't look at me. Not after he slung the towel over the rocks. Not even when he turned and held out his hand, muttering, "You need to eat."

*I need to eat?* I need to—my fist clenched at my side. I needed...

*Chaos,* the word stopped my rage dead. *Malevolent chaos.*

I swallowed hard as memories of last night reared inside my head. Dark power lingered at the edges of my mind, deeper than the burn that Unseelie bastard had put in my chest. I looked down at the green glow that spilled faintly through the black t-shirt. Something else moved through me now. Something so strong it terrified me. It wanted more...*it wanted all of them.*

Phantom's outstretched hand waited, until he slowly turned his head. "Carina?"

My belly let out a howl, forcing me to step forward and take his hand, letting him lead me into the next room. A fire was crackling in an improvised fireplace dug into the far wall, the smoke slipping through the cracks high above, sucked away by some kind of updraft of the mountain air.

Phantom's kill sizzled over the flames, its belly run through with a tree branch. My mind was cast back to that wet *splat* as Phantom shifted last night. A splat that had obviously been freshly killed. Food. Even after all we'd gone through last night, his primary concern was for me to eat. I swallowed hard as my stomach howled with fury. "That smells divine."

Church rose from the fire and headed toward me, carrying a well-filled plate. "I thought you'd be hungry," he explained, and briefly met my gaze before he looked away again.

A pulse throbbed through my body as I watched him move toward me, carnal and wicked as that savage voice whispered...*mine...*

Church's eyes widened as he stopped, the damn plate trembling in his outstretched hands. I clenched my fist, driving my nails into the flesh of my palm as that savage echo surged inside me, rippling with dangerous possession. *You are mine.*

He ran from me last night, ran like his life had depended on it, and that dangerous part of me didn't like that at all. *She* wanted him even more now...like he was a challenge—like he was *unclaimed.*

Phantom stepped away, pulling his phone from his pocket and tearing me from that dark, malignant lust. He swiped the screen and lifted the phone to his ear, turning away from us at the last moment before he spoke. "Doc, you know who this is. I have a man coming, Darkness Desire Club, you know the address. The Unseelie are bringing him to you. I need him fixed, fixed and ready. Call me when you get this message."

I caught the tortured look on Church's face and reached to take his offering. "Thank you, I'm starving."

"News from the Unseelie?" Vitold asked, striding toward the fire as I lifted a piece of meat to my lips.

"Better be good fucking news," Arran growled behind me, making me turn.

Flashes of last night rose instantly. Licking, nuzzling, fangs scraping tender skin. His tongue between my thighs...and his cock driving deep. My body clenched in response, desperate for him once more.

"Special agent." He strode toward me, still naked. Those sparkling, seductive eyes were fixed on mine as he grabbed me around the waist and yanked me close. "Good morning," he murmured, then leaned close and kissed me hard.

Gone was my hunger, gone was my fear, as his lips claimed mine. He was all-consuming, this Wolf, ravenous and ravening, stealing me from the real world in an instant with the promise of his body, until he pulled away.

A small smile curled the corners of his lips before he leaned down and they took the piece of meat from my fingers.

"That was for Carina," Church growled, watching intently.

Arran just smiled a little harder. "Then she'll have to go to you for more then, won't she?" he chided. "All meek and mild...begging."

A growl came from Church as he turned on Arran. The air crackled with unbridled tension.

"That's enough," Phantom growled. "We've got bigger things to fight about. Our absence hasn't gone unnoticed."

Church jerked his gaze to the Alpha. "It's been one fucking day."

"A day, an hour, a minute." Phantom strode toward the fire and yanked a chunk of meat free before consuming it in two savage bites. Juice ran down his fingers, then he licked them, taking them deeper into his mouth. "Makes no difference to our enemies."

*Fuck me, he was stunning.*

"The Vamps are gone," Vitold declared. "That leaves the Unseelie protecting the city."

Phantom nodded, his gaze fixed on mine. "Not gone...not yet, at least. I'll set up a meeting, damn if it doesn't feel all too fucking familiar."

I shifted from one foot to the other under his gaze, and

picked at the pieces of meat on my plate. They'd been chosen with precision, lean and seared. Only the best for me, while they gnawed and consumed gristle and everything else. *Set up a meeting,* the words grated on me...the Vampires...my pulse sped, and I tried not to conjure the image of Ruth in my head.

"We need to get back," Church added, "call in the others, strengthen the boundaries, use every favor and allegiance owed us."

"We do that and we're sitting ducks." Phantom shook his head. "From both sides of the river."

I snapped back to the moment. This I knew. *This* I was good at. "Harlan will sit back, but he'll get every other agency involved, police, Homeland. Hell, the CDC, which has more power than you can imagine. You want a section of the city shut down...they'll do it."

"Fuck me," Arran grunted.

"Finis needs to be our priority here," Phantom disagreed. "When he comes...*and he* will *come,* it'll be to finish us once and for all."

*Chaos,* that whisper moved through me, making me swallow a thick wad of meat. It hurt going down, but not as much as seeing the desperation in Phantom's eyes.

"He's coming," the Alpha repeated as he turned away from the others and me...and strode toward the opening of the cavern. "We need to be ready when he does."

He was gone in an instant, leaving the rest of us behind. Arran glanced at me, and shrugged. "Looks like I'm on patrol."

"Me, too," Vitold agreed, and headed for the opening, leaving Church and me alone.

Careful glances and awkward silence came next. I glanced at my plate as he just stared at me and shifted his stance. "Yeah, well..."

"Church." I swallowed that dark need whispering in my head. "Thank you for the food."

His nod was awkward as the muscles in his jaw bulged.

"Will they help us…the Vampires?"

He scowled for a second, deep in thought. "They'll help. Elithien won't stand by and allow another pack to move in…but if it's Ruth you're worried about—"

"I'm not," I cut him off, taking a step closer, that treacherous need slipping through my veins. "I'm not worried about her at all. I'm worried about…me."

He met my gaze, confusion shimmering on the surface, but underneath that was fear.

"I'm changing." My voice trembled. To be open and honest was all too raw. "This…*thing* inside me is making me change."

"Unseelie."

*"Unseelie,"* I repeated and that hunger swirled inside my head. "Chaos, Mojin called it. It scares me…Hell, *I scare me.*"

Images flickered inside my head. Church, naked, his grunt of desire followed by the slap of flesh on flesh. Need raging in those perfect blue eyes…*so much need.* Painful need. Humiliation. He was…*humiliated.*

His chest rose with deep breaths as I stepped closer. "It knows things about people…*senses them.* I want to belong to this pack, Church, and you're a big part of it. So I need you to tell me what I have to do."

In my head, Church half whimpered and half growled, desperate for release. *Please.*

That was what he needed…what he'd hidden from me…that was why he'd run. "Part of me is still real, and it's that part that'll do whatever you need."

His eyes were wide, his body frozen in place.

"You want me to submit to you?" The darkness rose faster, and even as I said the words, I knew that wasn't what he wanted.

He jerked his gaze back to me as sweat beaded on his top lip. *"What did you say?"*

And that *knowing* rose inside me like a deadly storm. Hunger. Lust. Control...*so much control.* "Just tell me what you want, Church." He flinched as I stepped closer, my voice deepening with that sadistic hunger. "You want *me* on my knees?"

"No." He was shutting down.

My throat tightened as that deep throb in my chest turned ravenous. "I will, if that's what it takes." My voice quietened as I lifted my gaze to his. "I'll be whatever you need."

Emerald green glowed in the center of my chest. I didn't need to look down to know. Desire lashed like a lover's tongue, swirling and marking, searing that Unseelie hunger deeper inside me. It wanted more, that need...*more* than the others...it wanted Church...

*His hand around my throat. Savage and terrified. That heady scent of lust in the air as I gave him what he needed.* I was rocked by the image, catching the panicked flinch of his body. He was wound tight, too tight...like he was ready to explode. "Church—"

"I *ahh*..." he started, then stumbled as he moved. "I can't do this...not with you."

He kicked a plate, scattering the picked-clean hare bones as he turned...and ran.

"I'm sorry." My tortured words burned like acid. "Church, I'm—" But he was already gone, leaving me standing there... alone. "I'm sorry. I'm so fucking sorry."

I don't know how long I stood there while the fire crackled and dimmed, until that darkness slowly sank down inside me. *My darkness. "Fuck!"* I screamed, and the word resounded inside the mountain.

Slowly, I strode toward the scattered bones and bent, gathering the rest of the meat and the plates, doing something at least, instead of feeling pissed off and sorry for myself. I didn't belong here, not with the Wolves, or with my own kind anymore. I belonged nowhere.

Bad apple…fallen not too far from the tree. Hell, all I'd need was a few bottles of the cheapest Scotch I could find and a piss-stained sofa right next to my old man. Maybe then I could slowly drown myself. Maybe then I could think of all the fucking ways this had gone so goddamn sideways.

*An accomplice to murder.* That's what they'd say. But I wasn't just that, was I? I was…

*Unseelie.* The thought was chilling. I glanced down to the glow in my chest. It was a lot more than lust now, a lot fucking more.

"He'll come back."

I jumped at the words and spun, finding Arran standing in the doorway. His hands were curled into fists, deep breaths drawing in the scent of chaos and hunger. My throat tightened, hardening around a lump. "Yeah, well…maybe if I'm gone."

"It's not you he's running from."

A hard bark of laughter tore free. "Could've fooled me."

"We all have our demons, Carina."

I snarled at those words, raging at the Wolf. "I *terrified hi,.*" I growled, hate and pain a fist in the center of my chest. I moaned and rubbed the ache. "I fucking terrified him. No wonder he ran."

"He ran because he can't get what he needs from us." The Wolf's tone deepened, sorrow tainting every word. "Because like you, he's desperate not to be what he is."

I lowered my hand, my body searching for cold clarity. "And what is he?"

"Tortured." Arran stepped closer and grasped the back of my neck. "Tortured is what he is, special agent. Just like you."

I fought the Wolf's hold, turning my head toward the cavern's opening. "A storm's coming, Arran. It's like nothing I've felt before. A darkness…" I turned back to his gaze. "Darker than this Unseelie hold."

He swallowed hard as that flicker of fear rose in his

midnight eyes. "Then we'll need to make sure we're ready, won't we?"

All five of us against how many? A shudder tore through me, blooming into pain that gripped my bladder tight.

"The cavern opens up through there." Arran lifted his hand to the back wall. "There's a stream, it flows away from the mountain. It's perfect if you need a little privacy, God knows you won't get much of that once you step outside the cavern. Here." He turned, bent, and grabbed a lantern. A spark of ignition came before the lantern grew brighter, throwing a flickering amber glow against the cavern wall.

The thought of stepping inside a dark cave with nothing more than a smoldering lantern was fucking disgusting...but then, so was relieving myself out in the open with the Wolves around.

"It's not far. When you're ready, you can meet me outside, and we can talk strategies."

"Strategies?" I mumbled, and swallowed hard. "Sure, we can do that."

He lifted the lantern toward me. "You're going to be alright, Carina. You're stronger than you give yourself credit for."

I took the lantern from his hand and turned, as that ache became desperate. "Thank fuck for that."

I left him behind, lifting the lantern higher as I headed for the far end of the cavern. There was a gap, just as Arran said, opening up to a deeper alcove. Darkness crowded in as I stepped inside and glanced over my shoulder, looking back the way I'd come. There was nothing but emptiness, a cold, dark emptiness that crawled along my spine.

The trickling sound of water was the only thing that kept me from racing back the way I'd come. I lifted my lantern high, seeing a small rivulet of water that flowed away from the opening, just as Arran had said it would.

I moved deeper, found a place to do what I needed to, and

washed myself in the icy stream. But I didn't leave…not yet. My throat tightened as I stared into the blackness…until the warm trickle of a tear slipped down my cheek.

This time, I didn't brush it away.

This time, I let myself feel.

There was nothing I could do to protect them.

*Not even from myself.*

I wiped the tears from my face and straightened my spine before grabbing the lantern and hurrying back the way I'd come. I'd spent far too long in the dark of this mountain. I needed sun on my skin…and purpose. That's what I needed… *plan, protect…fight.*

I killed the flame and stepped into the cavern, heading for the sunlight that spilled through the doorway. Trees surrounded us. In the light of day, I saw just how high we were, green treetops stretching out like a blanket below us.

I made my way down from the opening and looked around. Last night's storm had washed away the tire tracks, a pity it hadn't washed away a lot more than that. Phantom said I'd ache—my insides clenched, and that deep throb moved through me.

It wasn't the ache I was worried about. It was the *seething* inside me, that dark touch of Fae power that stoked deeper than the heat of lust. I ground my teeth, staring across the expanse of trees. I'd been overcome last night, inciting the Wolves to turn on one another. If I could do that without thinking, then imagine what I could do if I wanted?

I stepped down, finding a trail. Movement came from the corner of my eye. Arran stood there, leaning against the trunk of a tree, arms crossed, waiting for me. He glanced my way and his nostrils flared, scenting me. "Feeling better?"

"You know, that whole sensing if I'm in pain trick is going to get on my nerves pretty damn fast," I complained, my cheeks burning.

"If you're talking about your time of the month, we've already got that covered."

I flinched and jerked my gaze to his, my cheeks burning all the way down my neck. "What the hell does *that* mean?"

He just shoved off from the tree and gave a shrug. "We're Wolves, Carina. It's in our nature to scent, and nuzzle, and bite. Hell, I need to talk myself down from pushing you to the floor and rubbing my damn face in your crotch every second of the day."

The memory of that first morning bloomed inside my head. I'd woken in Phantom's bed...but I hadn't been alone. No, that green shit had hummed and burned in the middle of my chest and I'd woken with two Wolves at my back and Arran's face nestled between my bare breasts.

The Wolf strode toward me, his long, sleek strides quickly closing the distance between us. "Best sleep I'd had in years," he murmured.

I ground my teeth, wrenching myself from the memory. "You're in my head, in my scent, under my fucking skin. Is nothing private anymore?"

"No," Phantom growled behind me. I jerked my gazed over my shoulder as he strode up the steep mountain track without breaking a damn sweat. "Not when you're part of a pack. Every twinge of pain, every need to go to the bathroom, we'll know." He stopped in front of me. "And yes, when it comes to menstruation, we're going to anticipate your cycles better than you do. We've worked with women and we're used to knowing their needs. We make sure we're careful and distant, we make sure they don't realize we scent every single thing about them... but they aren't you, Carina. They aren't even close to you. We won't be able to stop ourselves, not from caring or from wanting you even when you bleed."

My body clenched as I swallowed hard. I didn't know a lot of women, and the ones I did closed down during their time of the month. But me? I hated it, *loathed it.* The heat, the heady, slick need, my body swelling with the urge to fuck. It sucked even more when you were lonely. So I worked, I trained, and I hated it.

"All you have to do is tell us what you want," Phantom continued calmly. "You want space, we'll give you space…to a point. You want chocolate and takeout and a binge session of some sappy TV show, we'll give you that, too. Whatever you need…Arran can give you."

Arran jerked his gaze to the Alpha, surprise written all over his face.

The coldness was back in Phantom's eyes, that distance which hadn't been there before. He was pulling away from me… he was pulling away. The sting was instant as Phantom tore his gaze from mine, turned, and strode away.

He was gone in an instant, heading for the cavern, leaving me standing there. "Arran can give you, huh?" Pain etched my words.

"He didn't mean…" Arran started.

I turned away from the Wolf. "I know exactly what he meant." I lifted my gaze once more toward the Alpha before he disappeared into the opening of the cavern.

Something had changed in him since the phone call from the Unseelie, a growing distance and a tormented mind. "It's alright." I tore my gaze from the cavern. I felt that darkness too…but it wasn't from a damn phone call, it was inside me.

"How about you show me the boundary…and tell me more about this Finis?" I murmured, and glanced at Arran.

"The boundary yes, Finis is a little more complicated." He motioned ahead along the worn track.

We made our way down the mountain, slipping on the loose shale until the ground evened out, and as I stared at the thick green forest all around me, this became all too real. I stopped and leaned over with my hands on my knees, sucking in deep breaths.

"Carina?" Arran called, concerned.

"I'm fine," I answered, and closed my eyes. Pain lashed the back of my head…but it was just a memory, the feel of the tire iron against my skull, and Murphy's hands around my throat. My fingers grazed my neck. The acrid scent of the smoke still seemed to cling to me, even though I knew it was no longer there.

*Chaos,* that animal part of me whispered. *Chaos and death…*

I opened my eyes, finding my Wolf standing beside me. "How the hell are we going to get out of this?"

Agony and guilt glinted in his eyes. He had no answers, none that were the truth, and I wasn't one for lies.

"Fight or run," he answered. "That's all it comes down to. We fight and ride it out, protect our boundaries, protect those we can…or we pack up and run."

"And what…become nomads?"

I closed the distance and felt his arms around my shoulders, pulling me against his chest. "Rogue packs survive. They might not be as strong, but we've endured before and we will again."

*Rogue packs.* No territory. No home. The midnight-colored Wolf surfaced in my mind. Out there, with Finis after us, we wouldn't survive for long, rogue or not.

"Looks like fight it is." I turned my head, pressing my cheek against his chest and slid my arms around his waist, taking comfort where I could.

"That's my special agent," he murmured into my hair. "Don't forget, you're the woman who shot our Alpha in the chest…*and* stole my damn Jeep. Fuck, I love that car."

A bark of laughter tore free from my throat. It didn't matter if the world was falling down around us, Arran was there to make me smile and make me fucking ache with need. "Stupidity or balls. I'm not sure which one possessed me in that moment."

Arran lowered his head and his lips brushed mine as he whispered, "Desperation, Carina. Never discount desperation. It's what brought you to us…and for that, I'll sacrifice every single thing I goddamn own."

My breath caught at his words as I stared into his eyes. I'd never seen the truth burn so brightly, never felt this kind of connection…not like I felt with the Wolves. "This scares me, Arran."

"Good," he growled, and lowered his head to nuzzle my neck. "'Cause it fucking terrifies me."

8

I let Arran kiss me, let him graze his fangs down my neck, and pull me against him, even as the faint rumble of thunder slipped into my ears. I felt that sizzle of energy, felt it spill from the clouds above to fill that hollow pit in my chest. I felt the urgency swirl in my soul, and amidst the violence, *purpose* found me.

*Claim them...all of them...and protect them with our life.*

"Chaos," he grunted, kissing that place behind my ear. "That's exactly what you are, special agent. I can feel the lust pouring from you. It makes me feel wild, Carina." He slid his hand up my front until he cupped my breast. "Makes that unrestrained part of my nature savage as fuck."

*Use him...*that desire growled. *Take him...here in the dirt and the trees, let him ride you out in the open.*

Arran dropped his head to the swell of my breast, his hand kneading and grasping as his body trembled, his muscles rippling with pent-up energy. Lust roared through me as the thunder grew louder.

*But it wasn't just lust, was it? It was Unseelie...and it was me.*

That dark, animalistic beast unfurled in my head, desperate

for me to claim *it,* as well. Arran lifted the bottom of my t-shirt as the sky darkened overhead, and exposed my breasts. He bent his head, lips and tongue taking one nipple. "Fuck, I can't get enough of you," he muttered, taking my nipple deeper into his mouth.

"That's because you're mine, Wolf," I answered, my voice deep and husky. "And I'm yours."

His hand slipped down my body and delved inside the waistband of my pants. A moan tore free as his finger slipped into the crease of my sex. He lifted his gaze to mine as a *crack* tore through the sky, stopping him cold, the heat of lust in his eyes. But it was turning to something else now. Something savage…something *possessive.* Something that whispered in my ear and lashed through my veins. His top lip curled, baring his teeth in warning. But still, he didn't slide his hand free, if anything, he pinned my gaze with his and started that slow slide again as movement came from the trees and Vitold stepped out.

"Don't stop on my account," he murmured, his gaze riveted to Arran's hand down my pants. "I'm just here to enjoy the show."

But it wasn't just a show…it was a storm. a storm that was crowding all around us. A *crack* of thunder sounded, punching my heart against my ribs. "The storm," I gasped as Arran slipped his hand lower, finding that part of me slick and ready.

"What storm?" the Wolf questioned, kissing my neck as I dropped my head to the side.

Darkness moved and panic followed. I could feel that hunger, but as I lifted my gaze, I saw only clear blue sky above. There was a storm coming, a violent eruption, but it wasn't from bruised clouds overhead…*it was coming from somewhere else.*

"Arran.," I cried as something gave a *snap.*

Vitold tore his gaze from Arran's hand down my pants and swung his gaze to the edge of the trees.

And in an instant, my two Wolves shifted. Arran ripped his hand back, and spun, his focus on a thick clump of trees in the distance as Vitold gave a terrifying snarl and stepped forward, the sound booming from his chest until he lunged.

Arran followed, lunging between trees on one side, while Vitold took off in the other, both Wolves heading in the same direction. *They're coming...*that darkness whispered in my head a second before a howl tore through the air.

*They're coming...*

The sound was deafening, rolling violently through me, chilling my blood. My Wolves were gone before I knew it, leaving me standing there with the Unseelie wrath boiling in my veins and no one to fight. I took a step forward, my senses on fire. The snap of a twig came in the distance to my right ... something moved through the trees, coming closer... *closer...closer.*

Fear moved through me, dark and fetid, making me step forward again. *Snap!* Another twig snapped, this time closer. My heart thundered, the sound filling my ears as I pushed forward, making my way around the thick brambles and deeper into the forest.

There was a second when a faint voice inside my head said *careful now...*but that whisper was gone before the thought took hold, leaving me to continue pushing ahead. *Crunch!* I jerked my gaze toward the sound, moving faster now as that whirlwind of Unseelie rage swirled like a tornado inside me, and for a second everything else just melted away.

I was alone in the forest...alone with no one around me.

*Crack!*

I swung my gaze right and kept on pushing, cutting between thick ash trees and moving deeper into the dark.

*"Carina!"* My name caught the wind, so faint now…barely there. So easily forgotten.

I turned away from the sound and pushed on, following that urgency. *Mine.* The word filled me, thrumming with my pulse. *My Wolves, my territory.* Something was coming, some foul sense of sickness that wafted through the air to slam into me.

I knew that sickness. I'd felt it before, amidst the terror and the panic as I ran from Murphy. It had been a moment just like this, one that made the hairs on my arms stand on end. I stopped running and darted my gaze around, scanning the trees.

A blur came at my left. I glimpsed white fur, spotted with brown. I caught my breath as I watched the unfamiliar Wolf slink through the trees and head past me without giving me a glance. It was stalking something…*or someone.* Arran and Vitold filled my mind.

I gritted my teeth and pushed toward the beast. *"Hey!"* My hand went to my hip…*shit, no gun.* "Over here, asshole," I snarled, and lifted my fists.

The beast turned on me, that sick, savage gaze filled with rage that was now aimed at me.

"Come on, you piece of shit," I taunted as it stalked closer, until a howl of agony and pain ripped through the forest, coming from the same direction Arran and Vitold had headed.

*It's not them…it cannot be them.*

The enemy Wolf's black nostrils flared, scenting something far more predatory than me. *Phantom.*

My pulse leaped at the thought as I spun, seeing a dark blur cutting through the trees behind me. *That's not Phantom.* My mouth went dry and my breaths slowed while my pulse spiked as the midnight beast slunk into a clearing and headed toward me head lowered. *That's not Phantom at all.*

I stumbled backwards. Rogue Wolves…that's what Arran

had called them. They were after my pack, coming for us just like Phantom had said they would.

*"CARINA!"*

My name was shrill in the air, making me tremble. I wrenched my gaze toward the sound, my heart slamming against my ribs. It took all my will not to scream for them. But one sound…one panicked call, and I'd put their lives in danger…*more than I already had.*

"You just stay right there," I forced the words as movement came behind the midnight beast. But it was the white Wolf, which was closer now…and more of a threat. It came at me, head lowered, top lip quivering and peeled back from its teeth.

There were more of them, brindle and gray, heads down, eyes catching every movement as they moved through the forest, heading for the cavern we called home. I focused on that black beast with the cold, merciless eyes. *Finis*…Phantom had called him.

"You stay the fuck away from him," I roared, my knees trembling as I took a step forward. "You hear me? *You stay THE FUCK AWAY!"*

*"Carina!"* Arran roared my name.

But the midnight beast didn't move, even as the others behind him slunk past him, heading toward the howl of my name.

"Finis," I whispered, and the midnight beast's ears twitched. Still it didn't move, standing too far in the distance for me to charge toward it and take the bastard out.

Instead, it watched me with a careful gaze as I took another step closer. A touch brushed across my mind, like a blanket of drowsiness. I knew without question it was the black Wolf. "You want Phantom," I warned, and stepped directly into the Wolf's path. "Then you're going to have to go through me."

Black lips curled, exposing long, terrifying fangs. "I don't give a fuck," I insisted, and held my ground in front of the enemy Alpha. "You don't get to hurt him, you don't get to hurt *any* of them *anymore*."

The Wolf advanced, low, sleek strides bringing it closer, cutting a glare toward the white Wolf before it settled those unflinching eyes on me.

Darkness swelled inside me. I forced myself not to move, not to let that *bastard* see the panic in my eyes. I forced myself to be, not the woman, but the *darkness* that spilled through the Unseelie power.

Chaos was there waiting, lingering at the edges of my mind. Dark and seething, whispering of all the things it wanted to do...*I'll start with this one,* she whispered in my head. *This fucking Wolf who thinks it can come for what's mine.* I opened myself to that raw power and let it flow through me, as a rumble came from the sky above, that oncoming storm I'd felt was more like a threatening growl in my head now. It was sweet and bitter in my nose, making the midnight-colored Wolf lift its head and sniff the air.

"That's right," I taunted. "Not so pathetically mortal after all, *am I?*"

The Wolf answered with a snarl of its own and stalked closer. I readied myself, widening my stance, my breath trapped in my chest. Movement came all around me in the trees, more Wolves hunting for my pack. I couldn't stop them...couldn't fight them all...but I could stop *this* one...*Finis.*

He came closer, head hunched between his shoulders, that vicious sound of warning rumbling in his throat to spill through his bared teeth. But it wasn't the midnight beast that I turned toward...that took the full brunt of my power. It was the white Wolf.

*Chaos* roared through me, spilling through that ache in the center of my chest, and I focused on that ache, driving the pain harder, until a *throb* tore free, followed by another.

*Throb.*

The White wolf stopped stalking toward me, the glint in its eyes flickering as it blinked and shook its head. I *had* it...had the connection, had the *chaos power*. A surge, and that connection became stronger. I pushed all my rage and desperation into that beast, then watched as it swung its head to the Alpha of its pack and let out a warning snarl.

The black Wolf stilled, nostrils flaring as it sniffed the air.

It scented something different now.

*It scented...me.*

*My* power.

*My* rage.

"Come on, you piece of shit," I hissed. "Give me your fucking worst."

The beast lunged in an instant, the black blur tearing through the air until it hit me with a *crack*. I was slammed backwards, flying through the air until I hit the ground. White sparks danced in my vision as that towering beast came closer, until it stood looming over me. White teeth were all I saw as the Wolf lowered its head, its gaze fixed on mine.

Rage rippled through my body, and the sky above gave a deafening *boom!* The storm...*the storm was me.* Lightning flashed blindingly behind the Alpha, showing the white Wolf just standing there, transfixed by the Alpha's attack. I clenched my fist and swung, driving my fist into the chest of the beast above me. "Come on, you fucking *asshole!*"

But it couldn't move, frozen between the command of its Alpha and the power that poured from me, trying to force it to bend to my will, desperate for it to *fight* for me...and to die for me, if need be.

The midnight beast was all rage and thick, matted fur, but underneath the pelt was nothing more than skin and bones. My blow hit its ribs with a hollow *thud*. Still, it didn't move. Instead, it opened its jaws and lashed out, its fangs sinking into my arm.

I screamed with the pain, kicking and punching with my

other fist as the Wolf thrashed its head from side to side, driving those wicked fangs deeper. Screams filled my ears, followed with the heady scent of blood. It took me a second to understand the screams were mine...and so was the sweet coppery tang in the air. But rage still pulsed through me, desperate for an outlet...until the vicious sound of a snarl slipped through the trees.

Crimson coated its white fangs as the beast released my arm and lifted its head. Its fierce gaze whipped to my right as, out of nowhere, it was slammed from the side. A howl followed from the midnight Alpha, the sound piercing and painful as it was knocked from its feet.

*Chaos,* that voice whispered in my head as the white Wolf advanced. *Savage, undeniable chaos.*

It poured from me, stinging and burning in the middle of my chest as I shoved against the ground and rose to my feet. Lightning ripped across the sky, blurring the day with a flash of neon white. A howl tore through the air, so loud and clear it stood the hairs on the back of my neck.

The midnight Alpha whipped its head toward the sound as a thunderous surge of power ripped from me and slammed into the white Wolf, forcing it to move.

It lunged, mouth open and fangs bared, and barrelled into the midnight beast. My ears were filled with savagery and the gnashing of teeth. Eyes were wild as claws slashed the air. End over end they tumbled as a splash of red sprayed against stark white. Blood. That's what it was. Blood...and the white Wolf howled with pain. Still it lashed out as I desperately drove that vengeful power into the beast.

*Fight.*

I clenched my fists and ground my teeth.

*Fight for me.*

A bark tore from the Alpha as it rolled away. The white Wolf pushed itself to stand, one paw curled under its body. But the air hummed with Unseelie power. It pulsed and throbbed like a living, breathing thing, and the midnight beast felt it.

"Carina!" Church roared. "Carina, where are you?"

I tore my gaze from the two Wolves and screamed, "I'M HERE!"

Seconds. That was all it took for the black Alpha to disappear, tearing through the trees to my left, head down, paws barely hitting the ground as he ran, leaving the injured white Wolf and me behind.

Church was terrifying, lunging through the air to slam into the white- beast. The Wolf never stood a chance. Transfixed again by the Unseelie power that spilled from my chest, he was battered by fists and fury as Church landed blow after blow.

The beast's jaw snapped shut as Church drove his fist upwards. He wrapped his strong arms around the Wolf's throat and twisted, slamming it to the ground with a sickening *smack*. Hard breaths consumed Church as he climbed to his feet and turned his head, looking for me.

Our gazes met, then he broke the stare, looking at the ground, then he turned to the Wolf once more. "You rise, and I'll kill you," the male warned, his knuckles coated red with Wolf's blood. "Stay there, and I'll let you live."

Terrifying howls of pain came from high on the rise above us. Church stilled, sucking in harsh breaths as he listened. "Sounds like the others in your pack aren't as lucky."

He took a step backwards, watching the Wolf the entire time as he neared me. "Carina, are you alright?"

Warmth ran down my arm in rivulets. The bite was deep, deeper than I'd thought. I licked my dry lips as the forest swam around me. "Fine," I whispered. "The others?"

Church swung his gaze toward the rise. He turned his head toward me at the last minute, and that's when I saw it, red marks around his throat...like the span of a hand. Terror punched through me as I stumbled forward and reached for his neck with my uninjured hand. "What happened?"

His brow furrowed and his brown eyes darkened. He almost lifted his hand to mine, then sparks brightened in his eyes. "Nothing," he snapped, and stepped away from me, his cheeks flushed and his breaths panicky.

The white Wolf gave a whimper and tried to rise to its feet. But it was hurt…badly. Still, all I could see were those marks on Church's neck…and the way he refused to meet my gaze. *Like he was embarrassed…disgusted, even.* "Church," I murmured as blood dripped from my arm onto his shirt.

My knees trembled a second before they gave way. Church was there, catching me, sliding his arms under my knees and cradling me against his chest.

Green blurred to gray as I tried to hold on.

"All my goddamn fault," Church groaned as his long strides jostled me from side to side.

"Not your…*fault.*" I gritted out the words, forcing color back into my vision. I gripped his shirt, my hands trembling with the strain. "You hear me?"

He met my gaze, but said nothing as the growl of an engine grew louder.

"Carina!" Phantom roared.

I tore my gaze from Church to find the Alpha. Terror filled his gaze. He was covered with blood, and filled with rage.

"I'm alright," I called. "Church, you can put me down." The male did as I asked, lowering my feet gently to the ground as my Alpha strode toward me with lightning in his gaze, then he saw the blood running down my arm.

The wince in his gaze made my throat tighten. "What the fuck!" He grasped my arm and turned it.

I whimpered at the movement, and grabbed hold of his arm as the pain made my head swim. Behind him on the rise, the Unseelie's black Explorer came to a sliding stop.

I heard her before I saw her. Commands were being barked before the door was flung open and my best friend leaped from the car.

"Chase!" Walker roared, her dark hair streaming out behind her as she raced toward me.

"The Wolf that did this...is it dead?" Phantom growled.

"No." Church shook his head. "But the bastard is damaged."

"This isn't the Wolf that did this," I denied, just as I was hit by Walker.

Her arms went around me and she pulled me close. "Jesus fucking Christ, Chase," she barked, hugging me against her. "You really know how to scare a woman to fucking death, you know that?"

She shoved me back and stared into my eyes. Her own were filled with terror and relief as I turned to Phantom. "The Wolf who did this was the one I saw before. Finis is here...and he came for me."

9

___

"What the fuck did you just say?" Phantom glared at Walker before he settled that focus on me.

"Jesus, Chase." She lifted my arm and turned it over. "What the hell did *this?*"

She examined the gash as the driver's door of the Explorer opened and the Unseelie, Mojin, climbed out. But it wasn't the moody, malevolent Immortal that drew my stare. It was the pale young male who climbed out of the back seat after Mojin and lifted his gaze to mine.

This Wolf looked *haunted and unhinged.* A mass of white scars savaged the base of his throat, and those big dark eyes swam with the look of someone close to breaking. *Wry.* My heart thundered as his name rolled through my mind. *Tormented,* Phantom's words followed. *Unstable.*

I flinched at the sight. One dangerous-as-hell Unseelie and an unstable Wolf. What the hell was Walker doing with *them?*

"What happened?" Mojin jerked his gaze toward a howl as it tore through the air in the distance.

"Rogue. Pack. Attack." Church sucked in great gulps of air

and swept fingers through his hair, eyes searching the trees. "Took us by surprise."

But it was Phantom who pushed Walker aside to grasp my injured arm. "Carina, *answer me.*"

"It was Finis." I winced from Phantom's grip and met his stare. "I'm sure of it. He was just the same as I remember, cold, chilling…and he wanted me dead."

A deep, chilling sound rumbled in the back of the Alpha's throat.

I looked down, finding his fingers. He wasn't hurting me, he was helping me, stemming the flow of blood even as he lifted his gaze to Church. One nod from his second, and Phantom was releasing his hold and turning away.

"What's going on?" I licked my lips. "Talk to me."

"I want you to stay with Mojin and tend to that wound," he commanded, and glanced at Wry as he took a step closer. Something passed between them; sadness, regret…and distrust *from both sides* as someone crashed through the trees.

Vitold and Arran strode out, both men covered with blood, and with identical savage looks of rage.

"We lost them," Vitold reported. "Three took off over the rise."

"They'll be back," Phantom glanced at me before he continued, "if Finis is leading them."

Arran's steps stuttered, smacking his boots against the ground as he swung his gaze to mine. "Finis is here?"

There was no answer from the Alpha. His silence said all they needed to know.

"Jesus Christ." Vitold looked at Church, but Arran's gaze was fixed on me as he took in the blood on my arm. "Carina?"

"I'm alright," I answered. "It's just a graze."

"It's *not* just a graze, Chase," Walker snapped. "It's deep. Probably damaged a tendon or two. You'll need stitches at the minimum, and I didn't bring my damn bag."

"Who the *fuck* are you?" Arran demanded, stepping closer with a possessive gleam in his eyes.

"Her goddamn friend," Walker snarled at him, and took a step toward him, fury rippling from her in waves. "The *only* one who's looking out for her, it seems. Goddamn Wolves, you just can't leave her alone, can you?"

Arran just growled and curled his lips, baring his teeth at the remark, then jerked his gaze to the Fae.

"Don't blame me." Mojin lifted his hands in surrender. "*This* one was at the goddamn club, screaming at the top of her lungs about *that* one." He stabbed a finger toward me and cut me an unflinching share. "*Your* doctor was a no-show…and she says she is one. *You're fucking welcome.*"

"Jesus Christ, let's just lead the entire mortal army here." Arran shook his head. "Every goddamn agent and cop will be up our ass before long."

"Give me a little credit, Arran," Mojin warned softly. He didn't raise his voice, and yet the carefully chosen words from the Unseelie chilled me to the bone.

"Wry." Arran stepped forward, making the young Wolf flinch and jerk his gaze upwards. I didn't know where he was…but it wasn't here with us. He had a look about him. Disconnected. Drowning. Dangerous. "You alright, brother?"

The young Wolf gave a slow nod of his head.

"Vitold." Phantom met the Russian's gaze. "You're east. Arran, west. Church will take the middle. We need to make a plan to get out of here and find somewhere close and safe."

"If it's Finis, he'll be long gone," Mojin muttered, and lifted his gaze to the trees.

But Phantom didn't agree. He just turned his gaze to me once more. I could see the fear in his eyes, see the rage…and the same haunted look that gripped the young Wolf next to us.

"I can fight," I protested, and took a step forward. "Give me a gun and I can hurt them just as good as any of you."

"Chase, no," Walker moaned. "No way. *You* are getting your ass into that goddamn car and letting this scary motherfucker drive us out of here."

My pulse sped at the thought and the chill of fear slipped in. But she didn't understand...not any of this.

Phantom's gaze bored into mine. "She's right. It's not safe here."

"No," I forced through clenched teeth. "No fucking way. You don't get to do this...you don't get to shut me out, not now, not when things have gotten real."

He lowered his head as he came closer. Those eyes held me... like whirlpools of amber drawing me in and under, until I lost all control. I wanted to be away from all this, to be back in that moment when the burn of lust was still fresh in my chest and his body was my only savior.

I wanted it to be just us...*all of us.*

*My Alpha.*

*My pack.*

"It's just for a little while." He curled over me, breathing in against the crook of my neck. "Until I know it's safe."

"Fuck safe," I snarled, and closed my eyes, my voice trembling. "We're a pack, remember?"

But there was no brush of his lips and no comfort from his arms. I waited for his touch, waited for his kiss to find me, for him to tell me it'd be alright...*as long as we were together.*

But the comforting words never came.

Instead, a pang of agony filled me as he breathed deep. In an instant, I realized what was happening. He was scenting me...*no, he was scenting Finis,* finding the smell of that bastard on my skin. I swallowed a shudder as the world crowded in around me. I could feel Finis there, his breath on my face, his fur under my fingers, his rage radiating from the steel of his eyes.

I opened mine and took a step backwards. The glistening amber irises of the Alpha darkened to the cold brown color of earth. It was all about Finis. All about Phantom's rage for the Alpha and retribution for his sister.

Was that why he looked at me like I was a stranger? Was that why he was pushing me away?

Phantom was changing, right before my eyes…leaving the man I was falling in love with behind to become the brutal beast.

"Phantom." *Please…*the word resounded in my head but it didn't make it to my lips. I was too proud to say it, and too fucking stubborn to stop him as his brows furrowed with a look of devastation and he turned away.

"You chased me, *remember?"* I froze him with the words. "You wanted me here, you wanted me as part of the pack."

"Maybe that was a mistake." His quiet words were a sledgehammer to my chest. "Maybe this was all just a…*mistake.* I need my men to be observant, need them to fight. Were they fighting when the rogue pack came?"

My breath caught as pain overwhelmed me. I couldn't move, couldn't blink, couldn't stop the agony from crashing down.

"No, they weren't," he answered himself as his head sank. "You're a distraction, Carina, one we just can't afford…not now."

He took another step, slower this time, then strode down the embankment, leaving me behind. I tore my gaze from that sight to Arran. Desperation filled the Wolf's eyes.

"No fucking way." The sting of anger choked out my ache of loss. "No *motherfucking way."*

"Carina…" Walker started.

But I was already leaving them behind as I charged after Phantom. The snap of a twig cut through the forest as I charged, forgetting all about the throbbing in my am. Nothing else mattered in that moment, not pain, not loneliness, not Finis… *just them…my Wolves…*

I raced down the steep embankment, catching sight of him

standing by a tree, his hand braced against the trunk as though he could barely stand. His slumped shoulders hit me harder than any words could have. It was the stance of a broken man, of a man beaten down by pain. Of a man hurting. My throat tightened, and panic fueled me. I lunged, driving my boots into the ground, running headlong toward him.

He turned in that moment, agony shimmering cruelly in his eyes as I slammed into him. His arms were around me in an instant, drawing me hard against him.

"No, you fucking don't," I roared, and pummeled his chest with my fist as tears filled my eyes. "*You* don't get to push me away, Phantom. *You* don't get to hurt me. Not ever, you hear me? *Not. Ever.*"

He held me like that, letting me pound my fist on his massive chest while agony and desperation raged in his eyes. His lips were on mine a heartbeat later. The heat of his desire was like an avalanche...and I just couldn't get enough, pulling him harder against me, yanking his shirt high to slide my hands against his chest.

One dangerous snarl, and he fisted my hair, yanking my head backwards, driving his mouth savagely against mine. I was spun and pushed against the tree that seconds ago he had used as a brace. His hands were at the button of my jeans and the zipper gave way before they were yanked down, exposing my ass.

"I won't let him touch you," Phantom swore before he licked the back of my neck and fumbled with his own pants. "I won't let him take you from me."

"Then don't let him," I commanded, stopping the Alpha cold.

His breath was a furnace on the back of my neck. He was so scared...so unbelievably scared...of losing me. I splayed my hands against the trunk and drove my ass back into him, feeling his cock press between my thighs. He was inside me with one unmerciful thrust, driving deep…connecting us once more. *This was where we were supposed to be…how we were supposed to be.*

Savage.

*Animal.*

No holds barred.

*"I'm not your sister,"* I growled as he gripped my hips and thrust deep, spearing that thick length inside me. *"And I'm not weak."*

I closed my eyes at the feel of him…sliding and *thrusting.* I twisted and reached backwards, winding my arm around his neck. "I…I love you."

He stopped mid-thrust for a second before he let out a growl of desire.

"I love you," I repeated. "I love…*you.*"

He answered me with the strength of his passion, grasping my jaw with his blood-stained hand. He was all predator in that moment, all danger, all lust.

"I'd lose my fucking mind if I lost you," he growled against my ear. "I'd tear the entire goddamn world apart and every living thing in it."

I held on as his thrusts turned almost brutal, driving harder, lifting me to my toes with every inward surge of his cock. Heat flared inside me, making me buck and writhe, making me gasp with desperation as that dark, dangerous hunger flared to life. "Just like this…*always like this"* I demanded, and slammed my eyes closed.

Our bodies as one. Our rage…as one.

His was mine…

And I needed more.

My orgasm consumed me, driving my ass against each slam of his hips while I shuddered and quaked. My body clamped tight around him, drawing a savage sound from his lips as he came with a roar a second later. The sound ripped through the forest, and harsh breaths followed as we slowly came back to our senses.

He leaned into me, his hard chest pushing against my back as he sucked in air. I waited for a moment, hating the way he softened and slid from me. He was quick to bend and grasp my jeans, dragging them up my thighs.

Still, the darkness of his anger lingered between us, a palpable thing, sliding into me, thick and dangerous. He'd tried to drive me away out of fear. But it was more than fear that held us prisoner, it was a whole world set against us.

I turned, holding my jeans with one hand, and touched his cheek. Love blazed in his eyes as I issued my demand. "We *stay* together, we *fight* together, and the pack survives."

"The pack survives," he repeated, fixing his pants, and lowered his forehead to mine.

I buttoned my jeans, my body still hot and humming. I didn't smell like Finis now...I smelled like Phantom. His dark, masculine scent clung to my body with every move.

I knew what he had tried to do...and I knew what it had almost cost him.

A shattered heart on both sides.

Leaves crunched behind us. I didn't need to turn my head to know who it was. From the corner of my eye, Arran came into view, and Vitold was further behind him. Phantom lifted his head and turned to the others. My heart startled as movement came at my right.

Church came closer, slower than the others. I glanced at his neck, where the red imprint of a hand had been just moments ago. But it was barely visible now, nor was the helpless disgust in his eyes. There was only hope now. Only desperation. Only us.

"We're going to need the others," Church urged as he stepped closer. One nod from Phantom, and relief swept through him.

"Send out the call," the Alpha commanded. "I've got some favors to cash in. But first we need to get somewhere safe…safer than here, anyway."

Church dipped his chin in agreement as Phantom reached for my hand. "Come on, special agent. Let's have your doctor friend take a look at that arm."

The deep aching throb only pulsed harder. I swallowed the pain and let Phantom lead me back up to where the others waited, but as we walked, I risked a glance over my shoulder. But it wasn't the forest and the dangers it held that called me—it was Church.

## 10

Walker blushed bright red as I crested the rise with my Wolves close around me. Her gaze bounced between the silent Unseelie who leaned against the Explorer with his arms crossed and a slight curl to his lips and the young Wolf who stood motionless and stared at the ground.

"Everything alright?" I checked, meeting her gaze.

"Sure," she answered, scanning my clothes, then shifted that scrutiny to Phantom. "Not as good as you though, it seems."

It was my turn to blush. But she wasted no time as her focus fell to my arm. "You need to clean that…and properly. You also need—"

"Stitches." Phantom cut in. "And you need a med bag." He glanced at Arran and Vitold. "Take whatever we need and load it into the Explorer."

"We just got here," Walker protested, scowling at the Alpha. "Where the hell are we going now?"

He didn't answer her, just reached into his pocket and pulled out his cell.

"*Great!*" She threw her hands into the air as Arran and Vitold strode toward the cavern, leaving us behind. She turned her focus on me, taking in my face, then my body. "There's something different about you."

Heat burned my cheeks as the Unseelie smothered a laugh with a cough and looked away.

"Not *that*," she muttered under her breath, and strode toward me. "You do know that half of the CCPD and all of the damn FBI are out looking for you, don't you? Apparently, they're under the impression you've been taken hostage by these Wolves."

"That's fucking ridiculous." I shook my head, but there was no sign of a damn lie on her face.

She pulled out her own cell phone and swiped her thumb across the screen. A second later, and Harlan's voice echoed as she handed me the phone. Harlan was there, standing in front of what was left of the Wolves' burned down nightclub with police tape stretched around the scene. *"We know Special Agent Carina Chase is alive, and that's all we're prepared to comment on at this time. The death of Special Agent Murphy and the events that led up to that discovery and after are under a full internal review."*

A reporter pushed a microphone closer. *"And if someone who knows of Special Agent Chase's whereabouts is out there, what would you like to say to them?"*

Harlan looked directly into the camera. *"I say, bring her back where she belongs. We want her safe, we want her protected. Carina, if you're watching this, know that we won't stop until you're found and those who are responsible are brought to justice."*

A chill raced along my spine with the sincerity of his words.

"He's telling the truth," Walker murmured. "They are tearing through every building the Immortals own on our side of the city, and soon they'll invade past the bridge."

"They can damn well try," Mojin growled. "They may just find they've bitten off way more than they can chew."

"Listen to me." She grabbed my arm, drawing me back to her. "I've been dating this guy, nothing serious, but he's high up in the CCPD. He says Harlan's sent out a call to arms to the highest level. He said things are going to get ugly, *real ugly.* He said that if there was any way this was going away...even part of it, would be when you come back."

*Come back.* I swallowed hard at the words and looked at Mojin. The Fae shifted his eyes and that bottomless, soul-searching gaze met mine. One look said it all. My heart pounded and heat spread into my cheeks as that darkness shifted under my skin.

Not Immortal.

And now not even myself.

I never asked for this, hadn't charged into the warehouse that night knowing my life would be forever changed. But still Mojin stared at me, pushing me to face the truth. *If I had... knowing all of this, would I have changed a single thing?*

"Let's get everyone inside until we're sure it's safe." Church glanced from the Unseelie to me.

"Maybe the smartest thing you've said yet, Wolf," Walker muttered.

She followed him, as did Wry, leaving me and the Unseelie in that battle of stares. "Fuck you," I growled.

He just lowered that cold focus to my chest. "If it'd been me who'd found you that night, you very well could have. Then again, I might've been the one fucking you, fucked you so well you'd never want to crawl from my bed. Fucked you so well you might even have forgotten who you were. No more special agent, no more daddy's girl. Think about that the next time you wonder what would've happened if it hadn't been Phantom to your rescue that night."

"Carina?" Church called.

I wrenched my gaze from the Unseelie as the cold slither of

truth snaked its way along my spine. I wanted to run, to stumble backwards and scramble to get away from him. But even though my knees shook, I forced myself to turn slowly and stride away, biting my lip until I tasted blood.

Church scowled at the sight, and lifted his gaze to the Fae. "Everything alright?" he asked as I passed.

Heat rushed to my face as I looked up at him. "I don't know, Church. *Is* everything alright?"

He met my gaze, following my eyes as they drifted to his neck. Anger swelled inside me like a midnight storm. I was hurting in that moment, desperate and in pain, and it made me want to lash out. This was about more than just sex, this was about honesty and pretense. This was about acceptance and the pack. This was about shoving me back out into the cold, when seconds ago I'd been wrapped in the loving embrace of their warmth.

They all wanted me…*except him.*

He paled as I stared at the faint imprint of a hand around his throat. "You left," I stated, and met his gaze. "Where did you go?"

He flinched as though I'd slapped him. His muscular chest rose with a breath, but there was no warning growl rumbling in the back of his throat, no baring of his teeth.

"You think I'm the enemy here." I pushed the point. "Like I'm somehow here to take what's yours. I don't want to take anything from you, Church, I'm just trying to survive."

"This is all you have to eat?" Walker queried behind me, and lifted a dusty bottle of bourbon. "No wonder all you do is fight and fuck."

Church's gaze seared into mine until a tremble tore through him. Something was happening here, some remnant of the truth was coming, spilling from his eyes and almost from his throat. His lips parted, the words right there on the tip of his tongue.

"Is anyone going to say anything? Or are we just going to

stare at each other all fucking day?" Walker snarled, and strode toward me, the bottle in her hand. "You. Hold out your arm."

Her command shattered our connection. Church looked away and took a step backwards. I felt the heat of Walker's gaze, heard her voice in my head as I turned to her. The splash against my arm was instant, and a blaze of agony followed.

"*OW! Jesus!*" I roared, and grabbed my arm.

"*That* is because you didn't fucking call me," she snapped, then looked around and gave a sigh. "And because who the hell knows what kind of infection is in this place."

I tightened my grip around my throbbing arm as Walker took a swig from the bottle, then gave a shrug and stared at the dusty label. "Not bad…not bad at all."

"We wait until nightfall, then we'll make a move." Phantom strode into the cavern behind me. He glanced at my arm, then at Walker as she helped herself again.

*Smack.*

I flinched at the sound and to face the young Wolf.

*Smack.* He punched himself in the base of his throat.

"You're alright." Phantom strode toward the young male and reached for him.

But Wry flinched from the movement and took a step backwards, lips curled, teeth bared. His eyes were impossibly wide.

"Alright," Phantom soothed him, lowering his hands. "You're alright. You're safe with me. You know that, right, Wry?"

The young male just stared at nothing.

"*Wry!*" Phantom commanded his attention.

Only then did the young Wolf meet Phantom's gaze. There was something wrong about him, like he was coming apart at the seams. I sucked in a hard breath, catching movement as Walker took a hesitant step forward. "Maybe I…maybe I can help?"

The young male's fangs grew longer as he whipped that

savage stare to her. Panic tore through me as Walker froze. There was no warning growl from the male. No caution in the way she moved, no sound at all. Just chilling, savage, silence.

"Alright." Phantom stepped between them. "She's not going to touch you. No one's going to touch you."

"I'll go make myself useful and keep watch with the others," Mojin declared. I saw the look he gave Phantom and the small motion of his head.

"I'll be just outside." Phantom spoke to Wry, but I was sure the comfort was for us. The glance my way was at least, as the Alpha followed Mojin outside.

Footsteps crunched, fading as they left. Walker took one look at me, then drank from the bottle again. "You want to tell me what the hell happened now, or do I have to guess it all for myself?"

I turned and paced, the relentless throbbing in my arm demanding movement. "Well, I wasn't abducted, that's for sure."

"That much I figured out on my own."

I glanced at Wry. He'd settled into that faraway look once more, focusing on the ground.

"I don't want to scare you," I said softly.

"Chase," she sighed. "I think we're well past that. Spill, and leave nothing out."

"There was a photo in my locker." I slowed my steps, pivoted at the stone wall, and slowly walked back toward her. "That last day at work, there was a photo in my locker. It was Dad, tied to a damn chair. Lenny was in the photo, too. He'd been shot."

"Jesus, Chase," Walker gasped, her brow furrowing as she tried to make sense of it.

"It was proof Dad didn't do it. Proof he was tied up, so how could he have shot Lenny and left him for dead? The photo had a note to meet someone at this farmhouse just outside the city if I wanted an explanation."

She flinched at that, and the color in her face drained away. "No, Chase. Jesus…"

I swallowed hard. "I had to go, Walker. You would've too, if it'd been you. So I went, and drove out there to meet with whoever. It had to be an agent, or someone in the building. I mean, who else could get into the locker room, right?" I glanced at the bottle in her hand.

"Want some?" she offered, lifting it toward me.

I shook my head. I didn't to be dulled, not anymore. The pain and terror I'd felt were all in the past. "It was Murphy waiting for me at the farmhouse. He attacked me, tried to…" my throat thickened. "He tried to…"

"Oh Jesus, Chase." Walker strode forward and wrapped her arms around me, hugging me to her. "Motherfuckingfucker."

A hard bark of laughter escaped from my lips. "You always had a way with words, Walker."

"You're here, and you're safe, and I hope that piece of shit got what was coming to him. Good for the Wolves for killing him. I would've killed him, too."

"But it wasn't them," I protested.

Walker stilled for a second, then pulled back. "What do you mean?"

"There was someone else." I lowered my voice. "Another Wolf. The same one who attacked us earlier today. The same one who did…" I glanced down at my arm, "this."

"Jesus, Chase." She grabbed my shoulder. "Wolves attacking Wolves. You're going to get yourself killed out here."

"Which is why we're moving her to some place safer," Phantom said as he strode in. "As soon as it gets dark."

"Where the hell is safer from a pack of Wolves?" Walker exclaimed.

But Phantom just kept walking. "Grab anything you don't want left behind, Carina," he directed with a wave of his hand. "Alcohol, as well."

I left my best friend's side to stride after him into the room. Ice cold water trickled down through the cracks in the mountain and raced away through more cracks in the stone floor. I glanced at the spot where Phantom and I had kissed and washed each other only hours before. It felt like days, not hours. We'd barely gotten here and now we were leaving again. "Where are we going, Phantom?"

He grabbed as many clothes as he could, not meeting my gaze. "Somewhere with more protection. Somewhere safer than here."

"I saw the news broadcast, saw Harlan. Why didn't you tell me it was getting this bad?"

He glanced my way, and there was sorrow in his eyes. "I wanted to protect you."

I closed the distance between us, grasped his hands, and turned him toward me. "You don't have to shield me from this, any of it."

"What do you want me to say here, Carina? That I'm scared? That I'm fucking terrified of what's going to happen next?" He gave a soft snort. "I have Wolves that can protect us, but not here. So I *have* to get you someplace else, then I can think…then I can try to figure out what the next step is. Finis is out there, and he'll come back, maybe tonight, maybe tomorrow. But he is coming, and the next time…the next time, we may not be as lucky."

"What the fuck does he want with us?"

That haunted look moved deeper in his eyes. "Me," he answered. "He wants me, begging and hurting, knowing my place as the Alpha of Crown City and no more."

"Jealousy?" I exclaimed. "He's hurting you out of sheer jealousy?"

Phantom swallowed hard and looked away. I saw it then, saw how someone like Phantom could be dangerous to an Alpha like Finis. Break the competition. Make them weak…

make them vulnerable. Make them broken.

The words resounded inside me. "Whenever you're ready, we'll leave," I assured him.

But inside I was trembling with rage...and that dark voice whispered...*no one hurts what's mine.*

11

We waited until dark. Church, Vitold, and Arran stayed outside until the last moment, while Phantom divided his time between the forest, the cavern…and me.

"It's time," he announced as the sun sank below the horizon.

"We'll need to make two trips," Mojin decided. "Carina, Doc here, Wry, and one more. I'll come back for the rest of you."

Phantom just gave a nod and looked at me. "I'll go with you. The rest will wait behind."

My heart squeezed with the words. *Wait behind.*

*Thud!* Wry punched his own chest. His eyes slammed shut. His skin was so pale in the dim light, he was like a ghost.

"Carina, you and the doc get in the car," Phantom commanded, not taking his eyes from the young Wolf. "I'll be right behind you."

Mojin strode toward the opening of the cavern and I turned to follow. But Walker didn't move. Instead, she muttered, "You go, Chase. I'm good here."

There was a gleam in her eye when she watched the frightened young Wolf. The savior complex was burning bright in her, and it had ever since she'd arrived here with the broken male. She licked her lips and took a step closer to Wry. "You know, I have a sister who's deaf."

The harsh, rasping breaths from Wry stopped for a heartbeat, and that was all Walker needed to get an in. She turned toward Phantom and murmured, "It's alright, fluff-ball. I got this."

"Fluff-ball?" the Alpha repeated, his brows rising before he scowled.

But it was Wry who aimed his focus her way, fixing her with a hesitantly interested gaze.

She just gave a shrug and continued, turning her attention to her patient, and I was reminded of why Walker was one of the fast-rising doctors in the Crown City Hospital Emergency Department. She was demanding, a perfectionist in all things that mattered...*and she cared.*

Like, really cared.

"Ebony is..." Her voice trailed off as she searched for the right word. "Blinding. That's how I can describe her. She is a million watts of energy and love, and I love her more than I love any other human on the face of this earth. She was born with a chromosomal abnormality known as Down Syndrome. Mom and Dad found out before they had her, and even though the doctors warned them she could be born with some severe abnormalities and might not even survive the birth, they chose to have her anyway. It turned out she's a fighter, probably would've refused the abortion procedure and marched out of my mother's womb and kicked the doctor in the nuts anyway. That's just how she is."

Phantom was dumbstruck.

But I knew Walker. I knew the way she operated, the way she talked and kept talking, turning this way and that, lifting her hand to brush her hair and giving a loud sigh. She was drawing the Wolf in to her, making him focus on her and her words.

She was weaving her own magic and, as I caught the spark of

a connection in the young Wolf's gaze, I knew to trust her. My pain in the ass Doc knew what she was doing.

"So she survived, thrived even, and became the best little sister I could ever have hoped for. But as time passed, we found out she was deaf. I mean, my constant nagging probably hadn't helped the situation, maybe she turned deaf because of it, I dunno. But while my parents were devastated with the news, I wasn't. I knew who she was, even at three years old. I knew she was a fighter, knew she'd never give up. Any obstacle to her would be seen as a challenge. So that's how I looked at it, as a challenge. And seeing as how I was quite a few years older, well, I just decided to learn sign language." I took a step away as she lifted her hands, but turned back as she continued. "We spoke like this, and before long it became as natural as speaking without our mouths. So what I'm trying to tell you is that there is a way to communicate, just in a different way you never expected."

Phantom stayed for a second longer, until he was sure the young male wasn't going to tear her throat out, before be followed me out into the darkness.

"What are we going to do with them?" Mojin enquired.

"I'll stay behind." Church stepped out of the darkness and strode toward us. "You can be there and back before we know it, and maybe by then they'll be ready to leave."

"Are you sure?" Phantom cocked his head.

"You sure?" I echoed, not liking how that sounded at all. "I can stay."

"No." Phantom shook his head. "I'm not risking you being here a moment longer than you need to be. Church will come with the others." He lifted his gaze to the stars that sparkled faintly in the sky. "We need to leave now."

Why the damn hurry?

A chilling whisper crept across my skin as Phantom opened the back door to the Explorer for me and waited. Arran and

Vitold were there in an instant, climbing into the back seat from the other side. Vitold leaned out across the seat and peered at me through the open door. "You coming, *lyubovnik?*"

I didn't know what that meant, but from the glint of desire in his eyes, I had a fair idea. I took one last look over my shoulder at Church and the dark interior of the cavern before I turned and went to the SUV.

The Explorer started with a growl, and even though this had been our first real place in solitude together, I wasn't upset to leave it, just the same. I felt a restlessness, one I feared would stay with me. Only my Wolves felt safe to me now...*all of them.* I climbed in, then Phantom closed the door behind me and slipped into the front passenger's seat. We were moving almost before I knew it, the headlights cutting through the trees as we drove forward and started the trip to wherever we were headed.

I pulled the seatbelt around me, leaving Vitold to clasp it closed. He met my gaze, then leaned close to kiss me. "It'll all be alright, just you wait and see."

Up and up we went, winding around to come out onto the same dirt road we came in on. Moonlight spilled into the cabin of the four-wheel drive, splashing across my arm as we traded the gravel road for asphalt. But instead of turning back toward Crown City, we headed further west.

Vitold grasped my hand, clutching it tight as we picked up speed. Excitement filled the car for some reason. I felt it like the north wind that blows in the spring, making me restless... making me pace.

But I couldn't pace now, only sit and watch the white lines on the road blur as we left Church, Walker, and Wry behind. I shifted in my seat, working the muscles in my neck until Vitold released my hand to work on the tension in my muscles.

"Turn your back to me," he instructed. I shifted in my seat, letting him find the knots and work them with expert hands until I sighed with relief.

"Better?" He kissed my shoulder and pulled me against him.

I gave a nod and relaxed a little. "Much."

He rested his arm across my chest, holding me. I took comfort in his embrace as we raced through the night until we veered east and before I knew it, we pulled up at an eight-foot electric gate and waited.

Seconds later the gate rolled aside, letting us through. I shifted in my seat, letting Vitold's arm slide from around me, and looked out at the high fence surrounding the compound. I had a strange feeling someone was watching us as we drove along the lengthy driveway, following the thick tree line until the towering ash trees fell away and revealed a spectacular mansion in the middle of nowhere.

"Wow," I muttered. "Your Wolf friends have a lot of money."

No one said a word, not until the four-wheel drive slowed and stopped in the driveway behind the house. It was gorgeous, almost Mediterranean, with sharp edges and sheer, flowing curtains that fluttered out of the wide-open doors. I caught the sparkle of a pool to one side and a separate guest quarters at the back, along with its own helipad.

"Nice," I muttered as Phantom opened the door for me. But the Alpha didn't meet my gaze, only stiffened as the dark silhouette of three men came striding from the darkness…and behind them the swaying stride of a woman.

"Wolf," one of the men greeted Phantom coolly.

*Wolf?* I lifted my gaze as they stopped.

All three men had pale skin and unflinching eyes standing in the shadow of the house. Not even the moonlight reached them, leaving me with nothing until one stepped toward Mojin. I stilled, the warmth of protection fading in an instant as the faintly familiar face dawned on me.

"No," I whispered. "No fucking way."

"Hello, Carina."

My fucking stomach dropped at the sound of her voice as

Ruth Costello stepped around her protectors and strode toward me.

The sashay of her hips was grinding. She looked perfect...*so fucking perfect.* I didn't bother to respond, just turned to Phantom as he winced, and gave him a glare.

12

It was my turn to curl my lips and bare my teeth before I wrenched my gaze from the Alpha and turned away.

"Well, well, *well*. How the mighty have fallen," Ruth. "How does it feel to be on the other side of the badge, Carina?"

My hand automatically went to my hip, fingers searching for the bite of steel, and found *nothing*.

"Looking for something?" She cocked her head to the side, her gaze following the movement. "Your gun and badge won't do you any good this side of the bridge, special agent."

"I don't need a gun, or a badge, to kick your ass, *Costello*," I spat her name like a filthy word, and caught her flinch. I jerked my gaze to Phantom. So this was his big goddamn idea? Jesus. I turned, needing to get out of there, needing to get away from both of them before I did something I'd regret...thoughts of shooting him in the goddamn chest surfaced...*again.*

"Don't be pathetic, Carina." Ruth called, her voice filled with fucking glee. *"At least come inside and give me the opportunity to kick your ass to the curb!"*

"Ruth.," the Vampire beside her warned. "You promised."

His answer was a low, throaty chuckle from the bitch. I

curled my fingers into a fist as the image of that black and white photograph filled my head. *Costello*...all I could see was the black pool of blood...and the look of terror on my father's face.

I spun on my heel, determined to shove those words down her goddamn throat, and stilled. Pain slashed across Phantom's gaze, pain and desperation. The memory of a broken man pushed to the surface, and stopped my words cold.

Still, Phantom stepped into her view of me, unleashing the bite of anger with a cold, ruthless tone. "Ruth, pleasurable as always."

"I'll be back with the others," the Unseelie spoke, striding toward the Explorer and climbing inside.

I wanted to call out, *hurry.* But the engine roared before the words slipped out, and the Fae was gone with a squeal of tires that made me wince.

"How about we continue this inside?" the Vampire lifted his hand, those stony fucking eyes settling on me.

He didn't like me, didn't like that I was there...and, with one glance toward Phantom, I *knew* he didn't like me with the Wolf. I stepped toward Phantom, sliding my arm around his waist possessively, and gave the Vampire an arctic smile. "Let's."

Vitold and Arran sauntered inside first, totally oblivious to the viper in their midst ...even if she did wear perfect makeup and a lipstick the shade of blood. My heart ached as I turned to look over my shoulder at the flare of the Explorer's taillights.

"They'll be fine," Phantom assured me, following my gaze. "And be back before you know it. Then you'll have a whole other battle on your hands."

"Oh yeah?" I met his gaze. "How so?"

"Walker..." he jerked his gaze toward the others as they disappeared through two massive open doors and into the mansion. "And Ruth."

My steps stuttered as I winced. I hadn't thought about that situation. I mean, why the hell would I? For all intents and purposes, Ruth Costello was a case...a purpose. She was a name, a vile, corrupt name. But as I followed the others into the house, a chilling cold swept through me.

Walker...and Ruth in the same house.

*Someone was going to end up hurt or dead.*

We left the cool night air behind and stepped through the double doors. Movement came from the end of the hallway as the familiar sight of Ruth's bodyguard headed our way. His gaze cut to Phantom with a nod, before he swept those icy blue eyes in a critical stare over me.

"Russell," my Alpha greeted.

"Phantom," he answered back, not shifting that gaze from me.

I knew him, knew him from watching her, knew him from the background checks I'd run in the past. He was a loner, quiet, with a spotless record and an impressive military history. For all intents and purposes, he was a nice guy...such a pity he was with Ruth.

The doors closed with a *thud* behind us. I lowered my gaze to the spotless shine on the floor and caught movement behind me as Phantom entered at my back. Slowly the events of the last few days faded, pulling me back to the old men, and *the better, new and improved, yet older version of me.*

Footsteps resounded as we made our way along the hallway and into the expansive house. It was breathtaking, but I didn't really see any of it. I kept my focus forward and slid my walls up around me. Phantom had known where we were headed... straight into the bitch's den. Yet he hadn't felt the need to warn me...*curious.*

I dropped his hand. "Carina," he murmured.

I lengthened my stride, pulling away from him. I narrowed in on the Vampires and...*her.* Glasses clinked and were passed around the room. Arran held out his hand with a tumbler holding Scotch. I shook my head and narrowed my gaze on the Vampires as they spread out in the dimly lit room.

Through the glass doors, the beautiful pool sparkled. *Perfect.*

Perfect fucking house. I lifted my gaze to the Vampires at her side, taking in the gorgeous, towering male at her side. Dark hair, perfect lips, and a body to die for. She noticed my analyzing gaze and moved closer, marking her territory. Her brown eyes flashed at me as I turned my gaze to the Vampire at her other side. He was smaller than the leader, but no less alluring.

He met my stare with his own, giving nothing away, until Ruth gave a sigh and stepped toward me. "You going to stand there and ogle, or are going to get to business?"

"Sure, seeing as how we're all here because of you and your family." The venomous words slithered free.

She stilled for a second, then threw her head back with a deep, throaty laugh. "Oh, that's *so rich.* How long are you going to blame me for every little thing that's gone wrong in your life, Carina?"

"When you and your family start coming clean," I answered as the seething, Unseelie darkness inside me came to life. "What's left of them, that is."

Gazes snapped toward me, *all but hers.*

"Carina," Phantom hissed.

But he could no more stop what was coming than he could hold back a storm. *Because this one had been building for an eternity.*

"Ruth," the Vampire Alpha growled. "We have an alliance with the Wolves."

"But *she's* not a Wolf, *is she?*" The bitch's eyes glittered with amusement.

Phantom edged closer, as did Arran and Vitold, and their movements didn't go unnoticed and spoke volumes. Ruth's eyes widened. I didn't miss the flinch as she watched Arran. It was my turn to leaned against *him* possessively.

"When we're quite finished with the pissing contest," the commanding Vampire muttered, and cut Ruth a glance with one brow raised.

I rattled her cage.

*Yeah, well, she rattled mine as well.*

I stepped closer to Arran. "On second thought," I murmured, taking the Scotch from his hand. Arran just watched me with a hunt of amusement in his eyes. "I'll have *your* drink."

I knew something had gone down between them, I'd even watched them from the bushes as they sat in his Jeep at the edge of the river. *My Jeep now...as was the Wolf.* I turned, pressing my back against him.

"Elithien," Phantom addressed the Vampire. "You said there were *updates.*"

One glance my way, and the Alpha downed his glass and strode toward the bar.

"You want to do this here?" Elithien questioned, not bothering to look my way.

"Why the hell not?" I growled, pushing him. "Let's lay it all out on the table, shall we?"

There was a twitch in the corner of the stuffy dead-dude's mouth as Phantom gave a slow nod.

"Very well then." Elithien exhaled nice and slow. "Finis has been spotted." Phantom jerked his gaze toward the Vampire as he finished softly. "Over two thousand miles away in the city of Innana."

The silence in the room was deafening.

"That's a lie." Phantom gave a shake of his head.

The tension grew more desperate and savage as Elithien's voice softened. "I'm afraid it's not. My men tracked him there four days ago and he hasn't left. They watched his every move, hoping he was going to show his hand and finally lead us to your sister."

Pain slashed across Phantom's gaze. In that moment I forgot all about my own hate and loathing as the floor fell out from underneath me. All I saw was desperation...*cruel, clawing desperation.* "But I saw him, Phantom...I saw—"

"I know," he answered, his voice growing darker. "I know you did."

The room spun around me, tilting and darkening. It *was* Finis...*it had to be.*

"He's been there all along," Elithien assured. "They've been tracking his every move."

"And you trust these men of yours?"

The Vampire gave a nod. "Absolutely."

Phantom took a step toward him, leveling him with a dangerous stare. "Because if they're lying to you, I'll fucking tear them apart."

"Me along with you, brother." Elithien's voice hardened. "But they assure me, on their lives, that it was him. They watched him coming and going, even sent images and video as verification for you to view. Rule," he glanced to the massive Vampire at Ruth's side. "Send the footage to Phantom's cell."

One nod from the Vampire and he was digging into his pocket and yanking out his own phone.

"Damn right I'll be viewing them." Phantom inhaled hard as a slash of agony cut through his gaze. "Because if they're telling the truth, E, then we have a real problem."

It was the first time I'd seen the Vampires up close. The leader of this clan was firm and strong. Danger clung to him in the way he moved, the way he watched, the way he *existed.* I shifted my gaze to the one beside him. He had *protector* written all over him. Barrel-chested, his suit jacket concealed the two pistols in his shoulder holster. He looked at me like I was nothing, and Ruth smiled.

"Then who was the Wolf who attacked us and was the only other Wolf who knew we left that piece of shit alive before he was murdered?" Phantom asked.

"I wish I knew, brother," Elithien responded. "I really wish I knew."

"He was the tie." I shook my head. "The only one we had to getting us back to Crown City. You know what that means, right?"

"That we can't go back," Phantom answered bitterly.

*We can't go back.* The words hit me like a blow as Harlan's warning filled me. *We can never go back.*

"Jesus, this is fucking bullshit." Arran raked his fingers through his hair. "There has to be a way to find that damn Wolf."

An icy draft ruffled the sheer curtains and swept across my skin. There was. Twice the Wolf had come for me. I had no doubt he would again. There was a subtle shake of Phantom's head before he jerked that piercing gaze toward me.

"He came for me before," I declared. It was all I had.

"No," he denied. "That's not happening on *any* fucking level."

If the Wolf wasn't Finis, then he was somehow connected to him. It was a simple play. Bait. Wolf. I gave my Alpha a nod. "It makes sense."

"No, it doesn't," Ruth disagreed with an eye roll. "If he even thinks Phantom or any of your Wolves are around, he'll be gone faster than you can blink. And anyway, what makes you think it's *you* he's after?"

I clenched my jaw until the muscles bulged and whipped my gaze toward her, lifting my hand. "One, he came for me at the farmhouse when I was on my own. Two, there's this problem of the four-inch gash in my arm from his damn fangs."

She had the gall to curl her nose at the sight of the throbbing wound. He *had* come for me. *I knew it.*

"There has to be a better way," Arran insisted, and drained

his glass. "We call in the rest of the pack and track him down. If we can get ahead of him, and behind, we might have a chance."

"He could be anywhere." I pointed out the obvious. "Hell, he could be out there watching us right now. There was no way we'd know it."

"In the meantime," Elithien gave the bodyguard a nod. "You have the use of the guest quarters, there's fresh linen and access to the pool. Anything else you might need, don't hesitate to ask." He lowered his gaze to the bag in Phantom's hand. "I see you've brought some clothes."

"Just nothing for Carina," Vitold cut in.

"I'd give her some of mine, but she's a little bigger in the hips." Ruth's gaze was a dagger. "And a little too *flat* in the chest."

We just stared at each across the room. her insults weren't anything I hadn't heard a hundred times over. "You didn't ask why I was there," I growled.

"What?"

"The farmhouse when we were first attacked. You didn't ask why I was there."

She said nothing. I made the Wolves nervous when I took a step toward her. "I was given a black and white image, taken from inside one of the Costello warehouses. You want to know what it showed?"

"I'm just breathless with anticipation," she answered dryly.

"My father bound to a chair, his face bloody after being beaten, and his partner lying in front of him with a gunshot to his head. The one piece of crucial information to clear him."

She flinched.

*Gotcha.*

It was her turn to close the distance, and she promptly did with that seductive stride, until we faced each other. "And where is that information now, special agent?"

Hate raged inside me, venomous and hungry.

"Ruth," Elithien cautioned. "Carina is our guest."

"You better stay away from me," I warned as that burn in my chest pulsed to life.

"Oh, you don't scare me, Carina," she returned with a sneer. "I've been holding my own with you for years."

I felt the heat of that anger burning a hole through my damn soul. My damn eye twitched. "Don't think *any* of this is going to stop me from coming after you."

She turned her head and hit me with a chilling stare. "Not in my wildest dreams. You, Carina Chase, are the stubbornest, most singleminded, most vindictive and delusional woman I've ever met. I'd say you need a good fuck, but by the looks those Wolves are giving you, I'd say you had that already. So I'm going to go with plain 'ol jealousy. *You*, Carina, are just green with fucking envy, aren't you?"

The bitch had the gall to lower her gaze to that seething burn in my chest. I couldn't breathe, couldn't think. "Jealous? You think I'm fucking jealous *of you?*"

She took a small step closer, until we almost touched. "You're quite literally glowing with the shit."

The room was silent, until there was a muffled cough from the bodyguard in an attempt to break the tension. I wanted to break it alright, all over her smug fucking face.

"Now, let's see if I can find you something of mine to wear," she sighed, and broke the stare and gave me her back.

The slaps of her bare feet on the polished floor resounded like the countdown to a fucking bomb.

I hated her…*no, I fucking loathed her.*

"I knew this was a bad idea," Vitold muttered.

"No shit, Russian," I answered, watching her as she left. "Now, pass me the fucking Scotch."

13

"They should be here by now." I looked out the double glass doors of the guest quarters. The *quarters*, as Elithien had put it, was more than a whole other house, it had its own gym a smaller lap pool, and an open-plan living area. The only dividing walls were the ones to the bedrooms and the massive bathroom. The same design as the main house left long sheer curtains brushing against my face like a caress. I turned from the doors to Vitold as he reclined on a thick, plush sofa. "Something's wrong."

"Nothing's *wrong*, Carina.," he denied with a shake of his head, pushing up from the gorgeous plum-colored sofa and heading my way.

But there was a flicker in his eyes, one that said he was thinking the same as I was. It was getting close to midnight, more than enough time to have gone back to the cavern, picked up Walker, Church, and Wry, and hauled ass back here.

I *knew* we shouldn't have left them. *Damn you, Walker, and your savior complex.* I wrung my fingers until my knuckles burned.

"Hey." Vitold reached out, grasped my aching hands, and pulled me close.

My arms went around him instantly, my splayed fingers sliding up the corded muscles of his back. *Wolf.* Even under the delicious scent of expensive soap, he still had that delicious, unmistakable scent of danger.

His hand slid around the nape of my neck and even though that low throbbing heartbeat of panic still thrummed inside me, I was filled with the image of him kneeling at my feet.

*That's it. Cum on my fingers, Carina.* I shivered with the memory of those words.

"You cold, beautiful?" he asked, that thick Russian accent turning husky.

"I'm worried," I answered with a sigh. "Just worried."

"You worry too much." He brushed my temple with his thumb and pressed in, circling in slow, languid movements as he lifted his other hand to follow suit. "So tense." His dark eyes sparkled. "I could help with that?"

I swallowed hard, my body humming with tension. I was wound tight, like an overwound spring.

"You want me to take care of you?" he murmured, that accent getting thicker by each breathless second. "Steal your thoughts, make you moan and writhe, make you pant with need."

I pressed harder against him. His accent wasn't the only thing getting thicker.

I moved my hand, sliding it along the inside of his thigh until I cupped that hardening length. "If they come…"

"They won't." He leaned down, his lips heading for mine. "Not until we're done. I'll make you cum fast, I promise."

Sweet Jesus. Heat flared between my thighs. "If something was wrong, we'd know about it by now, wouldn't we?"

"Mhmm." He dropped his hands from my temples to my

breasts and kneaded them. "Flat, the Vampire's lover called them. I say they're perfect." He lifted the hemline of my shirt, the backs of his scarred knuckles grazed my stomach. I trembled under his touch, lifting my gaze to his.

"You want the Alpha, you crave the second. Arran is comforting for you. But you will come to ache for me, as well," he promised, lifting my shirt over my head.

"I *do* ache for you," I protested, and lifted my arms, letting the shirt slide free. "My protector. You saved me that day in the morgue, came to my rescue."

He flashed me a wicked smile when I said *'my protector'* and a possessive rumble echoed in the back of his throat. The sound sent a charge of excitement through me. I'd never get used to that sound...*never be unaffected.*

"I did," he lowered his head, murmuring against my lips. "I wanted to kill him for touching you like that, wanted to puncture his gut with my claws and watch him to bleed out while I took care of you. I *wanted* to take care of you, Carina, To kiss these perfect lips, and taste this perfect pussy." He brushed his hand between my legs, making me shiver. "Fuck, I love the taste of your cum sliding down my throat. I could spend all day showing you what a Wolf's tongue is made for..."

I couldn't bite back the whimper. Instead I rocked against his hand. I knew now he'd *always* protect me...even from the danger I didn't see coming. My own personal bodyguard in the shadows. My own brutal hunter.

"That's the way, *my* special agent." His voice grew husky. "Ride my hand."

Soft footsteps rang out, coming closer. My pulse sped as I turned, watching Arran as he headed this way carrying two bottles of Scotch. "You better do her right, Russian, or I'm stepping in."

Vitold just turned his head, showing teeth as he grinned and let out a rumble in warning. "Sit back and watch, Arran. You might learn a thing or two."

My shirt fell and hit the floor beside us. But Vitold was already sinking to the floor and taking my sweatpants along with him.

"Wide hips." He leaned closer, kissing the jutting bones as my pants hit the ground. "Perfect."

I closed my eyes, my hand reaching to his head as he slid his hand along the back of my calf and lifted, urging me to step out of my pants.

"Kneel," he commanded.

I wrenched open my eyes. "Here?"

He didn't answer, just waited for me to do what he wanted. A flare of confusion tore through me. I inhaled hard, while he just waited until I slowly sank to the cold, polished concrete floor. The bitter surface bit into my knees.

"Open your knees, Carina." Vitold murmured, his gaze riveted to my body, drawing down my breasts, and my nipples hardened in response. "Let me see you."

But we were out in the open, with no walls for privacy...*anyone could walk through and see me.* I stared into his eyes as they glittered.

"Fuck me." Arran sank to the sofa, his gaze riveted on me.

Electricity tore through me with the focus. This was what they wanted, that moment where I bent to their will, where I became more than *a* woman...*I became* their *woman.* My thighs trembled as I forced the movement, sliding my knees open as I rested my ass on the back of my heels.

Cold air caressed me, sliding like a greedy tongue between my thighs as I opened. A tortured sound came from Arran, but Vitold was riveted by my crease. He leaned forward, his cock twitching inside his pants.

"I'm the only one naked," I whispered. "Not fair."

"Oh, I beg to differ," he whispered, and slid a finger along my crease. Calloused fingers rubbed against my clit, making me shiver and shake, my nipples tightening even more.

"Fuck, you make me want to kill something," Vitold growled, leaning forward to take my nipple into his mouth.

Fangs scraped tender flesh. I felt my pussy lips swelling with the graze as he lifted his hand and caressed the shimmering jewels embedded into the flesh over my heart. "Does this hurt?" he enquired.

I shook my head. There was no pain now with the Unseelie burden, only that savage hunger, that unrelenting *need.* Vitold bent lower on my chest, lowering his head to lick the green jewels. But it was his fingers that kept my focus, those same languid movements he'd used on my temples before now took center stage at the entrance to my pussy.

"Fuck me," I whimpered as Vitold took my other nipple into his mouth, then slapped two fingers straight against my crease hard enough to make me flinch with shock. My desire died.

Round and round, his fingers drew out that heat again, slow…achingly fucking slow. I shuddered and dropped my head forward, watching his fingers working.

*Slap!*

I flinched at the sound and let out a whimper. The sensation didn't hurt, if anything, it felt…*good.* Vitold pulled away, but his focus stayed laser driven. *Round and round,* until he slipped inside. I let out a ragged moan, my hips jutting forward, desperate to gain an inch.

On the sofa, Arran opened the button of his jeans. The zipper parted, releasing his cock. He was hard, and twitching, delicious and achingly perfect as he wrapped his fist around the shaft and slowly pumped.

"That feel good?" Vitold asked, starting those circles once more. Heat burned me, slicing through my core. I found myself rocking with the movement.

*Slap!* His fingers hit harder this time. I was no longer flinching, but growing wetter with the sudden contact. "More," I whispered.

"Fuck me, you're so wet," Vitold growled, slipping his fingers inside me again.

Desperation filled me, burning through the tension in my muscles. I felt pliable under his hand, blinded by the heat in my body. I lashed out, grasping his wrist. *"Please, Vitold."*

His eyes narrowed, and there was a catch in his breath. "Say that again."

"Vitold, please, I'm going to…"

He rose in an instant, the movement drawing my gaze to the thick bulge of his erection. One hard shove and he pushed his pants low. His cock sprang free, making me catch my breath. A bulging vein running under his gorgeous length pulsed, catching my attention.

I licked my lips as he straightened. "Come closer," I urged.

He did, bringing that bobbing member closer. I let go of his wrist, then wrapped my grip around his shaft and opened my mouth.

*"Trakhni menya."* He gave a guttural growl as the smooth head slid along my tongue. "Arran," he called the Wolf as his fingers speared through my hair.

My lover obliged in an instant, rising from his viewpoint on the sofa and circling me before kneeling. I focused on the slow slide of my grip, taking Vitold in deeper. The Russian's fingers tangled in my hair, driving the thrust deeper. But it was the slow slide of Arran's finger down the length of my spine that drew my focus. He kissed my shoulder blade before sliding his hand around to my front.

I gave a groan as he found the place where I needed him to be.

"Vitold's right, you are *very* wet," Arran agreed, making me clench my entire core and rise against his fingers as he circled my clit and slipped inside. "And I'm so fucking close." With a snarl, he left my heat and gripped my hips, lifting me. I splayed even wider as his thighs slid under mine.

I reached around, gripped Vitold's ass, and drove him harder into my mouth. He groaned and muttered more Russian as his hold on my head turned into a vise. But it was that length against my core that made me rock my hips.

"Carina." Arran let out a groan as he gripped my hips. Now it was my turn to go round and round.

"Fuck me," Vitold snarled, and pulled my mouth deep against him, holding my head there. Saliva spilled from my mouth as his cock kicked and pulsed, and warmth shot down the back of my throat. I held him against me as he emptied.

"That's my special agent," he moaned, easing the pressure on the back of my head. Instead, he mussed my hair and pulled out just a little, leaving me room to swallow.

A gentle brush of his thumb across my lips spread remnants of his cum around my mouth. Still I rocked, leaning forward, sliding my core along the shaft of Arran's length, until he angled his hips and that blunted head slid in.

My breath caught, and my eyes closed, savoring the feel of him as I drove slowly down.

"So tight," Arran sighed, his hand sliding down my back. "So fucking perfect."

I focused on the sensation, grinding and driving. I lowered my head, Vitold's hand still fisted in my hair. "That's the way, *krasivaya*. Ride him, take all you need."

I closed my eyes as that aching darkness licked deep, leaving a trail of fire inside me. The taste of Vitold lingered on my lips, as I felt the thrust of Arran deep inside me.

"Use me," Arran whispered. *"Use...me."*

I ground my hips against him, picking up the pace as the chaos in my chest demanded more. More Wolf. *More them.*

Always more, thumping against my thighs, buried deep in my sex. Aching. I ached…and ached…*and ached.* Darkness moved through me, finding the marks on their bodies. *My marks.* Through the connection, I unleashed my power and let out a cry as Arran growled.

"Take it," he bellowed. *"Take it!"*

With a final hard slam of my hips, I tipped over the edge, falling headlong into endless bliss. My body clenched, released, and clenched, squeezing Arran's cock. He let out a roar and drove my hips down, thrusting his cock deep inside as he emptied.

I stayed like that, with Vitold's fist in my hair, as harsh breaths savaged my chest.

"Fuck me, what the hell was that?" Arran let out a ragged groan.

"Her," Vitold answered. I lifted my head, our gazes colliding. There was more than love in his eyes. There was *utter devotion.*

*They would kill for me.* The thought filled me as Phantom's desperation rose once more. *They'd tear apart the world.*

My body twitched and pulsed, and I knew unequivocally, I'd kill for them too.

The sound of footsteps drew us from the heat of love. Vitold slid his hand from cupping my head as Arran steadied me, his cock sliding out as Phantom strode through the sheer curtains and lifted his gaze to us.

There was a flare of his nostrils, scenting the heady remnant of passion, as he narrowed his gaze. "Has my special agent worked out her frustrations?"

"Depends on what *'frustrations'* we're talking about," I answered, and pushed upwards.

My legs trembled, warmth cooling on my inner thighs. Phantom lowered his gaze, finding Arran's seed on me. "Alpha," I murmured.

He jerked his gaze to mine. Heat burned between us. I'd had him deep inside me mere hours ago, his cock claiming my desire, his scent on my skin, invading my lungs with every breath, and still it hadn't been enough. *It'd* never *be enough.*

"They want to talk to you," Phantom growled.

"They?"

He swallowed. "They want to know what the FBI knows about the warehouse. Apparently, there was DNA testing."

I stilled in an instant, my thoughts colliding as memories slipped in. Then it dawned on me. I forced a breath, the corners of my lips curling. "There was."

Phantom had never asked, even now he wasn't asking. He was giving me the option to play nice to our hosts. "Can you give me five?"

One nod of his head and I turned to Vitold, leaning close to kiss him. "Thank you."

Arran was next, his body hot against mine as I cupped his strong jaw and kissed those perfect lips. "You are perfect to me."

"As you are to us," Vitold answered, giving the Alpha a nod before striding toward the small kitchen and yanking open the fully stocked refrigerator, still bare-assed and gorgeous.

I headed for the bathroom and closed the door. I hurried to use the toilet and wiped. Then I grabbed the washcloth and shoved it under the faucet. So she wanted to talk, eh? Wanted to find out what dark secrets the FBI knew, secrets like her inhuman DNA. I lifted my gaze to the mirror and smiled. Check. Mate.

I washed quickly, swiping the cloth between my legs, and hurried to use the towel before yanking my clothes on again. Wonder how much her Vampire knew? I guessed there was only one way to find out.

I dragged a brush through my hair and winced at the knots, resigned myself to having to deal with them later, and strode from the bathroom. "I'm ready."

But Phantom was waiting, pouncing on me as soon as I stepped out, and pulled me close. "Seeing you like that, my pack's cum all over that perfect pussy of yours, you have no idea what that does to me. When Walker and Church return, I want you in here instantly. No all-girls' night, no catching up. Just you, naked, legs spread, waiting for me."

My heart thundered. "That sounds like a command, Alpha."

He took a step even closer, pushing me up against the doorway, his tone all dark seduction. "Female, you don't want to find out what will happen if I have to hunt you down."

My pulse sped at the words as he inhaled hard and adjusted himself. "Your body is mine tonight…*all fucking night long.*"

He turned and headed for the entrance, that powerful body slicing through the sheer curtains as they flapped and danced in the constant breeze. I followed, licking my arid lips, remembering the time I'd crossed the bridge, to find myself in Phantom's bed. The night he fucked me until I forgot who I was…and found a new purpose.

My bare feet were quiet on the concrete as I followed my Alpha into the mansion once more. I took more notice this time, taking in the minimal and expensive furniture. So the Wolves hid out in a cave with no hot water, and the Vampires got this? I turned the corner and lifted my gaze to the living room and the crackling fire.

Shadows moved in the corner of the room. The Vampire leader, Elithien, stepped closer, handing Phantom a tumbler of Scotch before he turned those piercing dark eyes on me and lifted a snifter. "I hope brandy is suitable?"

"Fine, thanks" My fingers skimmed the cool touch of his as I took the glass from his hand. A flare cut across my mind. An instant headache, pressing in, desperate to find a way…

*I don't think so, Vampire.* That dark whisper rose, obliterating the pain with a rush. The Unseelie power throbbed. I didn't think there was a way for his cold gaze to get any colder, but it did, dulling the glint until there was just *nothing...endless, unfathomable nothing.*

I was normally good at reading people. I could even get a bit of a handle on the Wolves. But these Vampires were a whole other ballgame. I lifted the glass to my lips and sipped.

"Your quarters are suitable, I take it?" The Vampire aimed the small talk at me.

"Yes, thank you," I answered. "I appreciate your hospitality."

"The Unseelie should be here any moment. I take it your friend will be with him, as well? We've taken the liberty of making up a room for her in the house."

The brandy was liquid fire, sliding down the back of my throat. "Thank you."

"I know this must be all quite confounding," the Vampire continued, searching my gaze. He was trying to read me, trying to find out if I really was a bitch. I'm sure Ruth had had plenty to say about that matter...and speak of the she-devil.

She strode into the room, looking very different from before. Her long red hair was tied up in a messy ponytail and her bare feet were quiet on the cold tiles. There was a worried look on her face, one that lowered her brows and carved lines in her forehead. Something was happening, more than what hovered on the surface.

"Everything alright?" I asked.

She jerked her gaze to mine, suddenly aware of my presence, and the walls behind her eyes slammed down. "Fine," she answered coldly.

But she was lying. It's what she did. I shifted my focus behind her to the darkened hallway and lowered my own walls, letting that *other* part of my nature roam. *Blood. Pain. Desperation,* rose swiftly, invading my mind like an avalanche at full speed. *No, don't do this...no, don't do this. NO. DON'T. DO. THIS!*

"Carina?" Phantom called my name, snatching me from the panic.

I flinched and jerked my head toward him. Those darkened eyes shimmered with a glint of silver. He swallowed and held my stare. A flicker of something danced between us. A plea...a careful, *desperate* plea. *Please...*

"We know about the DNA," I answered, holding my Alpha's gaze, then I cut to the Vampire. "The blood splatter from the warehouse came back a few days ago and the lab was able to match it to the dead, and those of the living we tracked there with CCTV footage."

He was careful, keeping his voice calm. "And the profiling obviously shows..."

"That Ruth's DNA markers indicate she's Immortal."

I caught the wince, before it was smothered by the lift of his glass as he murmured, "Interesting."

"I sure thought so," I added, toying with him for just a... second longer. "But in my haste and incompetence, I hadn't yet entered that into the database. I mean, I'm sure it's still there, buried under a mountain of paperwork on my desk. Organization has never been one of my strong points."

The Vampire whipped his gaze to mine once more, and his brows rose. He shifted his attention to Ruth as she poured herself a brandy and strode toward him.

"So, they may not know," she said hopefully. "Not yet anyway."

"It gives us time...and *options.*"

"I take it you're worried about someone accessing that information?" I sipped the brandy again, letting that burn spread through me. Still, I found my focus wandering, slipping to that darkened hallway and the unmerciful terror that spilled out from whatever darkness lingered in the depths of this beautiful mansion.

"You could say that" Elithien commented.

I swung my gaze his way. "Then I guess it's a good thing the focus is on us then, isn't it?"

The Vampire didn't answer. He didn't have to. The silence said it all for him. This whole shitshow was to their advantage.

"So let's get this straight." I prodded, or more like stabbed. "So, she's Vampire, and that's something you don't want released. I mean, why wouldn't you? Only..." I swung my focus toward Ruth. "She sure doesn't look like a Vampire to me. She looks almost...*mortal.*"

"I *am* mortal," Ruth snarled, but she wasn't sure about that. It was a heavy weight, shifting and closing in. She struggled under the thought of it.

"You obviously know about the attack at the warehouse," Elithien stated, "seeing as how you were there. But what you don't know is that the Vampire who came for us was very dangerous, very well connected...*and Ruth's father.*"

I froze, the snifter halfway to my lips, as the floor seemed to open up and swallow me whole. "Fuck me." I jerked my gaze to my enemy.

Now that weight made sense, as I saw her struggle and wrestle with the damn thing. "And she could be in danger?"

"Yes," Elithien acknowledged, never shifting his gaze from her.

Now *that* made a whole lot of sense. "Jesus, you really lucked out on the paternity lotto, didn't you? First daddy is a blackmailing, corrupt *thug,* and now you find out your real sperm donor is...a fucking Vampire. Makes sense, two monsters to make one."

"Carina," Phantom warned as the Vampire curled his lips and gave me his undivided attention.

Hate raged in that bottomless gaze. Untapped, pitiless...*hate.*

The words turned to ash in my mouth. "I'm sorry," I said, and glanced at Ruth. "That was uncalled for." She was pale...and shaking, the brandy in her hand sloshing against the sides of her glass. Now I felt like a true bitch.

"Forget it," she said, her tone wounded. "I expected nothing less from you, Carina."

Jesus, I really knew how to fuck shit up. The look from Phantom said just as much. My heart thundered as disgust flared in the silver of his eyes. I felt it like a punch to the heart. I took a step toward her and caught the shake of Phantom's gaze. Was he warning me, or protecting me?

I shifted uncomfortably. I wasn't used to this…watching my words, caring what impact I had. My heart pounded in my chest and with each boom, a fresh wave of disgust spread through me. "We've gone out of our way to hurt each other, haven't we?"

"I guess you could say that," she answered. "Although for me, it was always in self-defense. I can no more apologize for what my family has done than I can change my DNA."

Her words invaded me, driving home with a heavy thud in my chest. Heat rushed to my cheeks as she shifted her gaze to mine. Our energy collided. Opposite sides of the same coin, we'd danced around each other for what felt like an eternity. I'd chased and hounded. I'd done things I wasn't proud of, narrowing in on her with a singleminded savagery. Had I been wrong to pin every dark and foul deed her family had ever done on her alone?

I'd never thought that before…so why now?

*Because we're now standing on the same fucking side.* Heat carved through me. My throat thickened as I drained my glass and shrugged. "Well, look at that. I think that's my cue to leave."

I turned, scowling at the floor, and took a step.

"Wait," Ruth called, stopping me.

But I didn't turn, just focused on the floor while thoughts raced through my head.

"The image," she started. "You said there was an image of the warehouse, the day your father was framed. Can you tell me about it?"

I spun then, fixing my gaze on her. There was genuine interest, more than just a passing exchange of information. She wanted to know more...*was almost desperate to know more.* Looked like I wasn't the only one wanting to unearth the truth. Now wasn't that a kicker...

I swallowed and steadied myself for unfamiliar territory before answering. "What do you want to know?"

14

This wasn't how things were supposed to be. Not between me...*and Ruth Costello.*

She just turned and paced, processing every scrap of information I'd gleaned from that one image.

"And you're sure this *Murphy* had a contact?" she questioned, glancing my way.

"Someone was feeding him information," I answered. "Someone who was either there, or knew someone who was. That kind of stuff isn't freely passed around."

"No, no, it's not," she mused.

Phantom and the Vampire watched us with nervous attention. It wasn't like I was gonna throw her on the floor and arrest her...*right?*

"Could it have been someone on a case he'd been working on?"

I stilled, my mind working. "It could have been. I didn't think to look at his previous cases."

"If we cross-referenced, maybe we could find someone connected," she suggested hopefully. "I know most of my father's contacts...well, the ones he didn't hide from me, that is."

I swallowed hard. Working *with* Ruth. Never in a million fucking years had I ever thought. "I mean, it makes sense…"

*Thud.*

The sound came from behind me. I spun as a monstrous dark wave of terror slammed into me. I stumbled with the feeling, throwing my hand out as that *thud* came again and the Unseelie darkness inside me let out a shattering scream.

A shadow crashed into the room, falling through the open door. Blood…all I saw was blood as that scream of *chaos* inside me unleashed like a bomb. Panic rose, consuming, choking…*unforgiving.*

"*Mojin?*" Phantom roared and lunged, charging past me in a rush. "*WHAT THE FUCK?*"

"*Hurrow!*" Elithien roared. "*Russell!*"

The air quaked with brutal savagery that punched me in the chest.

"Attacked…" the Unseelie forced as he tried to sit up. Phantom was there, catching the Fae's shoulders in one sweeping lunge. "I got you, buddy. I got—"

"No," Mojin roared, and swiped his hands away, desperation etched in his gaze…"*need to get to them.*"

The male was a mess. His black shirt was reduced to nothing more than scraps that exposed rippling muscles smothered in blood. Long claw marks tore through his pants, leaving bloody streaks behind. He'd been hurt, that was easy to see. Bite marks marred his side, savaged in a way I'd never seen before—*and hope to never see again.* My stomach rolled as the room was filled with thunder.

But as the two bodyguards charged into the room, that sickening feeling inside me grew talons that clenched around my heart. "Phantom—" I whispered.

But no one was listening.

"*Phantom,*" I yelled.

My Alpha jerked his gaze to mine. My thoughts were screaming, howling with fury. *"Where are the others?"*

I stumbled backwards as a roar came through the door. Arran and Vitold were there in a heartbeat, eyes wide with rage, fingers curled in fists, ready to fight as Wolves. But my knees were buckling as the faint *whoop...whoop...whoop* slipped into my ears.

"Wolves" Mojin's gravelly voice made my stomach lurch.

There was only one way a voice sounded like that...*if there was a lot of screaming involved.*

"Walker," I whispered her name.

The Unseelie wrenched his gaze to mine. "She escaped...with the young Wolf."

"Wry?" Phantom jerked his gaze from Mojin to me. Concern flared deep in his eyes. Still that *whoop...whoop...whoop* grew louder, like a heartbeat pounding in my ears.

"Where is Church?" I whimpered, finally breaking free from the prison of fear. I stumbled forward, grasping the Unseelie, unable to care that I was hurting him. "Where is *my Wolf?*"

He didn't answer for a heartbeat...it may as well have been an eternity. "No," I screamed, shoving him away, desperate to unsee the slash of pain in the Unseelie's gaze.

"He fought them...fought while the doctor ran," Mojin explained in a voice filled with anguish.

My knees buckled, only there were no arms to catch me... there was only a free fall into agony.

"They took him," Mojin ended. "The black one...*the Alpha.*"

My breaths came too fast, and for some reason I couldn't slow them down. I couldn't do anything but listen to the *whoop... whoop...whoop.*

"We have incoming," Russell barked, turning from the double glass doors that overlooked the pool. Concern brightened his blue eyes. "Everyone out!"

*Incoming?* I jerked my gaze to Phantom.

"Ruth!" Elithien commanded.

She spun in a heartbeat, moving like a leopard before I knew it, running to him…like it was *instinct*. In a heartbeat, she was surrounded. *"Wait!"* She skidded to a stop, her bare foot squealing on the tiles. "I can't leave Justice!"

With long, wicked fangs bared, Elithien jerked a burning gaze to the bodyguard. *"Friend or foe?"*

Russell gave a shake of his head and turned from the doors. "I can't tell."

*Whoop…whop…whoop…*the unmistakable sound of the rotor grew louder.

"Keys!" Phantom barked, and lifted his hand.

I caught the blur of metal tossed through the air by Elithien as the sound of the chopper's blades turned deafening, streaking through the sky overhead. The bodyguard wrenched his gaze to me, then back to Elithien. His lips parted in a soundless cry which was smothered by the thunderous roar of the chopper until it faded just enough to hear, "FOE! FOE! *FOE!*"

The Vampires moved in an instant. Russell charged, picked up Ruth in a sweep of his massive hands, and tossed her over his shoulder like she weighed nothing at all. I registered a heartbeat as I felt myself lifted, too. Arran's arms clamped around me as Phantom and Vitold charged from the mansion and lifted their gazes to the sky.

Spotlights blazed as the blast of hurricane air whipped strands of my hair into my eyes. They blurred with the sting, but I didn't need to see as the voice blasted over the speaker.

*"You're surrounded! Let Carina Chase go!"*

I jerked my head upwards, panic mingling with the rush of blood headed for my face.

*"STOP OR WE WILL OPEN FIRE!"*

Arran turned, watching the chopper as it shot across the midnight sky and circled back. "Put me down, Arran!" I yelled and shoved against his ass.

He gripped my hips and yanked, letting me slide down his body, falling before he caught me with strong, quick hands. Our gazes connected as my bare feet hit the concrete. There was real fear in the darkness of my bartender's eyes. But it wasn't fear for them. *It was for me.*

"There's nowhere you can run, Phantom!" The familiar voice blasted through the speaker.

I lifted my head as Arran turned, protecting me with his body as I caught Harlan's face over the dark blue FBI windbreaker. The blinding beam of another spotlight carved across the Vampire mansion behind me. I reached up, grasping Arran's arm, and turned to find another chopper closing in.

"Run!" Phantom grabbed me, hauling me from the safety of Arran's body and dragging me with him. *"We have to run!"*

Darkness blasted through the air, slamming into my back and pitching me forward before Phantom caught my fall with massive hands on my shoulders. I shot a glance over my shoulder, to find the bloody and pissed-off Unseelie staggering outside.

He lifted his hand, driving his body through the vortex of the rotors until he was beside me. He jerked his gaze toward me and, with one savage glare, his rough, vicious snarl tore through my mind, *where's your chaos now, special agent?*

*BOOM!* A shotgun blast blasted free, smashing into the ground in front of us. Vitold curled his lips as the midnight blur of an Explorer catapulted toward us...*two of them.* Car doors were thrown open as they skidded to a stop. Phantom shoved me forward before I could think. I lifted my hand, desperate for that animalistic Unseelie power to rear inside me. Anything to save them...*anything to save* us—and the back window of the Explorer exploded with a *crack!*

I threw my hands up, protecting my face. But I didn't need to, as Phantom moved in a blur, stepping in front of me as shards of glass sliced through the air. Slashes of blood bloomed across his face and arms.

More shots were fired…like the sky unleashed a hail of bullets. I was already lifting my hands as I met Phantom's gaze.

"No," he cried, shaking his head, as the two helicopters descended. Agony bloomed in those dark eyes as the helicopters hovered, effectively surrounding us.

"There's no way out." Tears blurred my vision as I took a step backwards. "Like you said before, I'm a liability."

He gave a tortured moan as my gaze shifted from my Wolf to the shattered window behind him. Pain ripped through my chest, like I'd taken all those shards straight to my heart. He didn't move, just stood there, watching me like this wasn't happening.

*Maybe it wasn't.* Maybe this was all just a bad dream. One fucking nightmare. I took another step, the wind from the rotors kicking my hair around my head.

"Carina…*no!*" Arran roared, and lunged for me.

But I caught movement in the hovering chopper as a sniper leveled his rifle on my Wolf at Harlan's command.

"No!" I flung my arms into the air and stepped in front of Arran. Tears streamed down my cheeks, drying in an instant from the wind of the rotors. "I'll go…*I'll go!*" I screamed up at Harlan.

In the helicopter, my commander's lips curled, baring his teeth in triumph.

"Find them." I wrenched my gaze to Phantom. "Promise me you'll find them!"

One nod was all he gave. He was broken, shattered…maybe it was the shards of his heart impaled into mine? My throat thickened as I stumbled backwards, my feet moving on their own as I turned.

Pain flared in the sole of my foot, but I barely felt it, just kept stumbling toward the looming chopper as it lowered to the ground. They were out in an instant, rushing toward me with jackets flapping wildly. Harlan was the first to reach me, reaching out to grasp my arm and haul me backwards.

Armed officers were beside him, training their weapons on the one I loved. "I'm here..." I cried, but my words were snatched from my lips as I was yanked backwards, and into the helicopter before I knew it.

Hard steel under my body, Harlan's screams in my ears as we lifted from the ground. But I felt nothing...

*I heard nothing.*

In that moment, I *was* nothing.

*Nothing but a liability.*

15

"You're safe now, Carina," Harlan roared in my ear, holding a windbreaker around my shoulders as we raced from the chopper to the waiting four-wheel drive.

Others were there, men waiting for orders.

"I want the entire county searched," Harlan barked. "Every goddamn rock...*I want those Wolves in shackles by the end of the night!*"

My heart shuddered with the words, but I didn't lift my head, only looked at the ground before I slipped into the midnight four-wheel drive.

*Run,* I sent the plea through my mind. *Phantom, you have to run!*

His pain was palpable, *a real thing* burrowing in my chest, desperate to punch through flesh and bone and out the other side. But I kept it caged within my heart, desperate to hurt like he was hurting. The back door opened and Harlan climbed in before closing it. The weak interior light washed over his stony features. He wasn't just my commander in that moment. *He was my enemy.*

"Don't worry, Carina." The way he said my name made me recoil. "You're safe now. It's all behind you."

He turned and muttered a command. A second later, we were rolling forward, pulling away from the helicopter as it refueled and reloaded, this time with a squad of the fiercest-looking and most heavily armed guys I'd ever seen.

*It doesn't matter,* I reassured myself. *They won't find them...*

My pack would be long gone, doing what they did best, slipping into the forest, never to be found again.

"Goddamn savages," Harlan snarled. "Goddamn fucking savages for doing this to you."

I flinched at his touch and snapped back to reality. Harlan's fingers brushed across my cheek, almost with a lover's touch. "I'm fine," I answered automatically.

"You're not fine, Carina," he said as he moved from the opposite seat to the one next to me, winding his arm around my shoulders. "You've been through a terrifying ordeal. Attacked, abducted, held prisoner. *Jesus,* to think what those animals have done to you."

*What. The. Fuck?* I tried to slow the thundering of my heart. My thoughts were lightning strikes, arcing through the darkness to hit the ground randomly.

"I would've hunted them forever," my commander murmured, his fingers digging into my shoulder in an effort to pull me against him.

I resisted, my spine ramrod stiff. My chest heaved with heartbroken breaths as my feet burned from the cold. I curled my toes, digging them into the carpet.

"Your poor feet, you must be freezing," Harlan snarled, and reached forward, grasping me by the calves and swinging my feet up to his lap.

I swiveled with the movement, unable to do anything other than stare at the stranger sitting next to me. The stranger that'd been my commander for the last eight years…who'd *never once looked at me the way he looked at me now.*

"Harlan," I murmured, my words burning in the back of my throat. "What's going on?"

"They won't get away with this," he growled, his focus on my bare ankles and feet. His touch was awkward and light, fingers traipsing down the top of my foot before he rested his hand over my toes.

His touch made me tremble. His look did more. I swallowed hard. "Harlan, the Wolves. Murphy—"

My commander gave a shake of his head. "I don't want you to worry about that. Not now. It can all wait. You're cold, exhausted, and God knows what else…" he started, then stilled, brows furrowing. Anguish crossed his face before he continued. "Did they hurt you, Carina? Did they…I mean, do I need to take you to the hospital? They have rape kits available…"

"*What?*" Heat rushed from my face. I hadn't been cold before…*but I was cold to my soul now.* "They didn't rape me, Harlan.

He gave a slow nod, and relief swept his gaze, smoothing out the creases in his face.

"Harlan, you're not understanding what happened between us. The Wolves, they—"

"We're here," he cut me off, lifting his gaze.

My heart was in my throat as the realization dawned. He didn't see me as other than a victim in all this. Didn't see me as anything other than a pawn in Phantom's game. The black four-wheel drive pulled up in front of a nondescript house somewhere in the suburbs. I knew a safe-house when I saw one. The address hidden…except to those in charge. "Harlan, I lov—"

He yanked open the door and climbed out, leaving my feet to slide from his lap and smack the floor. Panic rose inside me, sending shudders to rattle my bones. Something had changed in the days we'd been running from him. The cogs had shifted, and a new machine had been built. One that was armed to the teeth…and pointed at the Wolves I loved.

My body was slow to move as I shoved against the seat and scooted forward before stepping through the open door. Lights were on inside the house. The front door was open and waiting. I tried to think, tried to work out how to call off the dogs.

I crossed the sidewalk and headed along the pavement, climbing the steps to the door. Movement came from inside. Shadows spilled across the floor and splashed on the wall. Two towering guards I'd never seen before stood in the living room, armed to the teeth. They met my gaze and gave a small nod as I stepped in. I knew what I was to them; a job, a victim to protect. But I was neither of those things. Here, I was a prisoner…one who needed to be set free.

Harlan was in the bedroom, standing at the foot of the bed when I walked in. He turned and lifted his gaze. Something moved behind his eyes, something *hungry*. I had to set this straight right now.

"Harlan, I need to tell you this, and you need to listen to me. I wasn't *abducted*. I ran, freely. They didn't kill Murphy. They didn't—" He just looked at me with a deadpan gaze, one filled with sympathy. That Unseelie darkness whispered through my mind at the sight. "Don't look at me like that."

"It's alright, Carina," he responded, and stepped closer, grasping my shoulders. "I let you down. I accept that now. You told me Murphy was making you uncomfortable and, well…I left you to deal with it on your own because I was fighting these feelings for you."

"No," I whispered, and stepped away, forcing his hands to drop. "No, Harlan."

But resignation hardened his gaze. "I failed you. I see that now. But I won't fail you again. Starting tomorrow, you're back at the Bureau. I want you in there for a full debrief. Your protection will take you in and bring you back here. There's food, clothes, anything else you need, just let them know. They're here to protect you, Carina." *Why was he still calling me that? He never called me that. It was always Chase. Always.* "They're here to watch over you."

In other words, I was going to be forcibly detained.

"Rest now, it's late. We'll talk again in the morning." He stepped toward me and I couldn't stop the flinch. But he kept walking, moving past me to the door. "I won't fail you again. I'll keep you safe this time…and those beasts where they belong."

He left with that, striding through the doorway into the small living room. I heard him speaking to the two guards with quiet commands not intended for my ears. Exhaustion made me sway on my feet as I leaned on the doorframe. I closed my aching eyes and the tears came, the sting inevitable.

Seconds passed, or it could've been minutes, before the front door closed. I opened my eyes, my senses prowling, finding the two still in the living room. But there was no one else here. Harlan was gone…*just like* they *were all gone.*

Still, the tears didn't stop, even when I opened my eyes and crawled into bed, nursing that wounded look from Phantom close to my heart. I didn't cry, not ever. I just got angry…and then I got even. But with my Wolves, it was different, because I cared so deeply.

The sheets were cold as I shifted. The crisp clean smell sharp and jarring after living with the heady scent of my Wolves. I curled on my side and closed my eyes. So much had happened…*so much.*

Silver eyes shone in the darkness of my mind.

Walker's smiling face came a second later.

Blood from Mojin.

And under it all, those terrifying words….

*Where is Church? Where is my Wolf?* The Unseelie's answer

resounded, taking me into the endless dark. *He fought them... fought while the doctor ran. They took him. The black one...the Alpha.*

I looked through the window of the Explorer to the FBI building as we slowed at the entrance. Cold concrete against a brooding sky. That place no longer felt like home, no longer felt like anyplace I wanted to be.

In my head, I was with *them...*wherever *there* was. Caves. Strip clubs. The guest house owned by a Vampire coven. Even if we were running...it didn't matter as long as I was with them. I shifted against my seat as the Explorer turned, nosing into the parking garage, and stopped at the boom gate.

Through the windshield, Beth-Anne watched me in open-mouthed surprise. *Chase?* she mouthed soundlessly. I turned away from her as we rounded the parking aisle and pulled up close to the bank of elevators.

"You alright from here, Miss?" the agent asked, not bothering to turn and look at me over his shoulder.

I didn't answer, just opened the door and closed it behind me. I was walking in there in cheap clothes that weren't my own and with a gut full of rage. I wanted this over...changed. Hell, I wanted this *done.* I strode toward the elevator, remembering how before I'd usually watch for Murphy's car, how I'd hurried to this same elevator in fear, desperate to outrun his unwanted attention.

Only now I was hurrying for a different reason. I wanted my Wolves back.

I stabbed the button and waited, stepping inside as the doors opened, and selected my floor. My eyes stung under the harsh white glare. I rubbed the nape of my neck, the muscles bunched and corded with knots on top of knots.

I hadn't slept. Instead, I'd tossed and turned, my feet tangled in the sheets as I ached and wept. Church was alone...and probably hurt, and Phantom was running. They were *all* running. *Everyone except me.*

I felt that need stronger than I'd ever felt anything in my life. The steady beat of my heart sounded like the pounding of my boots against the ground. I wanted to run...and keep on running. *I wanted to be a hunter of my own.*

Hunt them down.

Protect what was mine.

The elevator shuddered to a stop and the doors opened. Sounds assaulted me. Frantic tapping on a keyboard, fax machines whirring, chatter from three agents standing in the hallway. Then silence as each one turned to look at me.

The hairs on the back of my neck rose as I made my way along the hallway to Harlan's office. I opened the door and stepped in, coming to a stop in the middle of the reception area. Tracey lifted her head, her scowling expression freezing as she saw me. I couldn't speak, just stood there, words would be like ash in my mouth.

There was no snarky bite to her words, no bitchy bark. She carefully chose her words as she met my gaze and said, "He's waiting for you, Carina. You can go right in."

I gave a small nod, but made no movement. Instead, I just stood there, until finally the door opened and Harlan walked out to meet me. He looked like hell, worse than I did, with bloodshot eyes and messy hair. The suit, although impeccably pressed, hung off him. He'd lost weight in the days I'd been gone...a lot of it.

"We're in the conference room," he said, carefully reaching out to grasp my elbow.

I lifted my gaze to Tracey with the contact. If she saw, she said nothing, seemingly preoccupied with whatever lay on her desk. I had no choice but to follow Harlan. He was my ticket out of here. The only one who could call off this...*Wolfhunt.*

We made our way out of his office and turned left, heading to the large conference room at the end of the hall. The door was already ajar. My senses pinged in warning even before Harlan let go of my arm and stepped forward to open the door all the way.

"Carina, this is Investigator Aleks Volkov. He's here at the request of Homeland Security and is an observer only, I can assure you."

I stiffened as the huge male rose from the end of the table and adjusted a suit that must've cost at least four figures. "Special agent." He held out his massive hand to me.

I just looked at his thick fingers, encrusted with rings, the handshake waiting…

"Homeland Security?" I turned to Harlan. "Why?"

"Just precautionary, I assure you." My boss eased out a chair for me and met my gaze. "I want to make it perfectly clear that *you* are not in trouble here." *But my Wolves are, right?* Harlan just gave a sigh when I didn't say anything, and continued. "We know you were under duress of some kind, Carina. We just want to make sure we have everything correct. We need to know what we're dealing with here."

"Dealing with?" I tore my gaze from my boss to the Homeland Security agent. "You're dealing with a fucking obsessed agent that attacked me."

Harlan just motioned for me to take a seat. "Carina, *please.*"

I wanted to stand there and dig my heels in. I wanted to be the same old pain in the ass Chase I'd always been. I wanted to get my way kicking and screaming, but as I stood here now, profoundly changed, I knew that wasn't how this was going to happen.

There was no rock meets hammer in this moment. There was carefulness. There was strategy. There were the lives of the men I loved on the line. So I did something alien to me. I stepped forward and sank into the seat without question.

Even Harlan stiffened with surprise above me, then with a long, slow exhale, he stepped backwards. "Alright then."

"Special agent," Volkov started. "I just want to reiterate what Commander Harlan has said. You're not under investigation. We just want a clarification."

"For what, why Homeland Security is here to investigate the unwanted advances of another FBI agent against me?"

Volkov looked confused. That made two of us.

"You don't understand what's happening here, Carina," Harlan said condescendingly, snapping my last fucking strand.

"No, *you* don't understand. Murphy attacked me. He lured me out to some fucking farm and tried to rape me. He would have, too, if Phantom and his pack hadn't been there. They weren't the ones responsible for his death. They were with me the entire time."

"It's not just about the death," Harlan continued. "There've been attacks all across the city. Wolf packs are moving in, and this time they're not staying across the river. We've allowed this to continue for too long. They're a pest, a *menace.* One we won't allow to invade any longer. It's time we put a stop to this invasion and, Carina, we need your help to do it."

"It's Chase," I growled through my teeth, snapping my gaze from Harlan to Volkov. "My name is Special Agent Chase. You don't get to be so...so...*fucking familiar.*" Heat rushed to my cheeks.

My body shook, wracked with tremors as I shoved to stand up. "They are *not* a pest, or a goddamn menace. And the reason why you have random fucking attacks happening all across your precious city is because you're hunting down the *only* ones who can stop it. This is *Phantom's city* and he defends it." I was unraveling, coming apart at the seams. "Only you're too fucking stubborn and prejudiced to see it. They aren't invading *our* world, Commander. *You're driving them from theirs.*"

I was already stumbling, already shoving the chair aside as I lunged for the door...with tears streaming down my face. This wasn't like me...*this wasn't going to bring them back.*

If I couldn't save them here...then I had to find a way to get to them.

*Any way I could.*

16

The *Wolfhunt* raged for days. Days turned into a week….and I was coming apart at the seams.

Food went untouched. Sleep backed itself into a corner and swiped at me with wicked claws when I tried to get near. I sat in that empty bed with the scratchy sheets and thought of them…*every second of the goddamn day.*

I felt sick, this was more than being nauseated. I was heartbroken, pining like some pathetic lust-consumed teenager on the brink of collapse. I wasn't normal. *I wasn't me.*

Harlan might've wanted me back, but no one else did. I was watched 24/7, unable to take even a bathroom break without someone needing to fix their goddamn hair while I sat on the toilet and tried not to break down.

There was no getting through to Harlan, no amount of explaining the real version of events that had happened. The case files of the fire and the homicide were blocked to me. I tried all my usual tricks, even asking the others. But no one was talking to me, let alone trusting me. I couldn't investigate it myself even if I wanted to. I had nothing. *Nothing.*

Bullshit duties and paperwork waited, piled high on my

desk. Underneath it all lay the DNA report of the bloodstains from the warehouse. I fingered the corner of the folder, touching it before sliding it back underneath the waiting mountain, and all the while, Harlan was there, the every-watchful, dutiful commander. Only, when he thought I wasn't looking, he wasn't watching me like a commander—he was watching me like a *man*.

I was uncomfortable with the attention and aggravated by the silence, the cold, empty silence. While inside, I was screaming and raging. *Chaos* threatened, that ache welling in the pit that had once housed my heart. There was only pain there now, only emptiness and the clinking of broken shards, remnants of what had been my heart. But still, they hadn't found my Wolves, hadn't found a single one.

*And they never would.*

My Alpha would run, he'd track Church and Walker, then he'd circle back.

My pulse quickened at the thought.

I kicked at the sheets, hating how the scent on the cheap cotton only smelled like me. There wasn't a whiff of them, not anywhere, not on my lips…or between my legs. I slid my hand lower, down my stomach to cup myself. *Closer.* If I could just reach them, just connect to them somehow. I cast a glance at the closed bedroom door.

*That's it, special agent, ride my hand.* A shiver tore free with the memory. I wanted more than their cocks, wanted more than their hunger. I wanted *them…all of them.*

Heat built with the memory of them. No matter what happened, my life without them would be worthless…*empty,* hollow like a fucking shell. They'd filled me…they'd claimed me, even when I'd claimed them. In that panicked thought, something pushed in. Ruth with the Vampires. I'd seen how she looked at them…and how they'd looked at her, all dark, dangerous, and possessive.

I knew how she felt now.

How faking her own death was better than losing them.

With a flare of frustration, I drew my hand away and rolled, then shoved up from the bed. My heart pounded as I lowered my gaze to stare at the floor. Something had to give here. Something...*that darkness shifted under my skin.* Something Unseelie.

My heart leaped with the thought. The Fae were still here, still right across the bridge. I crossed to the bedroom door, rolling my feet against the floor, and turned the handle as quietly as I could. The metal grated softly. I froze, heart hammering, and listened for movement outside.

The low drone of the TV drifted down the hallway. I turned my gaze right, to where the sparse kitchen lay with its barely stocked refrigerator, one more reminder that this was only temporary. I didn't want it to be temporary...*I wanted it to be over.*

I made my way toward the back door of the small house. I wasn't naive. I knew they'd be careful, probably deadlocked. Voices echoed from just outside. I neared, straining to listen. It was an agent, Asshole Adrian I called him, cold eyes and an even colder demeanor. I gripped the handle of the door, watching through the glass pane as he turned away and started walking, mindlessly pacing.

I turned the handle as his guttural tone slipped through the crack.

"She doesn't know. No, no idea. The others are ready. Yeah, they're in place. I agree, it's only a matter of time now, we just have to wait. You want me to force it? You want me to set it up?" *Set it up? What the fuck did he mean by force it?* Blood drained from my face.

Did he mean force the Wolves to come?

In one harrowing second, as my pulse roared in my ears, I realized that this was all wrong...so unbelievably wrong. How fucking stupid could I be? They weren't protecting me—*they were using me as bait!*

My hand trembled as I pushed the door open more, then wider still before I could slip out. I moved fast, turning to ease the door closed, and hurried into the shadows.

"Then we just wait. We have guys all around the city. We'll catch them...then we'll have them all."

*Have them all...*

I pressed my spine against the wall and listened. Agony pushed and throbbed at the base of my neck. They were setting them up, *setting me up.* There was no concern from Harlan. I clenched my fists as that Unseelie part of my nature let out a dangerous low rumble.

*Chaos...*

The seductive whisper echoed through me. I ground my teeth and lifted my head. Revenge was better than sex...and I wanted to fuck them all. *Totally* fuck them. *Let me out,* my demon in the dark whispered. *Let me make your desires come true.*

The quiet groan of a hinge tore me back to the present. I watched as Asshole Adrian slipped back through the door. The *clunk* of the lock behind him cut off any ideas I had of getting back in tonight. I turned and lifted my gaze, finding the moon full and heavy in the sky.

*The Fae...they could warn them.*

I sucked in a breath and craned my head, listening for movement inside. But all I could hear was the faint sound of the TV. Time to get moving...*anything for my Wolves.* I took a step out, leaving the safety of the shadows behind, and stepped on a twig, *snap!* I winced, my heart in my goddamn throat. Why of all goddamn times did this shit fall apart when I was barefoot?

I eased forward once more, scanning the backyard, and rushed to the fence. Memories of vaulting another reared, and pain followed swiftly. I gripped the pointed wooden pickets and leaped. I was feeling the few pounds I'd lost in the last week, lunging higher, feeling lighter—even if my hips jutted even more than they had before.

I hurried, gritting my teeth and praying there was no man-eating hound on the other side as I landed with both feet. I was in luck, there was just silence, and darkness. Head down, I hurried along the narrow strip between the house and the fence before I found myself on a footpath.

With a deep, soothing breath, I tried to still the tremble inside me and took a step forward. Hurrying even more now, I raced along the footpath, keeping close to the bushes and parked cars, making my way toward the bridge, feeling like I was moving excruciatingly slowly, even though I knew better.

A midnight breeze picked up, flicking my hair behind me as I kept low and ran from one parked car to another. I slipped down side streets, winding my way until I was fairly sure they didn't have enough agents to cover this wide a perimeter.

My thighs were burning by the time I'd covered three blocks, and felt like lead after the fifth. By the time the moon had sunk lower in the sky, I was in big trouble. I rested, leaning over to brace my hands on my knees, blowing out air like I was extinguishing a hundred candles. My face was burning, sweat ran down my cheeks, and my soles were stinging, and still the bridge was a long way away.

I glanced along the row of cars, spying an older one, one I could try my luck at hot-wiring...*Jesus, if Ruth Costello could see me now.* She'd fucking clap her hands with glee like the devil at my back and shove me into the endless freefall from the right side of the law.

I took a step, swiping the sweat dripping into my eyes, and registered the sound.

*Low.*

*Threatening.*

*And utterly familiar.*

I jerked my gaze as that low rumble floated on the air

toward me, standing the hairs at the back of my neck. *"Phantom?"* I whispered.

But there was no answer. I licked my lips and straightened. A flare cut through my chest. No, a pang...*but was it a warning?* I scanned the shadows and slowly took a step. Was it them? My heart suddenly came alive at the thought, shooting adrenaline through my veins like a drug.

But the shadows stayed still, not rushing toward me with open arms. Maybe I hadn't really heard it? Maybe I was starting to lose my goddamn mind? Grief was like that, letting you sink into madness. *This* was its own special kind of cruelty, one that crawled under my skin. I could still feel their touch, still smell their scent...still hear that thunderous snarl that did things to my body no sound should ever do.

I pushed on, convinced now it had been the wind, striding past the potential ride and instead kept walking, my pace slower by this time, and cut across the entrance to a park. If I was right, this would bring me out on Holland Street. I wracked my memory, and realized that only three more blocks and I'd be at the bridge.

I chewed my lower lip and looked around. There were no shortcuts after this...it was all houses and streets, the long way around. I turned back to the dark entrance to the park. It was even darker inside, the gloom consuming until there was nothing. *Come on, Chase, you've never been a chickenshit before, so why start now?*

As soon as I took a step, I felt eyes on me. A nervous scan of my surroundings, and I kept walking. My hand went to my hip by habit, and found nothing but sharp bones. *Idiot.* I let that dangerous part of me push to the surface as I crossed the street and crossed the sidewalk to the park's gated entrance.

I was sure that was supposed to be locked at night. But there it was, wide open. I focused on the murky distance and the spot where the gates were just outside my sight on the far side of the park. A shiver tore through me, standing the hairs on my arms the second I stepped through the iron gate. That low rumbling sound flanked me once more, making my pulse pick up pace.

I panicked, and my hold on that Unseelie hunger slipped. A streetlight blew with a loud *bang* on the street behind me. I jumped at the sound, nearly running now, heading for that dark blur five hundred yards away.

I'd made it barely fifty when something stepped in my path. Silver eyes glinted as a gray Wolf slunk forward, black lips curled, white teeth bared. A low growl echoed coming from my left...and then behind me.

I swiveled, stumbling backwards as I saw another, my heart thudding in my chest. Three of them...*three massive Wolves.* "E-easy n-now," I stuttered and lifted a hand. "I'm n-not here to h-hurt you."

But they didn't stop, edging closer with a slow, predatory gait. I wrenched my gaze around.

"Phantom." I let out with a rush. "I know Phantom."

The low, throbbing, inhuman sound grew louder. My guts turned to water at the sounds, panting breaths as they closed in, the scrape of claws. And that unmerciful, *savage* sound built... and built *and built.*

These Wolves weren't Phantom's pack...they were rogues, just like the ones from the forest. The ones I'd barely escaped from last time. I closed my eyes, my knees trembling so hard they were about to give way. I couldn't stop the chattering of my teeth, the clinking sound filling my head until the consuming blast of a breath came against my face.

I wrenched my eyes opened, and found myself face to face with a beast.

Silver glinted like reflections on a lake.

But there was no life in those eyes.

Only madness. Unhinged, *vindictive,* madness.

"You know, don't you?" The words spilled free in a rush of breath. "You followed me. Hunted me."

That glint only brightened. *Triumph.*

A whimper escaped from the back of my throat. I didn't have to ask what they wanted. *I already knew.* Three Wolves. *Three Wolves.* The Unseelie chaos in my mind was quiet. I swallowed hard. Even she'd deserted me.

"They'll come for you," I warned. "My Wolves, they'll—" The gray beast lunged through the air, and all I saw was teeth.

I threw my arms up, shielding my face. Pain lashed deep and cruel...all the way to the bone. I cried out and stumbled backwards as all three came for me. I turned and ran. My feet felt strange and alien.

But there was nowhere to go.

I was cornered...the iron gates glinted in the background, a cruel taunt.

Still that snarl echoed around me, no longer a warning now. We were well past that.

I turned slowly, agony carving through my arm at the heady scent of my own blood.

*I'll never see them...*

The thought hurt more than any bite ever could.

*I'll never see them again.*

A strange calmness came over me as I sank into that bottomless pit of pain. Nothing mattered now—not if I couldn't have them. My world closed in. There were no more gates in the darkness, no more Fae to help. There was only me...*and them,* the three who'd come for my death.

Their snarling faces were all I saw as I lowered my hands. Warmth slipped along my arm...trickling as I found my enemy's gaze and whispered, "They will tear you apart."

17

PHANTOM

**M**y chest was a wall of fire, blistering and raw. Torn down the middle between need...and want. I wanted to run...*was desperate to run*...But I couldn't. Not yet. Not until I took care of business.

*FIND HER!*

The beast threw back his head and unleashed a howl. One that made me desperate. *One that that made me dangerous.* A whimper followed...and it wasn't mine.

Spitting and gurgling came from in front of me like a split hose on an overworked engine. Droplets of blood flew through the air to splatter warm against my hands. I breathed deep and looked down.

*"No,"* he whimpered and lifted a hand to me. Broken fingers, blood steaming along a savaged arm, face blurred. They all looked the same in that moment. *"Please...no more."*

My body quaked as I stared at the silver of his eyes. There was only killing now. Only hunger to ease that consuming ache...the one I felt for losing her. "You attacked the wrong car." I breathed hard and lifted my hand, claws *aching*, coated with blood. "You hurt my second. You took what wasn't yours to take."

*"Mercy,"* the rogue Wolf pleaded.

There was no mercy left now. *Only a finality.* Claws and brutality won out, and in that moment that's all I was, a beast. A broken-hearted monster.

His blue eyes widened, droplets of blood shot high in the air…a second before I struck, tearing out his throat with one last blow. *Crunch.* Bones snapped, shining neon white in the darkness, before I dropped what was left of the male on the ground. The *beast* urged me on, strengthening my fingers and sharpening my senses.

The sound of an engine roared in the distance. The low growl of an SUV, drawing my gaze behind me. I left what remained of the Wolf at my feet and lunged away. A flash of white tore through the clump of towering fir trees ahead, head down, charging toward me, all teeth and savagery.

Howls of rage came from my right.

*Familiar rage...*

*Our rage.*

Arran was a black blur cutting across my path before he slammed into the white Wolf with a bone-cracking *thud!* Both Wolves rolled end over end on the ground in a ball of fangs and claws and unrelenting rage.

That same desperation rode my brother, loss of her driving him to attack with nearly crazed rage. The white male was on his back in an instant. Arran drove himself to attack with mindless fury, slashing with his claws until they sank into fur and flesh.

His enemy never stood a chance.

I spun, chest heaving, at the sound of a battle cry up ahead. The rogue pack's Alpha…it had to be. I scanned the dark, catching a glimpse of the Wolf as he tore from the trees and raced ahead.

*FIND HER.*

I readied my stance and crouched, muscles trembling with the change, then leaped. Charging through the trees, the blood scent of Church was fresh now...so close. I tucked my head and curled my shoulders, charging until that battle cry still trembled, even in the silence. *There.* I leaped, slamming my paws into the ground hard as gravel replaced the soft pine needle bed.

Eyes bright and white fangs coated red. I caught the Alpha from the corner of my eye, slinking out from behind a boulder. But he wasn't the Alpha I wanted. This one was older, battle-scarred, and rusty brown.

Still, no one lasted this long without his fair share of kills. I slowed, striding out until Church's gut-wrenching roar filled the air. I clenched my jaw, fingers curling into fists, and turned my attention back to the walking-dead Alpha.

*"Fuck you!"* Church howled in the distance.

But the Alpha came for me, his head lowered, watching his quarry...before he grew tired of waiting. He was all fire, all white-hot rage. But he'd never met me. I raced forward and wrenched my fist backwards before I lunged.

He twisted as we hit and punched out with his feet.

Pain lashed down my side as we hit the ground with a thud. I stumbled, the pain stabbing, and looked down as he slowly rose to all four feet. My shirt was slashed, and soaked with blood down my ribs. I lifted my hand, fisted the sodden material, and yanked.

Remnants tore free with a sickening *squelch* as I lowered my head and looked at the gouges across my side. Blood shimmered black under the moonlight, making me think of her.

*NOW...*the beast roared in my head. *GO TO HER NOW.*

"Not yet." I sucked in hard breaths and turned to the Alpha as he came for me again. "Not until we do what we came for."

My beast curled his lips, black fur shimmering with blood

before he swung that chilling gaze to our opponent. It was kill or be killed...*and we weren't ready to die.*

My beast pushed to the surface. I felt that ache, low, chilling, like a fever that wracked my bones. *No,* I growled, and shook my head. *Need to stay in control.*

But the beast was no longer listening, no longer cared about anything but the end result. And for him, that was always going to be *her.* The Alpha feigned a lunge, jaws snapping, a low throaty thunder in the back of his throat.

There were others...a lot more than we'd expected. I grabbed a breath and slowed my body, narrowing in on my beast. "Do it," I forced. "Be done with this."

The answer was a resounding *snap!* as I fell to the ground, letting the beast take over. He roared to the surface, and consumed me whole. I burned from him, then screamed and howled as my spine bowed and grew claws. The pain was blinding, until I didn't want to look. I just *felt,* just *burned.* Just... became what she needed me to become.

And pushed from the ground, standing on all fours, the beat of my heart the only thing familiar now. Through the beast's eyes, I saw my enemy. There was no curl of his lips now, no rage and hate in his eyes...there was only fear. *For him it was far too late.*

My beast hunkered, thick thighs trembling from the hunger before he pushed off. We weren't man and Wolf in that instant —*we were death.* We hit the older Alpha head-on with a bone-cracking *thud,* driving him backwards with pure strength. The Alpha twisted and bit, sinking his jaws into my right flank. But there was no agony in the moment, no sting, no cruel punishment. There was only that second when he let go and lifted his head to find my gaze.

Then I opened our mouth *and bit.*

Fur gave way to our three-inch fangs. I bit deep and was reward with a howl of pain. Claws and teeth, my beast took over, ripping my quarry from side to side until the taste of blood bloomed in my mouth...*and still it wasn't enough.*

I didn't see anything else in that moment. Just her face...her perfect face and sorrow-filled gaze. *"Like you said before, I'm a liability."*

*A liability.*

*A liability...*

*A liability.*

"PHANTOM!"

The roar brought me back to the moment. I sucked in a breath and smelled blood. I lifted my head...and saw only blood. The darkness shifted, and the scent was familiar. Church stumbled forward, limping, *broken.* "He's dead, Alpha," my second murmured, drawing my beast back from his agony.

One look from Church to what lay on the ground in front of me, and the male winced. "He's dead..."

Movement came from all around me. The scent of Vampire cut like a knife. My beast curled his lips, bared his teeth, and whipped his gaze right.

"Easy now, Wolf," Elithien growled, striding toward me covered with blood, all cold savagery. "They're gone...what ones we didn't kill, anyway. I don't think they'll be coming back."

"If they do, we'll be ready." The male next to him promised. *Not Vampire,* my beast inhaled hard, scenting. *Fae...dangerous,* a shiver tore through me as the blond male shifted his pitiless gaze my way.

"We need him back, beast." Elithien met my Wolf's gaze with a look akin to respect. One nod of the head and the Vampire took a step toward him, keeping his voice low. "He has things to do, so we need him back."

In the darkness of my mind, I pleaded, "Let me take it from here."

My beast gave a whimper as he shivered.

"I know," Church murmured, and met my gaze. The bitter scent of heartbreak stung the air. *I know.*

My second looked away then, lest I see more of the truth. But the look was all the beast needed. With a thunderous snarl, he relinquished his hold, letting my body fall to the ground, letting the fire of the shift stake its claim.

I pushed from the ground on shaking limbs. One glance at the mess in front of me and my stomach rolled. "I did that?" My whisper burned.

"You did that," Church acknowledged.

There was nothing left of the Alpha, no distinguishing parts I recognized. He was nothing more than tufts of fur covered with bloody pulp. They didn't look at me the same now, didn't quite meet my gaze as Elithien tossed a pair of jeans through the air. "They're bloody, but they'll do."

I caught them easily, my senses laser-driven, and looked down. They stank like Wolf...and not of my pack. But I lifted my foot, my body still shaken by adrenaline-induced shivers, and stepped in. "Wry?"

"Gone." The bodyguard turned to lift his hand and point. "I tracked him for about ten miles before I lost him."

"And the doctor?" I asked hopefully.

But silence filled the air as Carina's desperate plea roared through my head. *Find them. Promise me you'll find them!*

"I found blood," I heard Arran growl behind me. I turned, watching him stride toward me, his steps slower and controlled, dressed in the shredded black cargos, his chest splattered with blood. He looked drained...he looked *pissed.*

"How much?" I forced the question as my heart sank.

"Some, but not enough."

Some but not enough. That mean she was out there somewhere, hurt...and bleeding, a neon fucking sign for every predator in a hundred miles. "We have to find her."

Arran gave a nod. "I'll—"

I shook my head. "No, she's my responsibility. I'll go."

"Phantom…" Elithien took a step closer. "Let us find her."

But she didn't know the Vampires. Hell, the pain in the ass woman barely knew us. She'd be terrified…more than terrified, she'd be out of her damn mind with fear. "I promised her." I took a step. "I promised Carina I'd keep the doc safe."

"What about me?" Arran murmured, unable to disguise his need.

"Go," I commanded, the word resounding in the hollow of my chest. "Go find her."

Elithien tossed keys into the air. "Take the car. We have more incoming. Find your mortal."

"And hope it's not too late…" I finished for him. "For all our sakes."

## 18

The blur lunged, all teeth and claws. Death. That's all I saw...*my own death.* I closed my eyes at the last second, readying myself for the impact as a sickening roar filled my ears, a roar like I'd never heard before.

Animal.

Primal.

*Beast.*

Howling with agony and rage.

Until a gut-wrenching *thud* filled the air. My heart thundered, ready for the pain. But instead of my agony, the shrill sound of another's came. Sickening, savage sounds forced me to open my eyes. There wasn't one beast...*there was two.*

My heart pounded as I stumbled backwards. In the murky glare I saw him...the deep amber of *my Wolf.* A cry tore free, thick and choking. "Vitold?"

He thrashed his head side to side, driving the other beast backwards with sheer force, his jaws clamped around the bastard's throat...until he ripped it free with a sickening *squelch.*

Blood spurted from the beast underneath him. He opened those massive jaws and dropped the glistening chunk of bloody fur to the ground before swinging that terrifying gaze to his next quarry.

My heart boomed in my ears, the sound deafening. It was all I could hear...all I could feel. *But my Wolf was all I could see.* Vitold stepped over the twitching body of the Wolf and stalked forward, hunting like nothing I'd ever seen before. This wasn't stalking...wasn't just warning. This was an outright bloodbath. One my Russian knew well indeed.

I jerked my gaze to the two others, who flanked him on each side.

*No...*my heart squeezed. I took a step closer, fingers curled into fists, before Vitold swung that piercing gaze my way, lips furled as he gave a soft snarl. The command was unmistakable...*No.*

My fists stayed tight and strained, then slowly released. Only then did my Wolf swing that dangerous gaze to his left, finding the remaining two Wolves who closed in from his sides.

But he never let them behind him...and not anywhere near me. Instead, he strode forward, moving with that sleek, prowling gait of a predator—and he was all beast in that moment. *A beast among beasts.*

One glance from the third Wolf toward me, then he followed my Wolf.

*You want the Alpha, you crave the second. Arran is comforting for you. But you will come to ache for me, as well...*Vitold's words filled me as the two Wolves closed in, coming for him all at once. But he never turned until he was nearer the other side.

He was drawing them away from me, giving me the chance to run...*and survive.* Tears welled in my eyes. This wasn't just a battle. This was *him* ensuring my survival.

My throat thickened as that hit home.

My protector wouldn't just fight...he'd sacrifice, as well. The gray Wolf lunged, eyes glistening in the night, white teeth ready to draw blood. But as my Wolf swung to meet the attack head-on, the other Wolf sprang. In a blur of savagery, he landed on Vitold's back and sank his fangs in deep.

A howl of pain cleaved through the air, one that stopped my heart.

*"NO!"* I screamed and lunged. *"NO...NO...NO...NOOOO!"*

Blood and fangs were all I saw as they both attacked with blinding fury. Vitold fought, biting and clawing, using his sheer strength to drive them backwards toward the other side of the park...and further from me.

Tears blurred my vision. My fists trembled, clenched tight at my sides. Part of me wanted to turn and run...and another part of me wanted to lunge headlong onto the bite of the beast. He buckled as the gray Wolf sank his teeth into the back of his neck again. The soft *thud* was a sledgehammer to my chest. Bloodied and limping, he pushed himself to stand, onto to wheel to face the next attack. He lunged, keeping one bloodied and mangled paw off the ground, and hit the brown Wolf head-on with a terrifying *crack!*

Both Wolves tumbled, hitting the ground hard, and didn't move. Heat lashed my chest, burning all the way from my lungs to the back of my throat. I let out a pent-up breath and jerked my gaze toward movement as the gray Wolf limped forward, circling the two silent beasts.

Warm slipped down my cheeks. I never brushed away the tears. Never even lifted my hand from my side. All I could see was the blood-matted dark amber fur of my protector, fur that didn't rise and fall with slow, even breaths...fur that now didn't move at all.

The gray Wolf limped toward my silent protector, head low...lips curled. His intent was clear. The movement shattered the unseen bonds around me, tearing me from that frozen state. I stumbled forward, my knees knocking. "No...no, you fucking don't."

A faint whimper drifted through the air, The sound so quiet

I almost missed it, so focused was I on the gray Wolf advancing toward my Vitold...until the sound came again.

In a soundless movement, Vitold's beast slowly lifted his head, those midnight eyes blinked, fixed on me. He was making sure I was alive...making sure I was safe, then in one powerful move, he pushed upwards, standing slowly on shaking limbs.

"*You,* look at me," I commanded the gray bastard as I stepped forward, giving him my full attention. "Not him...*me.*"

The rogue Wolf bared his teeth and shifted his focus as I moved faster, clenching my fists...ready to do whatever was necessary. *Scrape...thump...scrape...thump...scrape...thump.*

I risked a glance to my protector as he dragged himself toward the brown Wolf. The rogue beast was still breathing, the low sickening gasps maing my belly clench. I didn't need to look a second longer to know what was coming.

When you become part of a pack...there is nothing you will not do to protect those you love.

That reality drove me forward and into the path of our enemy. "You want him?" I growled and lifted my, hands ready to fight. "Then you're going to have to go through me to do it."

The gray beast let out a low, threatening sound. One that raised the airs on the back of my neck. But I wasn't new to this world...and I wasn't just any damn mortal. I was part of a pack, and as that last, slow *scrape...thump* at my back turned into deathly silence, I readied myself to fight, not for my life...*but for Vitold's.*

The gut-wrenching sounds of tearing flesh came behind me and the nauseating smell of fresh blood wafted through the air a second later. Gurgling gasps followed, and I stepped toward the gray beast, giving my protector time to do what he did best.

"I warned you," I whispered. "I warned you what would happen when they found me. You should've listened. You should've understood."

The rogue Wolf shifted his focus behind me.

"A-ah…" I eased my weight onto my back foot, ready to lunge and fight with fists and rage.

But the rogue Wolf moved fast, lunging from a standstill to a terrifying monster in full flight. Darkness settled over me before it was gone once more. Vitold was a blur, a gruesome… barbaric blur. He hit the rogue Wolf mid-flight, all teeth and claws, crunching and thrashing where he could.

I could only stand there while both beasts rolled around on the ground in front of me, kicking up dirt and grass before a spray of blood shot high in the air.

Shrill sounds followed, yelping and howling, the sounds so loud they made me wince. The gray beast scurried backwards, blood spurting from an open gash across his neck. But Vitold never gave him an out, taking one deep breath before he pounced once more.

Tires squealed in the distance…and grew louder. But the fight was over for the rogue pack…and as Vitold limped forward and sniffed the air over the dying beast, I caught the flash of headlights in the corner of my eye.

A low growl, and Vitold swung his focus toward three unmarked cars as they skidded to a stop at the other side of the park. My heart was hammering, punching against my ribs as I took a stepped toward him. "Vitold."

Hard breaths ravaged his body. He shifted that focus to me and in the depths of those midnight eyes I saw longing and need, until he looked back at the dying Wolf once more.

I rushed to him, even as shouts from agents filled the air. My fingers sank into wet, matted fur and into the deep gouges on his shoulders before I wrenched my hand back. "You're really hurt," I whispered. "Tell me what to do."

He swung that massive head, piercing me with the silver shine of his eyes. His wet nose swept across the base of my neck as he drew in my scent. Footsteps thundered in the distance. Commands barked.

"Take me—" I started before he drew away, stepping backwards, his gaze locked on mine...as he sank into the shadows.

*"Chase!"* My warden barked. "Stop right there!"

I wasn't going anywhere, not in this second as my protector slowly disappeared amongst the thick, dark foliage on the other side of the park.

"Take me with you," I whispered as tears slid down my cheeks.

"Where the fuck did you think you were going?" the asshole agent barked.

A cruel grip on my arm wrenched me around. I thought I heard a snarl of warning, thought I heard my Wolf in my head as I spun and came face to face with the undercover agent assigned to protect me.

*"What? What do you WANT from me?"* I screamed, spittle flying to smack against his cheek.

"Jesus fucking Christ," another agent muttered, stepping past us to stare at the mangled remains of the Wolves before he turned on me. "You did this?"

Pain drove through my chest as tears slipped down. "There's no blood on me, genius. They did it to themselves."

The grip on my arms eased, but there was no getting away from Agent Dick-face, even if I wanted to. My mind raced, they'd found me too fast...and too precisely. The bastard had the nerve to flinch when it registered. "You bastards *put a tracker on me?"*

I looked down at my bloodied palms...*Vitold's blood*—then at my sweats and bare feet as a cold shiver raced through me.

*You want me to set it up?* The words returned to me as I met the agent's stare. *He'd* done this. He'd let the rogue Wolves come for me...and I'd walked straight into their trap.

"Get your fucking hand off me, agent, before I tear it off and shove it up your ass."

That Unseelie rage slipped through me as he released his hold. She bared her teeth, my dark bitch, and she wanted very much to play.

"Make a sweep of the surroundings, push it out to five blocks. If there was someone else here, we'll find him."

My jaw clenched, the muscle strained tight, but inside I was panicking.

*Run, my beautiful protector...run.*

## 19

PHANTOM

"We'll find the doctor." Elithien lifted his gaze to the dimming moon. "Russell will keep searching and track them, then at first dark, we'll get her back."

I sucked in harsh breaths as blood ran in a trail down my arms to drip onto the ground. The night still screamed…or maybe it was the ringing in my head. A permanent chorus…one I'd created.

Arran was there, striding through the dark, both hands covered in blood, one clenched around something at his side. He unfurled his fist, dropping a bloody heart to the ground. The muscle still quivered as it hit with a *splat*…still shuddering with the need for life, and that's where he left it.

"Go, Wolf." Hurrow swiped his forehead with a bloody hand, and splatter marred his pale skin. "We got this."

His crimson-smeared fangs were extended, his bloodsoaked shirt molded against the muscles of his chest. Ruth and the bodyguard stumbled out of the clump of trees at our backs, trying to keep up. I licked my cracked lips and tasted blood. *Not mine. It* looked like Rule was still out there, hunting. I turned my head, finding Church at my side. The brother looked bad, broken bones still healing…and a hollowness in his eyes. One I'd seen before.

I turned back to my brother in arms. "If you're sure."

One nod was all that was needed. He would hunt until the last moment, then find safety before rising once more at first dark. "If she's hurt…"

"I'll take care of it."

*"We'll take care of it."*

I turned at the sound of rolling thunder, watching as Mojin strode toward us, the Unseelie's dark eyes glistening with the kind of bloodlust no one wanted to see. The Unseelie took one look at Church and froze. He was unhinged in the most dangerous of ways…more than any of us here.

The air rippled as the Unseelie exhaled long and slow, taking another step closer before he stopped in front of my second.

"Church," Mojin sighed.

The Wolf beside me took a step, limping as he went toward the dark Fae and lifted his hand. The males clasped palms, before Church pulled the brother closer, arms wound around the Unseelie in the kind of embrace we all needed. We might be worlds apart genetically, but in Crown City, we were family. I lifted my gaze to Elithien, remembering not long ago when I'd turned my back on the Vampire…and what it'd almost cost.

The Vampire met my gaze and gave a slow nod. "We'll find them." He glanced at Church as he pulled away from Mojin. "Go find Carina…get her back."

Something inside me trembled at the words. My throat thickened, choking off my voice. All I could manage was a stiff nod before turning to Church and glancing at Arran.

I dug out the keys to the Explorer and met the Unseelie's gaze. "We'll return as fast as we can."

A nod was all it took, before Mojin turned and motioned for the bodyguard. Russell, Unseelie and…whatever the hell the Dark Fae, Kapre, created, strode into the darkness. I didn't waste a second later...my heart wouldn't allow it. I turned, striding into the darkness, feeling the claw marks and the broken bones shift and crunch as I moved.

But Church was right there beside me, matching me with his painful limp as we made our way back along the overgrown trail...and past the bodies we'd left in our wake. Arran followed behind, keeping watch to our rear.

This night was supposed to have been different.

I was supposed to have protected her...supposed to have kept her safe.

"Phantom," Church growled. "Slow the fuck down, brother."

I jerked back to the present, listening to the brother's labored breaths and the slow, uneven *thud* of his steps. A howl cracked through the air in the distance. I remembered the pack that had attacked us was still out there, maybe running in all four directions...but they were out there, just the same.

I slowed my steps, waiting for my second to catch up, as I scanned the trees and drew deep breaths. The stench of blood still clung in the air, permeating every inch of the forest. I looked down...at the dead. Bits of bodies were all that was left, the dull shine of silver no longer all-seeing.

"Alright," Church growled. "Keep going."

We moved forward more slowly, working our way back to where the four-wheel drives had been discarded for us to hunt on foot. I didn't look at the dead, nor did I follow the howl in the distance. I was no longer there as I pressed the button and unlocked the Explorer before climbing in. I was already hurtling into the city limits, desperate to find the cure for this hollow ache in the center of my chest.

I shoved the key into the ignition and started the engine as Church climbed into the passenger seat and Arran into the back. As Church slumped against the door beside him, I swung the wheel, crawling the four-wheel drive back through the thick brush until I found the dirt road that led us as close as we could get to the thick forest at the base of the towering mountains.

Silence consumed the cabin as Church closed his eyes and let out a hard sigh. The brother would sleep. That was what he needed. His body would be working overtime, healing, re-setting broken bones and re-stretching ligaments. So I focused on the trail, and finally, on the asphalt. But my mind was already with her. *Our Carina...*

The last look in her eyes haunted me. *A liability...*words spoken in desperation resurfaced. My hands tightened around the steering wheel as I ground my teeth. I was stupid...*fucking stupid,* saying shit like that, trying to push her away and keep her safe. "Fucking idiot."

Church grunted and shifted in his seat as the headlights splashed against the white lines on the asphalt. Arran said nothing, just glanced out the window as I pushed the Explorer as hard as I dared.

The reek of blood was choking. I drove until the flashing bright lights of a cheap motel sparkled in the distance. "Church." The brother shifted in his seat and cracked open his eyes. I motioned up ahead. "We need to stop and shower, need to find some clothes."

He lowered his gaze to my bloodsoaked shirt and the blood splatter all over my arms before he lifted his gaze and pushed up on the seat. I motioned to the lights in the distance, growing closer.

"You go in and get a room. I'll find us clean clothes," Arran suggested.

I drew in the sick stench in the fourwheel drive. "Look in the back. We never unpacked our clothes."

Arran pushed up, turning to glance over the seat. "Fuck yes," he muttered, hauling over the bags of clothes as I tapped the brakes and pulled into the dirt parking lot of the motel slash diner slash bar. The parking lot outside the bar had at least seven Bronco's and three Jeeps beside two semi-trailers. "We shower, change, and we're out of here."

"Absolutely," Church muttered, turning to stare at the vehicles decorated in Nazi flags, one complete with a set of buffalo horns strapped to the front grill.

We knew men like these...mortals, with an axe to grind... and rifles to aim. We wanted to no part of it...not tonight. Not when we were blood-sickened and exhausted. Not when we were adrift, our moorings untethered and left to slip away into the darkness. We needed our pack...and yet it wasn't complete without Carina. Not now. Not anymore.

I nosed the Explorer into the first empty space, then glanced at Church and Arran before shoving open my door and stepping out. Music drifted from the bar across the parking lot. I glanced down to my black shirt, then my hands, and winced. A slimy green pool was behind us, illuminated by a single floodlight that highlighted the *UNDER CONSTRUCTION - KEEP OUT* sign tied to the front of the gate with black cable ties. But beside the closed gate was a faucet, one I prayed still worked. I strode toward the damn thing, listening to the hollering inside the bar, out of tune with the blaring country music.

I twisted the water on and washed my hands before smacking my wet palms on my jeans and headed for the motel office. Thirty minutes tops...that's all we needed and we were out of there.

*Leave now...*my beast growled, pissed off. *Keep on driving.*

I yanked the door open and winced at the loud *ding* above my head.

"Be right there," called a woman from behind the doorway marked *Private.* I glanced around the dusty room at a corkboard covered with faded pamphlets of white water rafting and warm mud springs before the sound of footsteps drew my gaze.

She stepped through the doorway, wiping her hands on a

hand towel, and lifted her gaze to me. One careful scan, and she flinched when she met my gaze. Her voice lowered just a bit. "What can I do for you?"

"I'm after a room for the night," I answered, and reached for my wallet. "Paying cash."

One nervous glance out the window as she stared at the Explorer. "For three of you?"

"Just one." I pulled out a hundred dollars. "All we want is a shower, and we'll be out of here."

She licked her lips, her gaze moving somewhere else before coming back to the bills in my hand. But her gaze went straight back to the window behind me. I waited for the snarl as she told me to piss off. Instead, she took a slow step forward and dropped the towel on the edge of the counter, motioning her head toward an open register book. "Name and address…for the damn accountant. It'll be two hundred."

I flinched at the amount, glanced at the *Guaranteed 80 Dollars a Night* sign over the counter, then met the steel in her eyes. Like the fucking bitch was goading me. But I lifted my wallet once more and pulled out two more bills, stepping forward and tossing them on the counter.

She reached behind her, grabbed a key from a board, and placed it in front of me.

Fuck her register book.

*And fuck her.*

I grabbed the key and turned, striding from the office, and headed to the four-wheel drive. The sooner we were showered and out of there, the better. Church was out of the car when I neared, massaging aching muscles in his back. One glance at the brightly lit office and he muttered, "All good."

I gave a nod before I yanked open the door and tossed the key to the room to him. "We're out of here as soon as we can."

She'd given us room eight and by the look of the paint-peeling *1* on the closest door, I was betting we were all the way at the back in the shadows. "Meet you at the end," I muttered to Church, then climbed in and started the Explorer once more.

I backed the four-wheel drive into the parking space outside the room and glanced at the low needle on the gas gauge. First chance we got, we'd get out of this shithole, gas up, and get back to the city.

Church was already inside, the hiss of the shower echoing as Arran hauled a bag out of the car and into the room. But as I closed the door behind me, I couldn't help but peer through the curtains.

There she was, the goddamn clerk tottering herself across the parking lot...and heading toward the redneck bar. "You'll need to make it fast," I barked.

Arran stepped up behind me and looked over my shoulder. "Trouble?"

"More than likely."

"Damn," he hissed, and strode to the bathroom, giving the door a bash before yelling through it. "*Heads up!* We might have trouble."

I turned as choice words were muttered from the other side of the door. The shower ended seconds later and a very wet and pissed off Church strode from the bathroom, dripping all over the floor. "Can't even have a fucking shower. What is it with these people?"

I didn't know, but I watched the woman from the office open the door and disappear inside the bar. We'd danced this fucking dance far too many times to expect anything different. The shower hissed as I yanked off my bloodsoaked shirt and tossed it against the bed before pulling out a fresh shirt from the bag.

*Should've kept on driving.* "Shut the fuck up, beast," I muttered as I stepped out of my boots and shoved my ruined jeans to the floor, replacing them with fresh black khakis.

"Umm, Phantom," Church warned as he shrugged into a

clean shirt, still peering through the curtains. I stepped closer, watching as the bar's door opened once more and, lo and behold, a mass of inebriated idiots stepped out...and headed our way.

"Arran!" Church roared. "Shake it clean, brother!"

*"Fuck!"* Arran roared.

I yanked my shirt on and stepped back into my boots as Arran stepped from the bathroom, toweling his dark hair dry. "Drunks?"

"Drunks," I affirmed.

"Always the goddamn same," Arran groaned as the group of assholes stumbled their way across the parking lot.

*"Hey, MUTTS!"* one at the front roared.

"Motherfuckers," Arran yanked his jeans on and grabbed the bag, hauling it over his shoulder. "Alright, let's do this."

I was the first to the door, opening the damn thing wide and stepped out, meeting the drunken mob head on. "We came here in peace." I met each stare...every one was fucking vacant.

They didn't even know why they hated anymore.

Only *that* they hated.

"We don't want your kind here, *dog*." the fat bastard at the front slurred. The yellow-stained, wifebeater shirt he wore had seen better days...and a lot of mustard stains, by the look off it. It strained across a mountain of belly, leaving a nice gap of hair and fat to poke through at the bottom.

"We're leaving," I growled, and glanced at the motel clerk.

But the mob kept coming, swarming around the front of the four-wheel drive.

"You know the thing we hate more than cops?" the fat, ugly bastard lifted a massive fist.

"I know," Arran answered behind me. "Cardio?"

I winced at the answer, and stepped to the side, meeting the asshole head on. I towered over him...outmuscled him ten to one, as well. I lifted my gaze, finding every dead-pan stare with my own. "I do *not* want to hurt you."

One hefted a shotgun, and I sighed.

"Fuck it," Church growled, and stepped forward, his eyes glistening with savagery as he lifted his hands. Claws curled from the tips of his fingers as he stretched powerful arms forward. "We've killed plenty tonight...what's a few mortals to add to the equation?"

The goddamn FBI. That's what.

But the warning worked. The fat asshole at the front froze and watched as my second took a step closer and asked, "You first?"

The color seemed to drain from the drunken asshole as he stared at Church's wicked set of claws.

"Well?" my brother taunted. "Wanna see what you look like on the inside?"

"I d-don't want them here, Cleo," the motel bitch squawked from the side.

I jerked my gaze to hers. "Like I said...we're already gone. Just move out of the way. We don't want to hurt anyone."

"I do," Church disagreed, low and dangerous. "I want to hurt someone *real* bad."

The asshole with the shotgun took a step backwards. Then they *all* did...all except fat guy and motel chick.

"I-I know you," fat guy muttered, jerking his gaze from Church's claws. "You're the ones with your faces splashed all over the news."

"Not us, amigo." Arran stepped closer and shook his head. "You must be confusing us with someone else."

"No," the asshole shook his head and shuffled backwards with the others. "It's you. There's a reward, too."

Arran just moaned and shook his head. "It's no—"

"Get in the car," I commanded. "We're done here."

I moved fast, stepping up to the driver's door. Church and

Arran were at the car a heartbeat later. We climbed in, and I started the engine and pulled forward. They moved, just like I knew they would, shuffling out of the way before I punched the accelerator and peeled forward.

*"Fuck!"* Arran barked and punched the seat. "How the hell are we going to get to her now?"

*I told you...*the beast rubbed salt into the wound. *I fucking told you...*

## 20

"You gonna answer me?" I barked over my shoulder as they pushed me toward the safe house. "You put a tracker on me?"

"For your own protection," Agent *Asshole* muttered behind me and pushed me through the open door. "Now sleep. We'll *both* have to file reports in the morning."

"Fuck your report." I yanked my arm from his hold and strode toward the bedroom. *"And fuck you!"*

"You can't fight us *forev*—"

I slammed the bedroom door, cutting the bastard off midword. Inside, I was still shaking, still desperate for my Wolf. I stumbled to the window of my bedroom and stared out into the night. He was out there, limping…in pain and running for his life. I pressed my fingers to the cold glass. "Come back for me, Vitold. *Please*, come back."

Agony plunged into my chest. The kind of pain I'd never felt before and never wanted to again. Tears filled my eyes as I stumbled backwards and hit the bed. Footsteps sounded outside, slowing at my door. I reached across to the lamp on the bedside table and hit the button, plunging the room into darkness.

He was out there.

*Needing me...*

I was in here, guarded like a damn prisoner. *Used for bait.* I leaned back against the pillows in the dark and pulled my feet up onto the bed. I didn't want to sleep. I just wanted to remember him...every glint in his eyes, the way he'd lured those Wolves from me. I rolled onto my side and closed my eyes as warm tears fell.

I replayed every second, every growl, every howl of pain, and the desperation that lingered in his eyes as he melted into the darkness. I slept like that, dragged down into the emptiness by despair, kicking and screaming with teeth and claws, and desperation. I tossed and turned, wrestled with the sheets with the torture of his howl ringing in my ears. Until that was where I found them...that was where I found my Wolves.

---

Three days, and nothing. Three days of watchful glances while I sat in my chair at work. Three days I seethed and ached...and stared out the window.

"You going to do any work at all, or just sit and stare?" Niall muttered behind me. "I've watched you all damn day."

I jerked myself back to the present, then stared at the pile of papers on my desk and the clock on the computer that said 3 pm.

"You know they might be watching you, but you're still an agent of the FBI. You can still investigate, maybe try to help yourself."

I swiveled in my chair and came face to face with an icy stare. He was quiet this one, barely saying boo in the few years I'd known him. Niall never came to work functions, never joined in team operations, wasn't a *'team player'*, yet here he was handing out fucking advice when I didn't need it.

"Thanks for the pep talk, buddy," I muttered.

He just gave a shrug, those piercing blue eyes shifting to the open file on his desk. Blue eyes that reminded me of Church, and that fucking hurt. "Suit yourself," he muttered. "Sit there and wallow."

*Sit there and wallow.*

Anger burned inside me, running all the way along my throat and into my mouth, tasting like poison. I parted my lips, ready to snarl back in anger, then stilled...*he was right.* I looked around the mess on my desk. The same mess that had sat there when I came back. The same goddamn mess I'd left what felt like weeks ago. The same half-closed files, the same scraps of information.

My gaze went to folder tucked under all the others. *Ruth's folder.*

I looked around the empty office and reached under the stack, snagging the corner of the folder and tugging it free. The file with the blood work from the warehouse. But as I pulled it, another slipped out with it.

My *personal* file on Ruth and all the players in the game. Her father, her uncles, her cousins...and all their dirty secrets. My mind kept going back to that black and white photograph, the one where Lenny was lying on the floor and my father was tied in a chair.

A flare of power cut across my chest as I pulled both files free, glanced around the office, and rose. I was beginning to get used to that Unseelie power, beginning to tune in to the whispers inside my head when they rose, maybe they'd been there all along? Maybe that was the real me.

It was just a seed of a thought, just a flicker in the dark.

*A whisper...*

I tucked the files under my arm, and grabbed my jacket as I

headed to the door. That seed of an idea sprouted as I strode past Niall's desk and snatched his keys. "Thanks for the ass kicking."

He said nothing, but I felt his gaze on me as I strode from the office and headed toward the elevator. My mind turned back to the other night, to when I'd seen Vitold and realized they'd put a tracker on me. I'd slept that night, but in the morning, I found the damn thing embedded under the skin of my upper arm.

I hadn't noticed it before, not after they'd taken me from the hospital that night, still drowsy, and drove me to their *safe house*. I should've known there was nothing safe there, should've known they were using me to lure my pack into the city before they sprung their trap.

I turned my arm and glanced at the tiny scab underneath. I'd missed it. I couldn't believe I'd missed it. Then again, I'd missed a lot of things in the days after I returned. I closed my eyes for a second as the elevator sank.

I was changed—*my Wolves had changed me*—I snapped open my eyes as the elevator came to a halt. I was a Wolf with no pack…alone, desperate, hunting for the one thing that made me feel whole. *Them.*

I glanced at the keys, found the license plate imprinted on the keyring tag, and scanned the vehicles, stopping at a pristine blue Ford. It was nicer than any other car they'd given me. So I hit the button and climbed inside before starting the engine.

Nice and steady. I glanced at the rear-view mirror as the elevator opened once more. But there was no one there. Not yet, at least. I wasted no time, backing out of the space and heading to the boom gate.

Beth-Anne wasn't there as I pulled into the lane, just one of the other guards. One who barely looked up from his magazine before he hit the button and the boom gate rose. "Suits me just fine," I muttered, and signaled before pulling into the traffic.

Last time I'd seen Lenny, I was sure he'd tried to tell me what had happened that night. The image of Denzel Costello on the TV had triggered him. Now, armed with more information, I could finally piece it all together.

I drove the streets of the city like a damn zombie. There was no excitement, no flare of rage, just that constant aching *throb* in the middle of my chest. I rubbed at the pain and turned the wheel, making my way to the edge of the city, where Heather and Lenny waited.

Past fruit stalls…and flowers, until I passed familiar houses and pulled up out front. Fresh flowers sat outside the house. Still, it looked the same. I climbed out made my way to the tiny white gate, and opened it. My boots echoed loudly on the steps as I climbed to the porch.

The front door was closed. I pressed the doorbell and listened to the chime inside. A heartbeat later, Heather was there.

"Hey," I smiled.

But she didn't smile back.

Her face was drawn, dark circles under her eyes as she unlatched the screen door and pushed it open. "Carina. Come in."

Something was different. Something was *empty.* "What's going on?" I looked to the doorway and the living room before turning back to her.

"I tried to get in touch with you. The office said you were on leave, and they wouldn't divulge your location."

I stepped into the living room, finding vases filled with fresh flowers, so many vases…and condolence cards. "Oh no, Heather…" I shook my head and stepped deeper into the house.

"I'm sorry, Carina," she murmured and reached out, placing her hand on my arm. "I tried. I really tried."

I closed my eyes and lowered my head, squeezing my fists at my sides.

"Your father came to the funeral, still as stubborn and as cold as he's always been," she whispered as tears slipped from the corners of my eyes. I'd cried more in these past few weeks than I had in my entire life.

"But Lenny left something for you. A letter, sealed so I wouldn't open it. But it's addressed to you."

I opened my eyes at the words and met her gaze.

"I found it when I was cleaning out his things. Wait a second, let me go find it."

Her hand slipped from my arm as she left the kitchen and strode through the living room before disappearing down the hall. I followed her into the living room and glanced at all the familiar things. I could almost picture Lenny here, could almost hear his gasps and wheezes. I could almost see his sheep's eyes still brimming with life, almost feel his desperation as he'd tried to tell me about Denzel Costello.

"Here it is," Heather said as she returned, carrying a small white envelope. "I hope it gives you the closure you've been seeking all this time."

"Did you read it?" I asked, and took the envelope from her.

A smile and a shake of her head. "Lenny would've wanted that for your eyes only. He loved you, you know? In his own way. I think in a different life, he would've been an amazing father."

"In a different life," I repeated, and stared at the almost illegible scrawl on the front. *Carina,* Lenny had written. I looked at Heather and stepped closer. "I'm sorry I wasn't here," I said as I gave her a hug.

"Is everything alright?" She squeezed as she hugged me back. "I saw the news reports."

"I'm fine." I pulled away and forced a smile. "Just peachy."

How could I explain it? Not only was I being used as a lure for the men I loved, but my best friend was out there...*somewhere.* She could be hurt. She could be alone.

Probably scared to death and here I was...*pretending none of that existed.*

"If you ever want to talk..." Heather rubbed my arms and dropped her hands. "Well, I'm right here and if you hadn't noticed...my schedule is wide open."

I gave her a genuine smile that time. "Thanks, but I think I need to figure this out on my own."

She gave a smile and stepped away. "Well, you know where I am if you need me."

"I do, and thank you for everything." I waved the envelope in my hand as Heather went to the door, giving me an out.

I took it, leaving her and Lenny's house behind, but I took the memories with me as I made my way to the blue Ford once more. I unlocked it and climbed in before I yanked the door closed.

All I could see was Lenny's childlike scrawl on the front of the envelope. My fingers shook as I lifted the edge, tearing as gently as I could, and pulled out the single slip of paper inside.

*Costello did this.*

That was it. I flipped the letter over and then over again, all that was there was the one confirmation I'd needed all my life.

*Costello...did this.*

"Motherfucker," I hissed and leaned my head against the headrest.

My head and heart were at war, fighting, clawing...yet neither drew blood, and it was blood I wanted. *Had she played me?* That's what I really needed to know. *Had Ruth pretended to give a shit. Had she lured me in...made me almost...care?*

I clenched my jaw and slowed my breaths. It wasn't just the letter in my hands, it was something else. That *seed.* That goddamn *seed,* trying to sprout, trying to grow roots inside my head.

"Did you play me for a fool, Ruth?"

Of course there was no answer. Nothing about all that was

*ever* that fucking easy. My phone rang in my pocket. I winced at the sound, knowing too well what would happen if I didn't answer. So I pulled it free, stared at Harlan's number on the screen, and answered it. "Chase."

"You working, Carina?"

"You're paying me like I am. What's up?" I ground out the words.

"Just checking up on you, you're not in the office."

"Out investigating, it's what agents do, and I'm still an agent, aren't it?" *Please say no...tell me I'm on my own.* One word and I was out of here, loyalty or not, I was running to the Wolves.

"Of course you are," he growled, his breath a rush in the phone. "Careful, Carina."

"Why the fuck should I be, when you're watching me every second of the day and night anyway?" I pushed the point. "Tell me, Harlan. Tell me what the fuck you're waiting for."

But he never answered, just ended the call.

I let out a scream, throwing my cell across the passenger seat for it to hit the door and fall. *"Fuck YOU!"* My hands closed around the wheel, white knuckles burning.

I was losing...losing my grip on reality.

*Losing my Wolves...and there wasn't a damn thing I could do about it.*

After all...*I* was the liability.

# 21

My cell rang again. The phone vibrated against the passenger's door where it had fallen as I sat outside Lenny's house and tried to get my shit together. I didn't have to look at the caller ID to know who it was.

Harlan…

*Careful, Carina,* his words rang in my head.

I was tired of being careful, tired of being controlled. Tired of being *used.* This was what death felt like. A slow death, agonizing, consuming, like a rot that settled inside my chest and slowly spread outwards. Empty. That's how I felt inside. I stared at the tiny mark on the underside of my arm, then turned my head to the small, empty house I'd once known.

Lenny was dead.

Walker was in trouble.

My Wolves were in hiding.

Those pains cut deeper across my chest, and that deep Unseelie green flared to life. I rubbed the ache in my chest and glanced at the movement in the rear-view mirror as it caught my eye. A van, white, unmarked. My stomach sank. I knew who it was.

"Just can't leave me alone, can you?" I clenched my grip around the steering wheel as more movement came from the other side of the street.

I jerked my gaze toward it as a Wolf slunk out from the shadows beside the neat colonial's fence, the silver shine of his eyes glinting as he glared at me.

"Sonofabitch," I growled as another stepped out on the other side of the house.

In the space of a heartbeat, more stepped out, silver eyes gleaming as they watched me from across the street, their black lips curled and their white teeth exposed. My hands trembled as I yanked the door open and stepped out.

One jerk of my gaze behind me, and the white van still sat there. There was no way he didn't see them. No way this outright call to war hadn't gone unnoticed. There had to be at least five of them, stepping out from between the houses before they all lifted their gazes to the house behind me.

My blood ran cold. *Heather.* It was a threat...a goddamn threat.

"Fuck you!" I screamed and stumbled across the street. *"Fuck you...you pieces of shit!"*

The door opened behind me. "Carina?" Heather called.

I whipped my gaze over my shoulder, to find her standing in the doorway. "Get back inside, Heather!"

Her brow furrowed as concerned filled her gaze. "Honey, is everything alright?"

I jerked my gaze back to where the Wolves stood on the other side of the street. But they were gone...*all of them.* A tortured sound tore free as I lunged across the street, only to find the Wolves gone.

It was a threat. *A warning.*

They were coming for me...and everyone I loved. I swiveled and crossed back to the driver's door of my car.

"Carina," Heather called as I yanked open the door, my thoughts a chaotic storm.

"You need to leave this place, Heather. *Leave*, go somewhere safe. I'm sorry I led them to you…*I'm so sorry.*"

I was shaking as I slipped back behind the steering wheel and started the engine. My fingers danced on the wheel until I clenched them tightly around it. My phone started again, the constant vibration rattling against the door and further fraying my nerves.

I had to get out of here.

Had to find somewhere safe.

Somewhere I wasn't backed into a corner.

Somewhere I wasn't a *goddamn liability to everyone around me.*

"Gotta get out of here," I whimpered and glanced again at the mark on my arm, then I shoved the car into gear and swung the wheel, turning around, back the way I'd come.

The white van followed, just as I knew it would. I tracked the movement in the mirror, replaying the outright threat of the Wolves as they'd watched Heather's home. "I can't let this happen…not again."

I lifted my gaze to the setting sun and slammed my fist against the wheel. "Fuck you! *Fuck all of you.*"

I glanced at the rear-view mirror, watching the van make turn after turn behind me. An ache flared across my chest, like a knife carving deep. I was coming apart at the seams, unraveling, desperately searching for a way out of this mess.

I didn't know where I was driving…until I came to the shopping center down from the warehouse. The same place I'd given Arran the slip. Desperation made me turn the wheel and pull into the parking lot. I nosed into a parking space and reached across the seat, snatching Lenny's letter before I was out the door, hitting the lock as I went.

*Costello…did this.*

The words resounded in my head as I rushed toward the

entrance to the shopping center. I caught a glimpse of the van, but I was already gone, sinking into the crowd with Lenny's words ringing inside my head. *Costello...Costello...Costello...did this.*

*You should've let me take care of her,* Chaos whispered low and dangerous in my head.

I winced at the sinister sound and closed my eyes, trying not to let her claws sink in deep.

But Ruth had played me for a goddamn fool. There was no way she could grow up in that house and not know the fucking deeds her father had done. She had some serious gall to stand there and *pretend to care?*

Pinpricks of pain stabbed in my head. I winced at the agony and kept on pushing, driving myself harder and faster, through one store and out the back into the crowd again. I hurried, weaving and working my way from one side to the other, and all the while that stabbing throb in my head grew worse.

I was running out of time—I paused and scanned the crowd, spotting an outdoor store— And realized I was running out of escape routes. Desperation made me lunge and scrabble toward the store as a guy stepped up to the window and flipped the sign from *open* to *closed.*

*"Wait!"* I roared, and pressed my hands to the glass. *"Please, I'll just be a second."* I fumbled into my pocket and yanked out my ID. "I just need a knife, that's all, I promise."

The guy was tall, he'd even tower above Phantom. He peered over his thick-lensed glasses at my ID, then looked at me. I risked a glance over my shoulder, spotting one of my fucking wardens as he charged out from a store into the crowd of shoppers.

"Please." I turned back to the geeky dude on the other side of the door. He followed my gaze to the agent who shadowed my every fucking move.

One *click* and the door swung open. "Inside," he muttered.

I didn't need to be told twice, rushing inside, leaving him to close and lock the door behind me. "I just need a knife." I sucked in a hard breath. "The thinner and sharper the better."

"You'll be wanting a skinning knife, then?" The guy rounded the counter and walked toward the end.

I lifted my arm and grasped the flesh underneath. "As long as it'll cut this thing out, I don't care."

He stopped, leaned over the glass cabinet, and raised a brow. "Seen that kind of thing before...in conspiracy magazines."

"Yeah well, this is no damn conspiracy. I want it out...and I want it out now."

He peered at the mark on my arm. "Tracking device, right?"

I gave a nod before he glanced at the front of the store, then motioned with his head. "What you need is a scalpel. I think I have one in the first aid kit out back."

I didn't hesitate, just followed him as he pointed toward a back room. "This way."

I needed Walker more than anything right now, and as I hurried behind the counter to the doorway leading to the back of the store, she filled my thoughts. Days. Days without knowing if she's safe...or even alive.

The *thud* of a plastic case hitting a counter drew my attention. The guy was already rifling inside, lifting out bandages, plastic vials of clear liquid, and a small foil package. "I don't want to do it. The sight of blood makes me sick," he muttered and turned to meet my gaze. "But it's all there, everything you need. Just don't...don't tell anyone I helped you, alright?"

"Scout's honor." I licked my lips, grabbed the foil packet, and peeled back the corner, exposing the dangerously sharp blade. "Now, if you don't like the sight of blood...I suggest you look away."

One deep breath, and I lifted my arm and pressed the tip of

the blade to the mark on my skin. Then I closed my eyes, thought of my Wolves, and *pushed.*

The sting was instant as blood left a trail under my arm. I lowered the blade, then squeezed my flesh, feeling the hard tracker underneath. The white end slipped out, coated with blood. I yanked the damn thing free, grabbed a large hunting knife from the counter, and smashed the tracker with the steel hilt.

It shattered under the force. The plastic splintered, some shooting off the table to hit somewhere on the floor.

"Jesus," the guy muttered and blanched. "They stuck that thing inside you?"

"They sure did." I tried to catch my breath, but it was too fast…this whole thing was too everything. The room seemed to spin, the walls washing white…

"Hey, there," the guy exclaimed, grabbing my arm.

Something cool pressed to the wound before a bandage was wrapped tight. "You're alright now. You're alright."

I looked down at my arm, and the bandage stretched tight. "I gotta go. I gotta—" I gripped my arm and stumbled, smacking into a shelf before righting myself.

The world was a blur as I staggered, slipping through the back door only to find myself not in the shopping center anymore, but outside…in a parking lot at the back. I glanced down at the bright red patch seeping through the bandage. A car horn blared as I walked. I didn't look back, just kept on walking past cars and people, past everything, as the sun slowly sank…until I stood beside a taxi stand.

"You going?" an old woman muttered and motioned to the cab. "Well?"

I kept on walking, leaving them all behind. People, cars, buildings, they all blurred, and still I walked. *Costello…did this. Costello.* I wanted to hurt something, wanted to hit something. The Wolves, the Costellos, this whole fucking city.

*Ruth...Ruth...Ruth...*Chaos whispered.

It was all I could feel now. All I could see...*and all I could taste.*

My boots smacked the ground. I don't know how long I walked, or where. Time had no meaning wrapped up in the rage inside my head. Still I walked, long enough for the sun to set and the stars to come out. Long enough for me to realize I was lost. Long enough to know that I trembled with rage when I thought of *her.* Red hair, perfect lips. Fucking *betrayer.*

*Costello did this.*

*Costello did this.*

*Costello...did...this.*

The sound of a nightclub echoed in the distance. I glanced around in the darkness, feeling the bite of the cold. That same menacing green glow pulsed in front of me, drawing me closer. I moved like I was in a dream, step after step. *That's right, just a little further,* Chaos whispered. *Almost there.*

I stumbled forward, finally letting that savage anguish in. "I want to fight!" I roared. "I want to *fucking kill something!"*

I blinked into the green haze, seeing the abandon buildings. I knew this place...knew this feeling of malignant terror. I rubbed my chest and swiveled. Gone was the throb of the nightclub. Gone was everything I knew. In the distance, lights sparkled on the bridge. The bridge that divided the city...*and I was now on the other side.*

I turned, staring at this empty, menacing world. "How the fuck did I get here?"

*I carried you,* Chaos whispered and that Unseelie ache in my chest burned brighter. *Brought you to where you needed to be.*

I let out a moan and stumbled around some more, my gaze moving to the darkened club in the distance. *My Phantom's club.* That ache only plunged deeper, carving right through my heart. I looked over my shoulder to the dark wasteland that was the

Unseelie's domain. Chaos had called me here...and Chaos wanted me to stay.

But it was my heart I followed. I followed that *throb* of pain, stumbling forward and started to rise back out of the dangerous Unseelie world. I didn't feel the cold anymore now, didn't feel anything other than desperation.

I climbed, gripping the ground, and drove myself higher until I crawled out of the Dark City and headed for the darkened night club. I didn't remember crossing the bridge to this side of the city, didn't remember anything at all, nothing but the sting in my arm and the throbbing in my chest.

I wanted them...

Anything that reminded me of them.

Tears slipped from my eyes and raced down my cheeks as I drove myself higher, until the ground evened out and I slipped between the buildings to the pavement. Sirens blared in the distance. I jerked my gaze toward the sound and scanned the lights across the other side of the city.

They wouldn't come here...not with the Unseelie power thrumming in the air.

Police tape closed off the entrance to the Hunting Ground. I watched, staying in the shadows, and made my way along the front to the empty lot beside the building. The same lot I'd parked my car in just days ago...before my entire life went to hell.

A brush of power danced across me, standing the hairs on my arms as I stopped at the side door. *The cracked open side door.* My pulse thundered as I gripped the handle, glanced over my shoulder, and slipped in.

This could be a set-up.

Could be Finis waiting inside.

It could be Harlan...

I swallowed hard, unable to turn around even if I'd wanted to.

I needed them, *ached* for them, and this is where they were. The memories of that first night flooded back to me as I stepped along the hallway. Phantom had carried me over his shoulder. My shirt had been torn open, fingers delving under my bra, rubbing and pinching my nipples, desperate to ease that hunger inside me.

That sexual agony…

I'd wanted him more than I wanted anything else. I *still* wanted him with the same kind of fire in my veins. *I wanted them all…*My eyes adjusted to the murky gloom, making out the outline of the doorway that led into the club.

I reached out, grasped the handle, and turned it. The squeal of hinges cleaved through the darkness before I closed the door behind me. Silence filled the space. Cold, lonely silence. "Phantom?"

There was no answer, no sound of anything.

Just silence.

I moved deeper inside the club until the flicker of tiny white lights came to life from the floor. I froze, my heart hammering. The lights were barely there, giving me nothing to go on as I scanned the darkness.

"Don't be scared." Church's voice echoed all around me.

I spun, searching…and froze as the darkness shifted. "Church?"

I stumbled forward, but he lifted his hand, stopping me cold.

"The others? Where are they?" I asked, scanning the club.

"Doing what they do best," he replied as he lifted some kind of tiny black remote. "Hunting…keeping you safe. No one will harm you, Carina. Not after tonight."

Music came from the speakers, the beat slow and erotic as a man's voice echoed through the speakers. "Do you like it?" Church murmured as the beat rippled through the empty club. "It's called Wicked Games."

I couldn't speak, couldn't fucking breathe as he stalked toward me. The tiny white lights gave me just enough light to see…Christ, he was spectacular, with a long-sleeved open-collar shirt and pants that clung to every delicious curve of his body.

Lust tore through me. I didn't have to look down to know that deep Unseelie glow pulsed from my chest. I knew what he meant. Phantom would kill the rogue pack and everyone they worked with for coming after me—he'd kill them all. My heart clenched with the thought.

"He left me to take care of you. Left me…to explain." *Explain?* "You wanted to know where I went." Church stepped closer. "That day I deserted you in the mountains."

"You wanted to know…now I'm going to tell you."

He moved slowly, rounding the end of the bar, and stepped into the open, his head lowered, eyes downcast. "In my own way, Carina."

It was the first time I saw them…really saw them. I scanned the darkened area, praying this wasn't a dream.

"First, I'm going to tell you, and then…if you're still here, and if you…*want me,* then I'll give you what you need."

My heart hammered until it was all I could hear.

"Sit, Carina…*please,*" he whispered, awkward and nervous. How someone who looked like he did could be nervous, I'd never know.

I swallowed hard and stepped backwards, bumping against the rise of the platform where the dancers performed. But it was too late now, too late to do anything but what he wanted.

"If you want to run, I'll understand." He stepped closer, finally lifting his gaze to meet mine.

Pain blazed in his piercing blue eyes, the cutting stare illuminated by the tiny white floor lights. The kind of pain when you bare your soul. The kind of pain that made you desperate…desperate enough to bare his body…*for me.*

## 22

I sank onto the plush velvet lounge as Church stepped closer. His fingers worked the buttons of his shirt, revealing a sculpted chest as his hands moved lower. Still that song throbbed in time of his movements.

His muscles rippled in ways I'd never seen. I swallowed hard, mesmerized, as the floor lights captured the sleek, predatory way he moved toward me. "I went to the closest town, to a bar, and found someone who'd...use me."

Jealousy tore through me as that Unseelie power flared. I clenched my jaw, but that did nothing to hide the curl of my lip.

I shook my head.

He winced at the movement. "I let men *hurt me*, Carina, let them *dominate me*. I need them to control me, need them to..."

I slowly pushed up from the lounge as he stepped onto the dance floor, his shirt sliding from his massive shoulders to fall in a heap.

"Do you think you can handle that?" he asked, those blue eyes sparkling like crystals. "Think you can handle me searching for that..."

"Is it only men?" The words slipped free before I knew it. "That can give you what you need?"

He didn't answer, but there was a flare of desperation that collided with that predatory power inside me. He stilled as the power burned brighter. His nostrils flared, his eyes glinting with both fear and defiance. "I don't do it to be fucked by them, if that's what you're asking."

I guess that's exactly what I was asking. I stepped closer. "And what if I could give you what you need? What then?"

I knew now why his shirt was discarded on the floor, knew why this whole sensual, *erotic* display. Knew it wasn't just desperation that darkened those perfect blue eyes. *He needs us,* Chaos urged. Fear pushed to the surface, until it was cast aside.

There was no room for that now. No room to be anything other than what he needed.

That hunger flared to life as I stepped closer, pinning his gaze with my own. "I won't hurt you," I said. "That's one thing I can't bring myself to do. Don't ask me to do that...but *anything else is on the table.*"

His breath caught as he searched my gaze. Did he expect me to run? Expect that he'd scare me with the truth? He needed to learn one thing about me. *I didn't scare that easily.* "Come to me," I commanded, and inside my head, *Chaos* whispered *yesssss...*

Darkness moved inside me, that feral savagery bloomed like a noxious flower just as it had that night in the caves. But there were no other Wolves to fight with now. There was just *us.*

He moved closer, his thick thighs stretching his trousers. Fear leaked from his body and tainted the air. He had as much riding on this as I did. So much power. So much *raw, undeniable need.*

"Who do you want to fuck, Church?" I whispered as he stopped in front of me.

Darkness splashed across his skin. The pale white lights cast shadows across his face. He wanted not pain...but power, and that malevolent beast inside me was all about power. I stepped closer, letting that bestial part of me slip through the air and taste his skin.

He flinched at the contact, and his eyes widened, his lips parted. *That's it, Wolf,* she whispered in my head. *Nice to finally meet you.* I felt myself moving, reaching out to place my palm against his bare chest.

No matter what was happening outside these walls…this is where I was needed.

*Right here.*

Fingers splayed, I followed the contour of his chest, feeling the thunder of his heart under my fingers. "Dance for me," I ordered, and took a step back.

He licked his lips as that deep throb echoed all around me. I took another step backward, until the back of my legs hit the velvet lounge.

He moved, just like I imagined he would, corded muscles straining as he lifted his hand to the hard muscles of his stomach. His eyes were riveted to mine as I watched him and slowly sat once more.

Those thick thighs strained his pants until I was sure they'd rip as he rolled his hips and slowly thrust forward.

*Fuck me.*

For a second, the panicked beat of my heart almost gave me away as I stared at the way he moved.

But the hunger inside me was just as desperate, pulsing through me as heat licked between my thighs. I wanted him… wanted him on his knees, wanted him naked and writhing.

*Wanted him desperate for me.*

His hands moved to the black belt, and the large fingers slipped the leather free and through the buckle. The slow slide through the belt loops made me catch my breath. I was captivated by the deep, corded V at the center of his hips as the burn settled into my chest. One hard exhale and the cool air rushed in. I tried to gain composure…but oh, the way he moved, all predatory and powerful.

Silver glinted in his eyes as his own beast rose to the surface. A tremor raced through me. It was almost too much, almost too *everything.* My nipples puckered and desire licked deep as I dug my nails into the velvet.

This was no seductive, female tease. This was raw, *masculine* hunger…aimed at me. The belt hit the floor with a *clang* before he reached for the button of his waistband. I lifted my gaze, holding his gaze as that Unseelie burn flared brighter, lashing his body with sadistic need.

He trembled under the power and his pupils widened until the dark, glinting circles were blown. I slowly pushed against the sofa and rose, taking a step closer.

*Mine,* Chaos whispered. *You are mine.*

Church let out a soft groan, the sound like fucking lightning through my veins. I stepped closer and reached out, taking the button in my fingers, and murmured, "Do that again."

Chaos smiled, licking the air, as I unbuttoned his pants and pulled the zipper low. Christ, I'd never seen a body like his. Phantom was taller and stronger, but Church was *big.* I trailed my fingers down the hard muscle of his hips.

He lashed out and wrapped his fingers around my throat. The defiance and desperation in his eyes were almost painful. This was the dance, wasn't it? This was what Chaos was born for. She swept around him, that dominance making me even more powerful than this gorgeous Wolf in front of me.

"Give in to me," I growled, and slid my hand inside his pants and down, grasping that thick, hard length.

His grip tightened around my throat. He was fighting, just as I'd known he would, resisting the Unseelie power. But no matter how much he wanted to fight, that Chaos inside me rose harder and stronger, until I felt myself slipping once more…and *she* took over.

"Give in to me, Wolf." The words slipped from my lips.

But the words weren't my own, they were *hers*. My hand tightened around his cock as I fisted the length, driving all the way down to the hilt, then back again. The savagery inside me swept around him, deepening my voice. "Give in to me."

Church closed his eyes and let out a moan. The grip around my throat eased and his breaths turned shallow.

"Mine." Chaos claimed him and slowly pumped.

She looked down, finding that silky soft skin at the head of his cock, and the glistening drop of pre-cum beading. She lowered herself and kneeled on the floor, breaking the hold around her throat.

Lips to skin. I craved to feel him, to taste him…but it was all her.

All carnal and control. One lash of her power and he whimpered, his cock twitching in her grasp.

"Again," he pleaded.

She obliged, only this time the power didn't just lash like a whip, it *bit*. She opened my mouth, her tongue sliding along the length of him before she took him into her mouth, pushing him deeper…all the way to the back.

Fingers tangled in her hair, and he gave a slow, hard thrust, driving deeper. Saliva spilled out around his cock, the slide captured by a greedy mouth as she licked and sucked, working his length with her fist.

"I want you," he growled, and lowered his gaze.

Chaos just smiled, licking the tip of his cock with a flat tongue before she pulled away to whisper, "That's not how this works, Wolf. When I want you…*I'll take you.*"

He whimpered at the words, his blue eyes glinting as the song changed, moving to something just as erotic…something just as cruel as she pulled away, rising to stand in front of him. "Now take your clothes off. I want to see what you look like when I fuck you."

She stepped backwards, licking her fingers, tasting that salty precursor to the real thing. His lips curled as he stood there, hard as a fucking rock...desperate to cum.

"Dance," she commanded, her voice low and threatening.

He just stood there, chest heaving with savage breaths, with a dangerous glint in his eyes...then slowly he started moving, swaying his hips, that thick, jutting cock swinging, until he grasped it with his own hand.

She stepped backwards and sank to the velvet lounge once more, captivated by that brutal stare and the way he fisted himself. "That's my good Wolf," she whispered with a curl of her lips. "Fuck your fist for me."

One jerk of his head toward the door and a chilling rage slipped through the air. She felt it, an invasion. A vehicle, coming toward them, slowly...carefully.

A savage sound escaped Church's lips before he looked at her...at his *Chaos,* then with a threatening snarl, he shoved his straining cock into his pants and yanked up the zipper. "I'll kill them."

*Mortals...*three of them in the car.

They were familiar.

The men who *guarded* her.

The ones who kept her prisoner.

"No," she whispered with a shake of her head, and pushed off the seat to stride toward him once more. "You hide, you *survive.* Come find me."

She kissed my Wolf, slow and hard, driving her tongue into his mouth before breaking the connection. Headlights from the car washed through the club, shining through the front doors to splash against the ceiling.

*Let me out,* I demanded. Only, Chaos wasn't done. She ignored my plea and turned, leaving Church to snatch his shirt from the floor and walk behind the bar once more. The music ended with the tap of a finger. But Chaos was already climbing the stairs and yanking open the front doors.

Chaos stepped out of the abandoned Hunting Ground and walked across the pavement as the unmarked sedan braked to a stop.

She opened the back door in silence and climbed in, never once looking back. Not to her Wolf, not to her past. A tremor moved through me as she yanked the door closed behind her. *It's alright,* she whispered in my head. *I know what we have to do now.*

And I'd never been so scared in all my life.

*Let me out,* I yelled in my head. But that dark Unseelie bitch had her claws deep into me...

*And she wasn't letting go.*

23

PHANTOM

I opened my hand, letting the severed head of the Wolf drop to the ground and roll away. Vacant eyes stared up at me from what was left of the beast as I shifted my gaze to the darkness. "You come for what's mine…and this is how you'll end. Your Alpha is dead, your pack is weak. Leave now and I'll let you. But chose to stay, and this is your fate. You harm another," I snarled, clenching my fist. "You go after *another* in this city, and the next thing you'll see is me."

Silence drifted from the empty buildings, but I knew what was left of the rival pack heard me loud and clear. I turned my back, letting that sickening rush sweep over me. One last glance at the gray Wolf's head, and I made my way back along the street to where I'd parked the Jeep.

The Alpha wasn't who I wanted.

I wanted the black Wolf.

*The one I was sure was Finis.*

But no matter how hard I hunted, keeping to the shadows and the back streets and far away from any cop or FBI agent, I just couldn't find him. My phone let out a *beep*. I plucked it from my pocket and stared at the screen. *He's still in Cathedral City. E.*

Even though I saw the words, I knew they were a lie. I pressed the button and listened to the phone barely ring before it was answered.

"Short of a DNA test, how solid is that information?"

"As solid as you can get. They say he's still there, still attending the Inner Circle meetings, still going back to his home...*alone.*"

"Alone," I forced the word through gritted teeth.

"We don't even know if she's alive, Phantom."

I caught my breath at the words, my steps faltering. Only the Vampire would dare to say such a thing. "And we don't know she's dead, either."

"I'm coming back to Crown. We'll be there within the hour," Elithien murmured. "I want you and the others to stay with us. The mortals won't come through the fog, you'll be safe."

First Caedes and now Finis. How much more could our three packs handle? Still, the thought of the Vampire coven coming back sent a surge of determination through me.

"Have you seen her?"

My breath caught for a second before I exhaled and answered. "Tried to, but she has a number of sitters. Ones who don't care for my kind."

My pack was scattered to the wind; Arran was carefully watching the FBI building, Church the Hunting Ground, and Vitold prowling the streets, keeping an eye on the rogue packs who'd decided the woman they loved was fair fucking game.

"We're pulling every string we know," Elithien assured. "Putting pressure from the top down. We'll get her back, Wolf. Don't you worry about that."

I knew he would. He'd be using every source of power at his disposal. "Thank, you...*brother.*"

"You stood by me, even when you weren't sure I deserved it. This is the least I can do."

"And Ruth, what's happening with her and the Circle?" I

knew the battle for her didn't just stop at Caedes. The woman carried the strength of a thousand Vampires in her blood. They'd be after her, hunting her, just like those damn mortals hunted Carina. They wouldn't stop. They'd *never* stop. Not until *we made them.*

"She's safe, she's protected. That's all she needs to worry about. We're stronger when we fight together."

*Stronger when we fight together...*the memory of the warehouse flooded back to me. I hadn't thought we'd get out alive. But we did. "We are. I'll be looking for you, Vampire," I growled into the phone, and ended the call.

I strode toward the Jeep and pressed the button to unlock it before climbing in. My cell vibrated again, this time with a call...from Church.

I started the engine and swiped the screen, putting it on speaker. "What is it?"

"She was here." The Wolf sounded breathless. "Then *those bastards* came."

I jerked my gaze to the screen. "Did they hurt her?"

"No, but Phantom, there was something strange about her, the way she was acting. The...*power* she had. She just stood up, told me to hide, then walked out of the damn club and climbed into their car like it was nothing."

The words were a fist to my chest. "They didn't force her?"

"No, they barely pulled up outside before she climbed in. She...she's darker, Phantom, more Unseelie than she was before."

*Chaos.* That's what she'd called it in the cavern. That feral hunger rode her harder than I'd ever seen before. "It's the Unseelie." I answered, but even as I said the words, a chill swept through me. "Goddamn it. How was she when you saw her?"

The male didn't answer right away, making me focus on the silence. I lifted my gaze to the darkened houses through the windshield, and let the *Alpha* in me roam. I tested the boundaries of our bond, pushing deeper through the connection of Alpha and his second until I felt that charge of *lust* echo back. The kind of animal lust that only comes from one thing. "You…consummated the bond?"

He didn't answer at first. Jealously tore through me, making me strangle the wheel and fight the savagery in my tone.

"Not completely," he answered. "But it was enough. Enough to know she bonded with me…and I with her."

My lips curled back from my teeth, and my fangs shone white in the rear-view mirror. I closed my eyes for a second. That was a good thing. That was the *right* thing. I opened my eyes and leaned forward, shoving the four-wheel drive into gear. "Then it's done. She belongs to all of us."

My beast shifted under my skin and scented the air. *Need to mark her,* he growled. *Need to bite, need to rut…need to smother her with our scent. No other pack will come for her then…not when they know who she belongs to.* I found myself turning the wheel.

"You're angry," Church murmured.

"Not angry, fucking agitated," I answered, scanning the traffic before I pulled out. "I don't like her away from us. Don't like the way they have her locked up and controlled."

No, I didn't like it at all.

"I don't like it either," Church echoed through the phone. "Something doesn't feel *right.*"

I reached down, and my finger hovered over the screen before I ended the call. I scanned every car that drove past, always searching now for the enemy in unmarked sedans.

I turned the corner of the low-cost housing development and caught the flare of headlights of an agent's vehicle as I passed. His head turned, watching me, before I signaled and turned off onto a side street. I kept driving, watching the rear-view mirror, and stopped the Jeep three blocks away from where they were keeping her in the safe house.

If I could just get to her…just talk to her.

I climbed out of the Jeep and closed the door, locking it before I set off on foot. Mortals. I could smell them a mile away, the only problem was, they were like goddamn vermin right now…crowding around her.

I scanned the darkened houses, found one without the faint flicker of a TV through the blinds, and slipped along the side of it until I jumped the fence into the backyard.. The low, warning snarl of a big dog trembled through the air until I jerked my gaze toward the sound.

A whine followed before the Rottweiler cowered, sinking to the ground and rolling onto his back. I knelt beside the animal and scratched his belly, then his head. "Good boy. I'm not here to harm your family. They're safe from me."

He lifted his head and licked my hand as though to say *thank you* before I rose and kept on moving, leaving his home behind. I'd spilled enough blood that night…I didn't want to spill any more.

House after house, I worked my way closer to her, reaching through our connection, desperate to touch her. Church's warning rang inside my head as I leaped over a six-foot fence and hit the ground with a *thud*. I froze, scanning the darkness.

*Need her,* the beast inside urged. *Need to lick, need to taste… need to breathe her scent.*

"I know," I whispered, and kept on moving, my strides longer, my breaths coming harder.

I stepped up to the fence and peered over the brickwork to the back of the safe house. The lights were on inside, and the scent of a male lingered in the air, a male that guarded her like she was a prisoner.

*She is ours,* my beast warned. *Kill them, tear them apart.*

I closed my eyes for a heartbeat as that urgency grew. "No," I whispered to the beast. "We do that, and we'll be running forever."

I opened my eyes, gripped the top of the bricks, and as silent as the night, leaped over and into the backyard. I couldn't feel her, not like I should be able to, couldn't sense that darkness in her, couldn't smell her goddamn scent. I scanned the outside of the building, my gaze lingering on a bedroom window before it stopped.

*Her bedroom.* I was sure of it.

But the room was dark, and there was no life inside. I pressed my fingers to the glass and focused. Two...no, *three* agents, moving around in the house. Talking. I strained to hear.

"Harlan is just a little too interested in her, if you know what I mean," one of them said.

Another chuckled. "He pants around her like she's a goddamn bitch in heat."

A low, savage hiss spilled from the back of my throat. Was this why the change in her? That...goddamn Harlan? Was he turning her against us? Feeding her fucking lies? Making her *bend to his will?*

The scrape of a shoe wrenched me back to the moment. I jerked my gaze toward the sound as another agent pushed his hand through the gap in the fence and unlocked the gate.

I was already moving, stepping backwards into the shadows as the gate opened and the agent walked in. One fast, silent leap, and I hit the ground on the other side of the brick wall and hunkered down.

But my mind was racing. Imagining all the fucking things Harlan was doing to her.

My beast pushed toward the surface, driving his claws into me as I knelt behind the wall. He wanted blood...and he wanted Harlan. Before this night was through, he just might get both.

## 24

———

The office was dark and empty when I flicked on the overhead lights and headed for my desk. My steps were slow, and my feet were heavy, almost as heavy as my heart. The first grumble of thunder from an approaching storm came as I pulled out my chair and sat at my desk.

For a second, I couldn't move, just listened to that rumble above and stared at my darkened monitor.

*Dangerous, just how we like it,* Chaos whispered in the back of my mind. Her voice was so close now. So close, I could barely feel anything at all. Just *her.* Just *Chaos* and the sickening desperation of what I was about to do.

*Get to work now...*

I closed my eyes. She let me in, let me have control, but only to do what she needed me to do.

*Ruth,* she whispered in my head. *We need the files on Ruth.*

"No." The word tore free with a shake of my head. My fingers froze, hovering above the keyboard. "I can't do that."

*Can and will...*

"You know what this will do to them," I whispered as a shudder coursed through me. "I can't hurt them, not like that."

*The Wolves,* Chaos whispered. *Or the Vampires...you choose.*

Our thoughts collided. She became me, and I was left in the darkness.

A merciless Unseelie darkness that held nothing but rage and despair.

My hands moved on their own, firing up my computer and logging in. That grumble overhead grew bolder before the first flash of searing white light filled the widows. I took no notice, knowing that savagery spilled from Chaos, inside me. She was a whirlwind...*no, a tornado,* whipping and slashing, growing with every minute I sat there.

It'd been an hour since I'd left Church in the Hunting Ground. An hour since this battle raged inside me, and slowly, I felt my hold on reality slipping.

My fingers typed, dragging up file after file. Before I knew it, I was hunched over the keyboard, my fingers flying at a dangerous pace as I collected file after file. I opened the database we kept on the Immortals, researching as much as I could on all the major players.

*Elithien.*

*Caedes.*

*Phantom.*

*Finis.*

*The Inner Circle in its entirety.*

There wasn't much I could find. But by the time I'd finished my fourth cup of coffee and the thunder had grown deafening within the steel gray sky, there was noise drifting from the hallway behind me.

A *crack* of thunder sounded right over the building as a startled voice cried out, followed by retreating footsteps.

"You're in early," Jager muttered, wincing as lightning seared the sky outside the large office windows. "Eager to lock up those fucking *dogs,* are we?"

I stiffened at the words and lifted my gaze. Water dripped

from his hair and ran down his face and for a second…all I saw was blood. Blood down his face, blood in his eyes. Blood spilling from his neck as I tore out his—

He yanked out his chair and turned, meeting my gaze, and that sneering glint dulled in an instant, hardening to something close to *fear*.

A savage snarl ripped from that tornado inside me. Shadows splashed against the walls as the sound of shattering glass exploded through the air.

"What the fuck?" Jager exclaimed, and rose.

Those shadows grew bolder, crawling along the wall beside me as I followed his gaze. An agent stood In the doorway, holding the handle of what remained of the coffee pot. The rest lay in shards at her feet. Cutting shards…I fought that hunger inside.

Green spilled from the top buttons of my shirt as I turned to those shadows. They morphed and swirled, showing me Ruth's face, then my Wolves. My chest tightened at the image of Phantom's face, his hard jawline, those intense, piercing eyes, until the dark splash morphed into Church, then Vitold followed…and finally, Arran.

The roar grew louder all around the building, drawing every set of eyes toward the windows. Movement followed. Chairs slid backwards and expletives were muttered. I forced my eyes downward to the file and tried to hold on to the war inside my head.

I shoved up from my seat and grabbed the file off my desk. A tremor filled me, only this time it was no display of power…*only fear*. My breaths raked my insides like shards of glass as I turned and walked from the bank of desks, heading for the elevator.

Footsteps echoed all around me, the chatter of those staying behind at their desks rose. Those who I'd never really connected with. I was the odd one out. A lone agent, just like a lone Wolf. I pressed the button for the elevator and waited.

A lone Wolf always under attack…

Always watchful. Guarded, and ready to do what had to be done.

That's who I was here…*amongst these mortals;* a lone, guarded, *vengeful* Wolf.

The elevator gave a *ding* and the door slid open. I stepped in, turned, pressed the button, and waited for the doors to close. But they were wrong. I wasn't a loner. I was very much part of a pack. Just not *their* pack.

I watched the lights as they blinked, moving floor by floor, until it came to a stop and the doors opened. A chilling sense of impending doom washed over me as I stepped out and strode along the corridor heading to Harlan's office. My steps faltered, something inside me writhed under the strain of what I was about to do.

My mind raced, searching for any other way out of this mess. Voices echoed from ahead in the hallway. I glanced at the strategic door, which was cracked open, and listened as voices spilled out. I'd only ever seen that office used once. But here it was, the door open…and senior officials inside. I glanced at Harlan's office, then turned back to the open door. It felt like an invitation…just *begging* me to look inside.

*What the hell…*

I stepped closer, grasped the door, and eased it open before slipping inside. There was six…no, seven of the top officials and their chiefs of staff. Suits and ties and all the proper nods and smiles—and *now there was me.*

The walls were armored with rows of whiteboards, some covered with maps of the city peppered with markers, other boards with familiar faces. My stomach clenched at the sight of Phantom's face, and under it were Church, Vitold, and Arran.

My breath caught as I glanced at the other boards. More Wolves, more faces. Some were vaguely familiar, most weren't. They were only interested in the Wolves. I fought a wince as I scanned the boards and the faces. I'd suspected it before, now I knew for sure.

They didn't even notice me, so wrapped up in their thirst to *'rid our city of this vermin',* they failed to see me before I slipped the door open once more and eased back out.

A battle raged inside me as I lifted my gaze to Harlan's office. That uncomfortable *shift* inside me fought the images from that room. Right and wrong. Desperation and the fight to survive… the fight for my *Wolves* to survive.

I lifted my gaze to his empty secretary's desk and strode toward the door. Harlan's voice spilled out through the open door of his office. "I don't care what it takes…I want those men doubled along both sides of the river, do you understand me, Commissioner?"

I tried to control my breathing, tried to focus on the folder in my hand, tried to tear myself away from the war waging inside me as I neared his office.

He met my gaze as I entered, and his eyes widened, sparkling a little brighter as he motioned for me to come in. He didn't seem to notice my wrinkled suit, or the fact that my eyes had dark circles and were bloodshot. He just smiled at me, like I was exactly who he wanted to see, as he muttered a command into the phone and hung up.

"Carina," he started, then glanced at the open door before rounding his desk and closing it softly behind me. As he returned to his desk, he continued, "You gave me quite a scare last night, venturing across the river like that. You know how much I—"

"I came back, didn't I? Of my own accord, I came back." I tried to swallow the sour taste in the back of my throat.

"Yes, I suppose you did." He moved closer, not stepping completely around his desk, but perching on the corner to my right.

Too close…*too close.* My skin jumped with the contact as he brushed a stray strand of hair from my shoulder. "You came back to the office. Why?"

I turned, finding his brown eyes as he looked at me like I was some kind of broken thing in need of saving. Maybe I *was* broken, shattered to pieces, unable to fit back together the way I was. The way I *used to be.* "I saw the planning room," I started, catching the flicker in his eyes. "I saw the whiteboards, saw the sheer amount of manpower that's going into hunting down the hunters. But I think you're making a serious mistake."

*Yesss,* Chaos whispered. I felt that dark urgency like never before, pushing me, forcing me, making the words spill from my lips and fall to the floor. Thunder rumbled outside the building walls, making Harlan wince.

He didn't know. He didn't realize…*I was that storm.*

*Keep going,* that Unseelie growl sent a charge through me, a stab, a cut…the tip of the blade pressing against my heart.

"A mistake?" he asked. "What kind of mistake?"

The folder in my hand trembled as I closed my eyes. I couldn't do this…couldn't *say the words.* Chaos pushed harder, pressing against my skin, forcing my eyes to open. My voice turned deeper with her presence, more guttural. *More beast.* "You're failing to see the bigger picture here, the more dangerous Immortal than this city has ever known."

Harlan leaned closer. "And who is that?"

"Ruth Costello."

The corner of his lips curled into a half smile, until he realized I wasn't joking. "Ruth isn't an Immortal."

"Isn't she?" I murmured. My hand shook as I opened the file and took out the one page I'd sworn I'd hide. "This report from the bloodstains that night in the warehouse says otherwise."

He lowered his gaze to the sheet in my hand as his skin paled. "There has to be—"

"Denzel Costello wasn't her real father. This DNA test proved it and what I'm about to tell you is because I spoke to her a few days ago, right before you descended with your army, guns all blazing. Her *real* father was part of a secret and incredibly powerful organization known as the Inner Circle. A group of Immortals who govern all the others. Her father…*her real father,* was the Vampire Caedes, and that makes her a very powerful individual indeed."

"If she has Vampire blood, then why isn't she a Vampire?"

It was the same question that'd haunted me since I'd found the report from the warehouse. "I don't know. But her blood, and what she says, match. You're looking at the wrong type of Immortal, Harlan. You're focusing on the scapegoat while the real danger lurks all around us in the shadows. Always quiet, always hidden. I'm offering you the Vampires of Crown City in exchange for the Wolves."

"For your lovers, you mean?" he snapped.

"Yes," I said carefully. "You know and I know they didn't kill Murphy. You've had the lab run the tests, you saw that the cuts and the DNA didn't match."

"We haven't matched them *yet,*" Harlan forced through his teeth.

That black beast reared inside my head, all fangs and fury, all hate and rage. I knew *he* was the one who'd killed Murphy, knew he was the one who'd attacked Wry. My stomach clenched at the young Wolf's name. He was still out there, and so was Walker.

*Whatever it takes,* Chaos whispered, and that chill slithered along my spine once more. "And you won't match them, because it wasn't any of these Wolves. It was one of the rogue packs who entered the city, the same one who attacked one of Phantom's own crew, a young male Wolf by the name of Wry. He had his throat torn out and when he healed…he healed damaged. He can't speak, but everything points to this *Alpha Wolf who isn't Phantom.*"

"Jesus fucking Christ."

"So it's not any of Phantom's pack doing this. It's the ones *we've* allowed to come in and try to take what's Phantom's in the first place. But the real danger here isn't the turf war, it's the bloodlines. It's the Inner Circle. It's the one that will bring not just Crown City to its knees...but the entire country. Ruth Costello carries the blood of a powerful Vampire in her veins, and if you think her wrath is over...I guarantee you, it's barely begun."

Harlan straightened. His lips parted, and his eyes were riveted on mine. It took the wind out of his sails, snatched away every battle cry he had stored for the fight against his perceived enemy.

That flicker of his despair unleashed a cry inside me, that time part of me that knew what I was doing...*and hated me for it.*

Chaos rose, just as swiftly stealing away the thunder of my heart and that sickening feeling I was falling into a chasm of my undoing. *Eyes on the prize,* Chaos whispered, and Phantom's tortured face filled my mind. "I didn't ask for this."

"What?" Harlan questioned, drawing me back to the moment.

I lifted my gaze as that sense of hopelessness filled me. "I never asked for this." I rose from the seat and lifted my hands, my fingers working the top button of my blouse.

Harlan stiffened, his eyes going to the closed door behind us. "Chase, what the hell are you doing?" But there wasn't anger in his tone, quite the opposite. There was *hunger.*

The Unseelie glow spilled out as I opened my top as far as I needed. Shards of green jewels sparkled against my pale breasts, glittering and shining, embedded deep into my flesh.

He stiffened, stared, then jerked his gaze to mine, his words almost choking. "What the hell is that?"

"That is what happened to me that night in the warehouse. That, Harlan, is what Phantom saved me from. I was spelled by an Unseelie, given some dark power, an uncontrollable power that Phantom and his pack have helped me to control."

I took a step closer, the swell of my breasts in line with his eyes. He couldn't look away, captured by the way I moved. "Without them, this...*Chaos* inside me will consume me. It will tear me apart until there is nothing left of me anymore."

His chest rose and fell with hard breaths as he continued to fix on my plunging neckline. "This *spell* causes you to what?"

"Drive men to the point they want to hurt me."

He flinched, jerking his gaze to mine.

"At first it's the looks, then it's the comments, then it's cornering me in the building as they try to kiss me."

Energy crackled in the room. He knew now, knew it wasn't just his own emotions at play here. It was Chaos, as well.

"That night in the warehouse, I was attacked, and hurt. But I would've been hurt even worse if Phantom hadn't helped me."

"Helped you how?"

I didn't want to tell him the truth, didn't want that flare of jealousy to drive the final nail into my Alpha's coffin. "He helped me to control it, helped me to push it down until it seethes inside me. But without his power, without my pack around me, it takes over. It consumes and controls. You feel it now, don't you? That hunger, that...*lust.* It makes you want to touch me, makes you want to cross that line between being honorable and a savage."

He wanted to be a savage. I could see it in his eyes, and the way he clenched his jaw, and fisted his hands, as though the mere thought of touching me *might...just...bring...him...*

*undone.*

"The Vampires?" he asked breathlessly.

"Ruth Costello and the Vampires" I urged. "It'll be bigger than anything you've ever done in your entire career." I worked the buttons of my blouse, closing them one by one. "And you'll let the Wolves go, let them protect this city once more."

"I can't close the investigation into the murder of one of our own."

"I'm not asking you to do that, keep it open while we hunt down the real Wolf who did this. You said yourself, Phantom and the others weren't a match."

Harlan swallowed hard and nodded.

*That's it...*Chaos whispered, making my stomach lurch and roll.

"And you'll come to me." His words were almost a plea. "If you find out more."

"Harlan," I stepped closer and reached out, placing my hand on his. "You'll be the first."

He looked toward the door, his eyes glazing before he held out his hand for the file. My fingers clenched, and fear crowded my head. That battleground inside me stretched out, *right, wrong...betrayal, and protection.*

I loosened my fingers, and my nails gouged the folder as my glance caught the keys on the bookshelf, the *familiar keys.* "You kept them here?" My voice deepened, sounding guttural and raw as I rounded the corner of his desk.

"I knew you'd return."

Sparkling metal, the familiar burn as I grabbed them from the shelf. "You know what this means, right?"

There was no answer at first, until I clenched my fist around the keys and turned, finding his sullen expression. "We both get what we want," he muttered.

"You're doing the right thing, Harlan. The *only* thing you can do."

Then I left, yanking open the door, hurrying through his secretary's area until I was outside in the hallway, with the low drone of voices coming from behind the cracked open door of the strategic planning room. There was nothing here for me now. Nothing this office...or this world could give me that I needed more than *them.*

I hurried for the elevator, stepped in, and rode it all the way down to the parking garage. My heart was racing by the time the doors opened. I hadn't let myself look before, hadn't wanted that cruel torture. But now I scanned the cars parked along the far wall of the garage and stilled at the sight.

I had to stop myself from running, had to stop myself from crying.

*All for them...*

Chaos whispered as I hurried for that familiar black Jeep. *Damn, I love this car...*Arran's words echoed through my head as the downpour outside grew deafening. I pressed the button, unlocking my Wolf's Jeep, and climbed in.

*We're done,* Chaos whispered.

Those words plunged deeper than ever before.

There was no more safe house for me now, no more coming back here, no more future as I'd envisioned it. I gripped the steering wheel. *There was just them.* I fought that fear inside me and lifted my gaze to the rear-view mirror...*if they forgave me, that was.*

Doubt crowded my mind as I shoved the key into the ignition and started the engine. There was only one place I could go. One place where I could think about what I'd just done. I shoved the Jeep into gear, backed out of the parking space, and headed for Walker's apartment.

## 25

## PHANTOM

"Are you sure there's no sign of either of them?" I forced the words through clenched teeth and listened to that dreaded silence on the other end of the phone.

"I'm sure, Wolf," Mojin whispered.

The gasping rattle of his breaths told me more than his words ever could. He'd hunted, running until even that dark Unseelie blood in his veins couldn't keep him from exhaustion.

"I'm not giving up," Mojin growled. "But we need the Breeds."

*Will they come?* The question lingered a heartbeat too long. "I'll make a call."

"Already done it. Griffin and his team are on the way."

"Send in the Wolves," I muttered.

"Who more than the most brutal, bloodthirsty bastards there are...apart from you, that is." The Fae growled through the phone, making the corners of my lips twitch.

"It's only a matter of time," I muttered and lifted my head to the teeming rain from the steel gray sky. "Are you heading back?"

"Already on my way," the Fae answered. "I'll see you when I get there."

*Things have changed, brother.* I opened my mouth to say the words, but he was already gone, the line silent. I slid my phone back into my pocket and lifted my gaze to the dark windows of the Hunting Ground.

I scanned the rear-view mirror, catching a car as it rolled past and kept on going. The streets were strangely silent. No unmarked cars sitting outside my club this morning, no drive-bys on this side of the river. I glanced at the rear-view mirror again, waiting for a second before I opened the door of the white Ford sedan and crossed the road.

It was a different car every day for me and the pack. We were always moving, always changing, never staying in one spot for too long. Which is why I was here…at the last place Carina had been before she disappeared in the early hours of this morning. But that'd been hours ago now.

*You mean the last place she was here with Church?* my beast snarled, desperate and aching. Hungry. That's what he was. He was fucking starving, haunted and hollowed from the inside out. I headed for the back door of the club.

A club that should've been thrumming with life, only now it was in total darkness. Headlights of a car parked against the curb further down the road splashed against the wet asphalt before it pulled out and turned around in the empty road, heading away from this side of the river.

My steps stopped as the brake lights flared and the vehicle turned toward the bridge. Something felt wrong. I scanned the darkness and swiveled, my fists rising from my sides. But there was no one behind me, no rogue pack attack…no FBI agents in waiting.

There was nothing but the growl of thunder overhead. Thunder that'd been growing in the early hours of the morning until the storm was a living, breathing, destructive thing.

Rain splattered the side of my head. I turned back and stepped forward, lengthening my stride until I hit the back door of the club and punched in the numbers before the lock clicked open. I caught the faint scent of her still clinging to the air.

*Mine,* my beast growled, staking his claim.

I ground my teeth as his desperate pants followed, drawing the taste of her deeper into my lungs until her scent crawled under my skin. Jesus, that woman invaded me like no one else. I massaged the tight muscles at the back of my neck, stepped through the open doorway, and went into the back bar.

I walked through the place, moving behind the back of the bar, taking my time as the ache of the familiar cut deep. Memories filtered in. The night I'd found her in the warehouse…and brought her here.

*Stick it in, for fuck's sake.* Her desperate plea roared to the surface of my mind.

Jesus, she didn't understand, then…didn't realize just how much she called my beast. She couldn't fathom the kind of things he wanted to do to her.

*Stick it in?* My own reply rose swiftly.

I'd traced that swollen, sensitive nub between her legs before dragging my finger along her center until my beast let out a savage, unmistakable warning and forced my head lower, licking, *claiming.*

*I licked it,* my beast had growled between her legs. *So it's mine.*

We were happy here, weren't we? Maybe not happy, but secure, at least. My dancers were all taken care of, all protected by the outlying members of my pack. But for how long? I didn't know. I followed that seductive scent, all dangerous and feminine as it sent my heart racing. She was the storm that raged above me, violent and controlling.

Christ, I wanted her.

*Need her…*the beast growled.

I followed her seductive scent, coming back into the present as the light grew brighter outside, stepping up onto the dancer's podium. She'd been here...with Church. The male had left his marking scent all over here...and over her. I closed my eyes, imagining them together. Kissing, touching, her hand down the front of his pants, and that desperate look in his eyes.

As much as the thought set my teeth on edge, I wanted it just as much.

Wanted her with us.

*All of us.*

Time slipped away as I stood there. I didn't know how long I stood there, mesmerized by the fantasy in my head and the knowledge she'd just been there. My phone let out a *beep*, dragging me back to the moment. I yanked it from my pocket and stared at the message from Elithien.

*Meet me at the house. We have a problem.*

I let out a groan and turned away from the dancers' lounge and the scent of lust still lingering in the air. "What the fuck now?" I muttered out loud.

We were so close to getting Carina away. I'd secured a facility not far from here, had my men already working on the security. Seven-foot fences equipped with razor wire and spelled by the Dark Fae, it was a concrete fortress. One big enough for the entire pack...even the fringe members.

But that was still weeks away.

Weeks I was prepared to hide and fight and keep her far away from those who hunted us. It didn't matter, as long as we were together. I made my way back out of the club and locked the door behind me, before I stopped cold.

*Someone was here...*

The scent of another caught the wind for a heartbeat before it was gone. Rain smacked against my cheek as I froze. Still, a chill crawled along my spine. I scanned the darkness that stretched toward the Fae's compound with a predatory gaze and stepped out into the opening.

*Finis?* my beast growled.

Whoever it was was...*powerful,* and dangerous. The scent so *impenetrable.* I couldn't get a handle on it. Male...female, their standing...it was all convoluted. I stepped out into the darkness, scanning for movement.

Black shifted at the edge of the trees across from the Unseelie compound. My pulse sped as I scanned the grounds while water ran in rivulets down my neck and slipped under my collar. Was this the midnight Wolf who hunted Carina? The one who'd attacked and killed the bastard who'd tried to hurt her... the one who'd attacked Wry?

I lunged, driving my boots against the pavement as I crossed the parking lot, then across the street to the barren ground on the other side, and plunged through the brush-like trees beyond.

Head down, my arms thrashed sharp branches aside as I ran. Wet leaves slapped against my face as movement shifted ahead of me. Whoever it was...they were fast, racing through the thick brush like it was nothing. Twigs snapped, making my beast snarl and push forward, desperate to take over the hunt. But I held on, driving myself deeper into the dense thicket, until the scent faded.

Until there was nothing but the heady scent of the rain and sweet earth.

I stopped, drawing in the air, desperate for that scent, and swiveled, scanning the trees all around me, searching for movement...until that clench in my gut told me they were gone.

I retreated, working my way back to the street, watching all around me. No one would attack out in the open like this...not unless they wanted to die. I looked toward the flare of lightning across the sky.

I was sure that was Finis, even if the Breeds assured me the leader of the Wolves was hundreds of miles away. *They didn't know him...not like I did.* I worked my way to the street and scanned the cars once more before I headed for the white Ford and dragged the keys from my pocket.

The Vampires were waiting. But I couldn't shake that feeling that I was being watched…*and hunted.* I unlocked the door and climbed into the sedan, my clothes soaking the seats, making my shirt mold against my skin as I started the engine. Headlights splashed across the deep puddles, but that unnerving feeling stayed with me even as I shoved the car into gear and pulled out onto the street. I watched the rear-view mirror, tracking every car that passed and every set of headlights behind me as I turned left and headed into Vampire territory.

The road was slick, with puddles growing even larger under the thunderous downpour. I drove until the nondescript lane speared off from the main road. Thick fog seemed to spring up from nowhere, closing in around the sedan and growing heavier the further I drove. I gripped the wheel hard, fighting the need to turn around as the Vampire wards took hold.

The house seemed to rise out of the murky white gloom, a towering mansion. I pulled up alongside the gray Explorer and killed the engine. The house looked quiet. But I knew better than anyone that with Elithien, looks were always deceiving.

We'd grown closer in the last few days. Desperation had a way of revealing your true allies, and I had that with the Fae and the Vampires. I'd fought for Elithien in the warehouse, stood side by side with the Immortal, and he'd done the same for me when I needed it, coming to rescue Carina even if it caused tension with his own mate. Whatever was coming for Ruth after the death of Caedes, we'd face it together as allies.

I climbed out of the car and strode to the front door, lifting my gaze to Rule as he opened it and stepped aside.

"Vampire," I greeted the younger Immortal.

He just nodded in reply. But there was something cold in his gaze, some kind of icy edge that made me look toward the sitting room as I made my way deeper into the house. Hurrow stood at the front of the house, his double shoulder holster loaded with two Sig Sauers, as well as the one in his hand...the brother was armed to the teeth.

Something was going on here...something I wasn't getting. I glanced toward the window where Hurrow stood, then turned my attention to Elithien as he stood outside the study door, Rule now at his side, and Russell, the bodyguard, hovering in the background, crowding Ruth.

"E," I muttered, acknowledging the Alpha of the Vampire brood. "Everything alright here?"

The Vampire just pushed off the doorframe and uncrossed his arms, those dark eyes glinting like a starless midnight sky. "I was about to ask you the same thing."

The brother's voice was cold as damn ice, dragging that chill to the surface once more. I'd never felt fear around any of these Vampires before, but that's what was crawling through my bones as I stood in the middle of the Vampire den.

"No word on my end," I said carefully. "Only, I thought I saw an unmarked pull away from the Hunting Ground and make for the other side of the city." I decided to leave my brush with the midnight Wolf out of the conversation, at least for now.

"Funny about that," Hurrow muttered behind me.

But it was Elithien I focused on. "You want to tell me what's going on here?"

"Seems like the FBI are no longer interested in the Wolves."

I clutched hold of every word, unable to fight a rush of relief. "Jesus." My breath escaped as I sagged. "So we're able to come home? Able to re-open the clubs?"

"It seems so." That cold bite didn't leave the Vampire's tone.

Did the prospect of that piss the brother off? "I'm not understanding the pissed-off vibe I'm getting here, brother. You don't want the clubs open, is that it?"

"Quite the contrary," Elithien denied as he strode toward me, his blood red lips peeling back from his extended fangs.

The brother was riding the killing edge, ready to unleash any damn second...*on me.*

He reached out, grasped my sodden shirt, and yanked me close, until all I could see was the empty depths of his eyes, and those sharp white fangs.

My beast snarled a warning growl, but I fought the need to react and forced my hands to stay at my sides. "E, this is me here," I tried to get through to the Vampire.

Danger shifted through the air all around me. I felt Hurrow step away from the window and raise that damn Sig in his hand. I was about to be torn to pieces, or shot.

"You mean to tell me you don't know *why* the FBI are no longer interested in you...*Wolf?*" Elithien growled. "Lie to me... and I'll tear *your* fucking throat out."

I battled to control the beast inside me and met the Vampire's stare. "No, I don't know, so you want to fucking *enlighten me?*"

There was a flicker of...*relief,* before the Vampire eased his hold on me and dropped his hands. Hash breaths made his chest rise before he took a step backwards. "I *told* them you weren't involved in this, that there was no way you'd betray me."

*Betray?* A sickening sense of foreboding rose like a gathering storm.

Just like the one that had unleashed above my head.

"A deal has been made," Elithien started, looking away for a second like he couldn't bear to meet my gaze. "A deal that puts you and your pack in the clear." The bodyguard reached and grasped Ruth's hand, and the possessive stance couldn't be any more obvious as Elithien met my gaze once more. "And puts Ruth and us firmly in their crosshairs."

My lips curled as I shook my head. "That's bullshit. We'd never—"

"Not you," Elithien growled. "Tell me, *brother.* Have you spoken to Carina lately?"

Warmth slipped from my body as my smirk faltered, then fell.

*She's acting strange,* Church's warning rang loud and clear in my head. "No," I whispered. "She wouldn't."

But the look in Elithien's eyes spoke the truth.

*She had...*

## 26

I walked through Walker's empty apartment as I slid the key she kept with her neighbor into my pocket. Everything was the same, spotless, *lived in.* I went into the kitchen and trailed my fingers along the counter as my mind went to all the terror that was happening to her.

Lost, alone…probably hurt, if not dead…

*No. I won't think like that.* I can't. Tears threatened my eyes as I glanced at the fridge and the picture of Ebony smiling and reaching toward the camera, just as she'd reached for her sister all her life. *Just like I'd reached out to Walker, and now look what had happened to her.*

I turned around and made my way out of the kitchen, stopping at the cracked open door to her bedroom. I'd barely slept in the last two days. Sleep seemed elusive to me, as was any kind of rest. I made my way into the living room and slumped down onto the sofa.

This was torture, that was easy to see. I wouldn't *allow* myself to rest.

*What is rest, when we have everything we want?* Chaos whispered in the back of my mind.

I closed my eyes at her words and laid my head against the back of the sofa, sliding my hand along the soft material beside me. "Just go away," I murmured. "Leave me alone."

Agony carved across my chest as I spoke. Her anger was cruel and powerful, making me catch my breath and rock forward. I let out a whimper, and pressed a fist against my chest until finally, the piercing ache eased.

*You'd think you'd be a little more grateful.*

Tears threatened my eyes once more. I trembled at her words, hating her and myself. I didn't want to think about what I'd just done, or the consequences. *Maybe I should just leave?* Pack what few belongings I had and just drive away...and keep on driving.

That merciless ache flared again for a heartbeat. It was a threat, a warning, but then it was gone. She didn't need to speak, didn't need to do anything. Just the feel of her in my head was enough. I yanked my fist away from my chest then unleashed, hitting the bone with a *thud.* I was a prisoner in the confines of my skin, my thoughts no longer my own...and now neither were my actions.

A tremor raced across my skin, something raw and *savage.* Something that spilled through the air, setting my teeth on edge. I felt him before I heard the pounding steps, and rose from the sofa as the front door to Walker's apartment was thrown open.

*Phantom...*

My pulse leaped as the temperature in the air plunged to icy levels and the door was closed with a *slam!* I stumbled sideways from the sofa, desperate for the floor to open up and swallow me whole. Then he was there, striding around the corner from the hallway, all predator...and cold.

...and Phantom had never been cold.

*Not like this.*

He lifted his gaze, and those once haunted brown eyes shone with steel.

"Phantom." His name was a whisper. I stepped away again on reflex as rage became a beast, prowling the air all around him. "How did you find me?"

"Did you think I didn't know where you were every second of the day?" he growled, his tone cold and raw.

I backed up once more, until the heels of my boots smacked against the wall. I scanned the room frantically—*there was nowhere else to go.*

I waited for him to say something more, waited for the rage and the anger. I waited for him to lose control. But he didn't, only slowed his steps around the corner of the sofa and pinned my gaze with his.

Inside, I was panicking, desperate to find a way out of this. I licked desperately dry lips, searching that animalistic gaze, and asked myself a question I never thought I would—*was Phantom going to hurt me?*

He reached me and lifted his hand, bracing it against the wall behind me.

"I think we need a break." The words slipped from my lips before I knew it.

It was all I could think of. Run. Run away from the Wolves… run away from everything. I was better off on my own. *Never alone,* Chaos answered, dragging me deeper into that unfathomable pit.

"Sure we do." Phantom lifted his other hand, cupping my throat with his mammoth palm.

"I don't want to see you," I said, trembling.

"Of course you don't." He took a small step forward, driving me flat against the wall.

"Phantom. Don't push this."

"Not pushing anything, female." His voice was controlled,

*strained.* So why were the hairs on my neck rising? That hand moved from my neck, sliding down my chest.

God, his hand was huge, his splayed fingers spread across my breasts before he pinched the buttons of my shirt, working them open one by one.

*He wanted to have sex?*

A shudder coursed through me, and heat followed. My nipples tightened as I met his stare. There was nothing soft in the silver shine of his eyes, nothing *forgiving.* Just that ferocious need, that *burn* which had captured us from the very moment we met.

And it was here now, burning through my veins.

His fingers worked all the way down, until he pushed my wet shirt over my shoulders and tugged it free.

"I..." I started before he lowered his head, kissing the line of my neck. Then I forgot what I'd been about to say.

My bra was next, the straps slipped free by his massive fingers and sliding down my shoulders. "Wait," I whimpered.

The clasp at my back was released, letting the sodden bra fall to the floor. The Alpha was driven, moving to the button of my slacks, opening it in a heartbeat and pushing them low.

Cool air licked my thighs, but I shivered under the heat of his touch. He grasped the seat of my panties, his thick fingers shoving the elastic aside before he slid two inside me. Slick. *Wet.* That primal beast glinted in his eyes.

"Break, Phantom," I moaned.

"A break." He pushed off the wall and shoved his jeans down low. "Whatever you need, female. You know I'm all about that... whatever you need."

*Please.* The word surfaced in my mind, but it didn't make it to my lips. Instead, I let him manhandle me, yanking me from the wall and turning me. My hands rose and splayed against the wall as his fingers trailed down my spine.

I arched my back at the feel of his lips. His hands gripped

my waist, holding me still as he did what he wanted. I shuddered at the thought. That's how it was with Phantom, pure, primal desire. His breath was scorching against my skin, and the tips of his fangs pressed against my lips as he kissed me.

"A break," he growled again, as one hand moved, sliding over the curve of my ass. My panties were yanked hard, pulling me backwards until the sheer fabric ripped under the force of his strength. "You want a *break* from me?"

I dropped my head, my breaths coming hard and fast. But inside, I was sinking into that dark pit.

He stilled, closed his eyes and swayed as that chilling savagery lashed the air once more around him. When he opened his eyes once more, that blue was cold and hard, frozen.

He moved fast, lashing out to drive his fist into the wall beside me with a *boom*. Plaster cracked and gave way, leaving a fist sized hole in Walker's living room.

"I told you before, Carina. I'm no fucking monster. Tell me no, and I'll walk away," he whispered against my back. "Tell me you don't want me more than your next fucking breath, and I'll be out of your life forever."

Agony carved right to my heart at his words. I stood there, hands against the wall, desperate to say the right thing…*the only thing,* but words failed me. He didn't know what I'd done. He wouldn't be here if he did. He'd hate me. Hate and rage. It was only a matter of time.

"*Say it,*" he growled, that savagery spilling free as he rolled his hips against my ass.

His cock thrust deep, driving between my thighs. The tears that'd threatened to fall came now, spilling over and blurred my sight. I leaned my head backwards against his powerful chest as he reached for my throat once more.

"Say it, Carina." He clenched his grip, slamming me back against his body.

"I can't," I cried, rocking my ass backwards, meeting the jolt of his thrust.

His hold on my throat eased, fingers pressing against my pulses until the brutal grip turned into a caress. He lowered his head and his lips brushed against my shoulder before he kissed me beneath my ear. "That's right, *you won't say it.*"

He braced a forearm across my hips before he slammed his cock inside me, driving in to the hilt. The pain was sharp, tearing a gasp free at the brutality, before he eased out, teasing me before he pushed in once more. Only he was slower that time, taking his time as he slid his hand between my thighs from the front.

"You forget one thing, *female,*" he snarled in my ear. "You belong to *me.* There is no *break* where I'm concerned, no *forgetting* what we have, no *goddamn walking away* from us."

"You," he drove deeper. "Belong." His fingers found my clit, *circling.* "To *me.*"

I was blown apart by the heat, bucking my hips against his cock and his fingers. Tears slipped down my cheeks as savage desire burned in my veins. I couldn't stop myself from lowering my head, rocking back into the cruel thrusts.

I wanted him to hurt me...*like I'd hurt him.* "Harder."

Big hands gripped my hips, lifting me until my boots left the floor. He turned me like I weighed nothing, then took me to the floor in the middle of Walker's living room. With a frenzied yank of my boots, they were torn from my feet and flung across the room, hitting something with a *thud.*

My pants were next, shoved down and slid from my legs until I was bare beneath him. He was all I could see, rising above me like a god. Those piercing silver eyes found mine, flicking to the tears sliding down my cheeks as he flinched.

But he said nothing more, just drove his powerful body between my legs. I jolted hard against the floor with the impact and my hands went around his thick wrists, feeling the muscles tense under his thrusts.

There was no stopping this time, no holding back. I opened my thighs wider, lifting my feet to wrap around his waist. The curl of his lips made my pulse race faster. His beast was there, riding close to the surface.

That foul Unseelie hunger called to him, spilling from my body to lick the air. Phantom let out a growl as he plunged between my legs, riding the edge of pleasure with unforgiving, merciless thrusts. "Say it." He forced the words through clenched teeth.

I stared up at him, my body taking every brutal blow. "I belong to you."

His lips curled and his fangs grew long.

I knew there was no running from him. No matter what I said, there was nowhere this male wouldn't find me, nowhere he wouldn't hunt me down. Desire was a beast between us, making him roll his hips, drawing a heated gasp from my lips.

I was his…

Body, mind, and soul.

*My Wolves.*

No matter what.

My breaths deepened, catching as my orgasm barreled down on me. He let out a growl, driving me to the brink of no return. I gripped his wrists, clenching until I lost control. He lowered his head and let out a dangerous sound as he bucked and twitched, spilling warmth inside me.

He stayed like that for a moment as his heavy breaths eased, then he slowly pulled out.

My hold around his wrists slipped away, leaving him to ease back. I didn't dare take my gaze from his, watching as he rose from the floor in one fluid move and adjusted his jeans. He looked away as a tortured look descended. "I just have one question."

My heart pounded in my chest.

"Why?" He turned to me once more. "Why did you have to betray them?"

I flinched at the emptiness in his tone.

He knew.

*He knew...*

I opened my mouth to answer, but there were no words. None that would make sense to him...or me. Chaos ruled in that moment. "Phantom..." I started, then stopped.

There was a bitter chuckle before he turned and strode from apartment. Stunned, I just lay there, bare, cold...*and utterly alone.*

The door quietly opened and closed once more. He may as well have torn the damn thing from its hinges and slammed the remnants to the floor. I slowly pushed up to my feet as that cruel emptiness swallowed me.

I'd tried to run from him by coming to Walker's apartment, tried to hide from the things I'd done. Now they were right here in front of me. I picked up my clothes and went into the bathroom. What *was* that? He refused to let me go...then walked out. I hurried using the toilet and yanked my clothes back on.

I had to find him, had to explain what had happened. I yanked on my boots, grabbed Arran's and Walker's keys, and locked the door behind me as I ran from the apartment. But by the time I raced down the stairs and out of the building, there was no sign of him.

I raced for the Jeep, unlocked the four-wheel drive, and climbed in, starting the engine in a second and shoving it into gear. I pulled out into the traffic, working the gears as the rain beat against the windshield. The Hunting Ground, that's where he'd go. My pulse was racing, my frantic thoughts were all over the place, replaying every word he'd said to me.

We weren't over.

*But we weren't good.*

That much I knew.

I battled the erratic traffic, weaving my way toward the bridge. My grip squeezed against the wheel as I punched the accelerator, pushing the Jeep harder, and climbed onto the bridge. My gaze drifted to the darkness that hugged the other side of the riverbank. "I'll take it back," I whispered. "Call Harlan, tell him it was all a lie."

*And you'll find yourself in Federal Prison,* Chaos answered.

I didn't care, anything was better than this. I swerved in and out of the few cars that ventured across the river and exited at the off-ramp. I was already turning, desperate to track him down, and turned down familiar streets. Four or five cars were parked against the curb, but none were familiar. Then again, my Wolves had been in hiding.

I pulled the Jeep up hard outside the Hunting Ground and climbed out. My nerves still hummed from Phantom's body, and my will was weak and desperate where he was concerned.

I hurried around the side to the empty parking lot and raced for the door, praying it was cracked open and they were waiting for me. But as I neared, I saw it was closed. I turned the handle and yanked, but it was locked, and I didn't know the code.

Rain splattered against my face, sticking strands of hair to my cheeks as I spun. There were no tire tracks in the mud, no signs they'd been here at all. I turned away from the door and hurried for the front entrance, stepped under the awning, and peered into the darkened club.

Chairs, darkness. No sign of anyone.

I grabbed my phone and slid my fingers down the screen, finding Phantom's number. I hated to be the desperate, needy girlfriend. That wasn't me, but this was no lover's quarrel, this was poison, one that could kill us slowly, and it was all my fault.

"You've reached Phantom. Leave a message."

I hung up on the voicemail and lifted my gaze to the ten-foot fence around the Unseelie compound. Fear trembled inside me as desperate thoughts rose inside me. *No, I can't...not them.*

Movement came at the corner of my eye, I spun around, heard the sound of boots against concrete, and hurried after the sound. *Was it Arran?* I rounded the corner and stared along the gap between this building and the next.

The past rose like a fog to crowd my mind as I moved, following the sound along the side of the Hunting Ground and out to the back. The air grew colder, denser...*heavier* as I stepped from behind the club and into the Unseelie darkness.

Terror lingered in the empty buildings behind the Wolves' club. The kind of terror you couldn't escape, the kind a Wolf like Arran ran from. Desperation drove me forward, step after step. My hands shook with the cold, or shock, I didn't know. In that moment, I'd do anything to get my Wolves back.

"Such beautiful chaos you create, Carina. Must be the Fae in you."

I spun at the deep growl and found that beautiful and brutal Unseelie coming closer. "Mojin," I called his name.

But I was under no illusion. This *male* was just as dangerous to me as he was to any other mortal who found themselves on the wrong side of the river...and wandering around in his world. I straightened my spine and jutted my chin higher, even as tears rained down my cheeks. "I wish this never happened to me. I wish..."

The Dark Fae just smiled that chilling, foreboding smile and strode closer, pitiless and wild, and stopped in front of me. I flinched as he lifted his hand. It was reflex. One he enjoyed as those midnight eyes sparkled with cruelty. "Be *very* careful what you wish for."

My heart leaped as his fingers hovered barely an inch from my face. He searched my gaze, unmoved by my tears, then he lowered his hand and kept walking, making his way into the cloaking darkness of the Unseelie world...*and disappeared.*

I waited for a second, desperate for him to return and undo all the damage I'd done.

But he didn't return, just left me standing there…until the salt of my tears slipped between my lips. I turned, made my way back to the Jeep, unlocked it, and climbed in. I was done. *No, they were done.* Done with me…I'd sacrificed the Vampires for nothing.

*FOR NOTHING.*

I let out a shrill scream and punched the steering wheel, desperate to hit something, hurt something. *Desperate to hurt me.* Instead, I started the car and pulled back out onto the street, turned around, and headed back toward the city.

I wasn't done.

*I couldn't be done.*

The traffic blurred as I drove back across the bridge and headed for headquarters once more. I pulled the Jeep into the parking lot and drove along the parking spaces, pulling in beside the Ford I'd used before.

I hurried for the elevator, smashing the buttons until the doors opened. I pushed the up button, then lifted my gaze and watched the lights slowly climb. By the time the elevator stopped and the doors opened, I was already running, hurtling myself along the hallways toward Harlan's office, and barged through the door.

But the office was empty. No secretary…and the door to his office was closed. I strode forward, and yanked the handle, finding the damn thing locked. "No…*nonono. Don't do this to me.*"

I slammed the handle, but the damn thing held. The other offices. I hurried out and into the hall, hurrying to every door in the executive hallway.

But every one of them was locked.

"They've all left."

I jerked around, finding Tracey, Harlan's secretary, walking back with a glass of water in her hand. "Where?"

"Arcanium," she answered with a scowl.

I stepped closer, making her flinch. "What's in Arcanium?"

"Some kind of Vampire horde," she whispered, fear crowding in her eyes. "Harlan told me if you came looking for him that you were too late."

"Too late?" I repeated as the walls closed in. I closed my eyes. *"Too late."*

"He said they found more than just the Vampire blood in Ruth's blood. They found a lone Wolf, an Alpha that'd been terrorizing the city, searching for you. He said he left the file on your desk, and to tell you, that you're not done here."

"I'm not done?"

She shrugged. "It's just what he said."

I stepped around her, still holding her gaze. *A file on my desk.*

I hurried, running back to the elevator once more. But the damn thing was all the way in the lower basement...and I couldn't wait. I raced for the stairwell door, yanked it open, and plunged down the stairs.

A file...

*A file.*

The Alpha that'd been hunting me was here.

And now I had proof. Maybe this was the way back to my Wolves?

If I gave them Finis.

I drove myself faster and faster, until my thighs burned with the movement, and exited on my floor. I was gasping and my legs were trembling by the time I reached the entrance to our cubicles. My gaze lifted to the stack of papers on my desk, and the dark blue folder in front of my chair.

"Hey, Chase, you're back?" someone called.

But I didn't answer, I didn't care. Instead, I yanked out my chair, dropped onto the seat, and opened the file. The image was grainy, black and white, taken from a night shot. I scanned the background, finding the massive midnight Wolf.

*It was him...*

My fingers trembled as I slid the image aside and stared at

the report. It was from Agent Asshole, my warden, and taken on the night I left to go across the bridge to the Hunting Ground, where I met Church.

The safe house had been attacked and an agent had been slashed. They'd managed to get off two shots before the beast ran. The image was taken from a CCTV camera. The next page was a lab report. *High Priority* was printed across the top in bold red letters.

I scanned the details. The markers of a Lycan, and then I stopped cold... "No, that can't be right."

I jerked my gaze back to the image.

*No. No, that wasn't right.*

Even Chaos was quiet inside my head.

I shoved upwards, knocking over my chair as I felt the blood draining down my body, leaving me lightheaded.

*Not Finis.*

*Not Finis...*

*NOT FINIS.*

I grabbed the report and fumbled for my phone, praying harder than I'd ever prayed in my life that he would answer this time. *"Please, Phantom,"* I begged as the phone rang...and rang...*and rang...*

"You gonna hide here forever, Wolf?" Mojin muttered and stepped out of the shadows of the warehouse.

"I'm not hiding," I growled to the Fae.

"Sure you're not."

I winced at the condescending tone and jerked my gaze to his. I wouldn't ask him, wouldn't say the words. *I refused to.* The woman still clung to me, her scent, her power. *Her goddamn cruelty.* Jesus, and I'd thought Wolves were ruthless.

"Stay for as long as you want." The asshole waved his hand in the air. "Hell, move in, for all I care. We can even share a bedroom, be bunk buddies and braid each other's hair. Yeah, that'd be cool, right?"

"Fuck you, Unseelie."

The bastard just gave me a chilling smile, lips curled, revealing his teeth. His dark eyes glinted as he watched me. "You know it wasn't her, right?"

I stiffened, my jaw clenched until my teeth nearly cracked as Mojin took a step closer.

"Look at me," he commanded.

I stared at the damn wall.

*"Wolf, look at me."*

I jerked my gaze to his.

"What am I?" he asked.

"What the fuck is this? Twenty goddamn questions?" I snarled.

"What the fuck am I, Phantom?"

"Unseelie. Dark Fae, and a massive pain in my ass."

"Cold, ruthless, *a savage.* Those are our natural fucking emotions. I have to work to be this fucking nice. I'm positively a fucking saint."

My lips curled at the words. Mojin, a saint? The bastard could be downright feral, malevolent and downright scary at times.

"It's our nature to keep control, do anything we can to protect what's ours, and what has your FBI agent done?"

"Protected what was hers." Deep down I already knew that. I just wanted some way to prove she understood.

"Chaos rules her, brother, just like it rules us all. She's fought her damn nature for longer than I damn well hoped. For a pissant mortal, she's pretty fucking tough. It's more than sex for her, more than a *need.* You are hers, and no matter who or what threatens either one of you, expect her to come out all fucking guns blazing—Unseelie style."

"And where does that leave me now?" I muttered, desperation riding my every breath.

Mojin just stepped closer and clapped me on the shoulder. "In one very precarious situation, my brother, that's where you are. I can't tell you what to do, only remind you what she is now. Deal or no deal, you're stuck with her...unless you decide otherwise."

He left then, leaving those last words to echo in my damn head. *Decide otherwise...*the thought slipped into my head. Just walk away, let her leave.

*I want a break, Phantom.*

A tremor raced through my body before the low growl of my beast slipped through my head. There was no way I'd let her leave. No way I could spend one more fucking hour without her. So how the hell did I fix this?

I glanced over my shoulder, looking for Mojin. But the Unseelie was gone, disappearing into the shadows once more. "Figures," I muttered, and strode toward the warehouse's back door. Rain still pounded against the steel walls, filling the inside with noise.

A perfect fucking accompaniment to the day. I shoved the door open and stepped outside, made my way to where the white Ford was parked, and looked toward the Hunting Ground.

Carina was gone. One scan of the street outside the club, and I found the Jeep gone, too. It almost fucking killed me to watch her skid to a stop outside the club and raced around the side to the door only to find the thing locked.

Still, she didn't give up. I almost ran after her as she disappeared down the side of the club, venturing into the Dark City. That was not a place I wanted her to be. Luckily, Mojin decided at that moment to venture out of the Unseelie portal. Whatever the brother said to her made her run back to the safety of the club.

Then she was gone, tires squealing as she peeled away from this side of the city, heading for the mortal side once more. I climbed into the Ford and backed out, turning the car around and waiting for the gate to roll open before I eased the sedan through and headed for the empty parking lot behind the Hunting Ground.

I had to find a way out of this, a way that protected both the Vampires and Carina. I pulled into the lot and climbed out, heading for the back door. My phone ran as I punched in the code for the lock.

"Church," I answered.

"I just had a call from Griffin. The Breeds have a lead on the doctor and the young Wolf."

Hope flared through me as I yanked open the door and stepped inside. "And they're both alive?"

"Yes, and being held together, it seems. There's evidence of blood...the Wolf's, not the doctor's. Seems our young Wry is protecting her."

"Jesus," I muttered, remembering the detached gaze of the young male and the way he unnerved me. "You think he'll hurt her?" I turned along the hallway, flicking on the lights as I entered the living quarters.

"Who knows, the male is volatile, at best," my second answered. "Griffin will have them within the hour."

"Good." I flicked on the light to the office and stepped inside. There was silence on the other end of the phone, long enough to make me stand still.

"You found her?" Church asked carefully.

I couldn't hide the edge in my voice. "I did."

"Jesus, Phantom, how the hell are we going to get out of this?"

I didn't know, didn't know if we even *could*. We had Immortals on our side, but was it enough? If the mortals were ready to go to war with us, then this could be the perfect weapon, and there was no getting away from that.

"Does she at least understand what she's done?" Church growled.

Our pack was injured, the wound as close to fatal as it could get. *You forget one thing, female. You belong to me. There is no break where I'm concerned. No forgetting what we have. No goddamn walking away from us.* My own words rose again now as I answered. "She does, and she hates herself for it. I underestimated the Unseelie power inside her. I won't make that mistake again. She needs to be with us, where she doesn't make knee-jerk decisions that put our entire life here in jeopardy."

"You want me to find her?"

My stomach clenched. Had she suffered enough? "Bring her back to the Hunting Ground. We'll stay here until the compound is secure, then we'll all move *together*."

"Will do," he answered with a rush, and ended the call.

I wasn't the only one who wanted the agent under our roof once more. I yanked out the chair and sat down, staring at the paperwork scattered across my desk. "How the hell am I going to fix this?"

I pulled out my cell and scrolled through the numbers until I found the only one I dared call. Kol was more than an up-and-coming Master Vampire, he now owned one of the largest Vampire covens in the country. Arcanium was more than a mecca for the bloodsuckers. It's where the power resided. I pressed the icon, listening to the phone ring three times before it was answered.

"I don't know you." The remark was cold and biting. "If you know me, I have to ask why the hell you're calling me in the middle of the damn day."

"Because I know you're with the Breeds, and if so, you're in their underground compound this very moment and…I was hoping you'd answer."

"Wolf," the Vampire growled. "Who are you and what to you want?"

I told him my name and the predicament I found myself in. He listened, and muttered a subtle, "Fuck me," before a, "Jesus, what the *fuck* was she thinking?"

"She wasn't, it's the damn Unseelie power riding her," I explained.

"All this and you have a member of the Inner Circle after you?"

I leaned back in my seat. "I believe so."

"Wolf, you got yourself in some pretty deep shit, and I take it you want to protect this…*mortal?*" The way he said it made me flinch. "Yes, I want to protect her. She fucked up, but I understand *why* she fucked up. She's trying to protect us."

"Good answer," the Master Vampire responded. "Leave it with me, let me make some calls. Can I reach you at this number?"

"Yeah, night or day. You feel me?" The urgency was like adrenaline in my veins.

"I do, *very much.* I have my own mortal-turned-Vampire to contend with, as well. If there's something I can do, then rest assured I will. Take care of that mortal, Wolf." He chuckled before ending the call.

I didn't think Elithien would answer my calls right now. He was too busy fortifying his house, and calling in an army to guard the one woman he'd die to protect. "Women," I muttered as the faint *thud* of the side door reached my ears.

I looked at the clock. "That was fast, Church. I hope you went easy on her."

Hate rolled through the hallway. *Seething, rancid hate…*and the stench of Alpha reached my nose. I was already turning, pushing back the chair as darkness filled the doorway to the office and a savage warning growl filled the room.

Silver eyes glinted as the massive midnight beast stalked across the threshold. I shoved up from the chair. The thick, massive coat made the beast look even bigger. I dragged in the scent of Finis…and froze. My pulse thundered as the beast curled its lips.

But this was no male…

*This was female.*

Black coat, piercing yellow eyes shining under the silver as the beast strode closer. She moved slowly, awkwardly. My gaze tracked to the heavy swell as the past reared inside my head.

Screams descended. Screams from my past.

Screams that belonged to the only Wolf who had yellow eyes like our mother.

"*Marian?*" I whispered, calling my sister's name.

Before the beast that smelled like the powerful Inner Circle Wolf bared her fangs, and eased her weight onto her haunches. And with one unhinged, unmerciful snarl…*she leaped.*

*Want to know what happened to Walker & Wry?*
*I've written a bonus chapter just for you. Click here to read the*
*beginning of their story!*

*I will fight like never before*

---

Wolf's Obsession out now.